Grace had known ... fecting someone wit... practiced such naïv... giddy and filled with ... under her spell.

This was altogether different. Butterflies did not flit back and forth in her belly. No, from the feel of it, a tiger prowled within her, inspiring fear—and need.

He opened his eyes.

Grace suddenly realized that she'd leaned in and was staring at him, much too close.

"Grace."

His honesty touched her and urged her on. She swallowed hard, attempting to stifle her reply. It was no use.

"Do not ever regret those parts of you that are good, Mr. Clark," Grace whispered, lost in his eyes. "They're what separate you from men like my husband."

At that very moment, Grace felt she'd never expressed anything more important in her life. She needed him to understand. She needed, desperately, to touch him more intimately.

Grace continued to hold his gaze as she closed what little space existed between them and pressed her lips tentatively to his. For one brief moment, he went perfectly still. Then he responded to her touch with careful coaxing, returning her kiss while asking for more.

By Stefanie Sloane

The Devil in Disguise
The Angel in My Arms
The Sinner Who Seduced Me
The Saint Who Stole My Heart
The Scoundrel Takes a Bride
The Wicked Widow Meets Her Match

Books published by The Random House Publishing Group are
available at quantity discounts on bulk purchases for premium,
educational, fund-raising, and special sales use. For details,
please call 1-800-733-3000.

The Wicked Widow Meets Her Match

A REGENCY ROGUES NOVEL

STEFANIE SLOANE

BALLANTINE BOOKS • NEW YORK

A Ballantine Books Mass Market Original

Copyright © 2014 by Stefanie Sloane
Excerpt of *The Saint Who Stole My Heart* by Stefanie Sloane
copyright © 2012 by Stefanie Sloane

Published in the United States by Ballantine Books, an imprint of Random House, a division of Random House LLC, a Penguin Random House Company, New York.

BALLANTINE and the HOUSE colophon are registered trademarks of Random House LLC.

ISBN 978-0-345-53116-2
eBook ISBN 978-0-345-53888-8

Cover design: Lynn Andreozzi
Cover illustration: Alan Ayers

Printed in the United States of America

www.ballantinebooks.com

9 8 7 6 5 4 3 2 1

Ballantine Books mass market edition: April 2014

For the girls

The Wicked Widow Meets Her Match

"It is not permitted," Langdon patiently reminded his younger brother, Nicholas, and their friends Sophia and Dash.

Nicholas rolled his eyes and grunted in disgust. "Well, of course champagne is not permitted. That is why we should most definitely try a glass. Each."

The festive sounds from his parents' dinner party floated up the main staircase of the stately townhouse and down the hall to where the friends sat on the floor, illuminated by the glow from the beeswax candles in the wall sconces. Conversations intertwined, making it difficult to understand anything that was said beyond a few words here and there. The men's deep voices rolled roughly through the oak floorboards. The women's laughter tinkled like so many bells and occasionally made the children laugh themselves. And fourteen-year-old Langdon wondered if he was the only one of the four who pictured himself downstairs, among the adults, doing what adults do.

He could not remember a time when his father had

not been preparing him for his future as the Earl of Stonecliffe. Langdon would inherit the title and manage the family estate and fortune just as the current earl had taken on the responsibility from his father. He would marry Sophia, as their parents planned. She would give birth to an heir. And Langdon would find the person responsible for the death of Sophia's mother. His future was meticulously planned out—and much too far away.

"One person cannot possibly carry four glasses of champagne," Langdon advised his brother. "Besides, you know as well as I that Greaves will be watching very carefully. Not one drop of the quality wine will be spilled on his watch. I heard him say so with my very own ears."

Dash and Sophia dutifully nodded in agreement, their overgrown shadows upon the wall doing the same.

Nicholas did not. "Really, two servings could be carried in one glass, and one glass in each hand. As for Greaves, we've managed to get by the butler before. Who's to say we can't this time? He is getting on in years. Surely his hearing or vision will be going soon—maybe both. Tonight, if we're lucky."

Sophia gave Nicholas an admonishing look. "Really, Nicholas. Rather mean of you to wish such a plight on a man—even someone as prune-faced as Greaves. Take it back."

"Oh, all right," Nicholas grumbled, his face reddening with shame. He dug his fingers into the Persian runner and clawed at the carpet. "I take back either the blindness or being struck deaf. But not both. It's champagne, Sophia."

It was well past their bedtime. And Langdon felt sure his parents would be most disappointed to know that the four were not asleep.

"Be reasonable, Nicholas," Langdon pleaded. "Mother is frightfully out of sorts because Lady Denham refused to come to the party. And Father is on edge because Mother will not stop discussing Lady Denham's refusal—even though she knows the woman is angry with her for having ordered a dress in the same fabric."

Dash playfully punched Nicholas on the arm. "He is right, as usual. We're young. There will be plenty of time for champagne. We needn't be in such a hurry."

Nicholas hung his head as he was wont to do whenever he did not get his way. "And if we die in our sleep tonight? What then? There is no champagne in heaven. Only angels and endless singing."

"I believe he is right—about the champagne, that is," Sophia chimed in sheepishly.

"*Et tu, Brute?*" Langdon asked the girl. "And after agreeing with me about Greaves?"

Sophia held up a finger in warning. "I agreed that four glasses could not be carried by one person. That was all."

"If it helps, I agreed with everything," Dash offered amiably. "Greaves scares me. He's all beetle-bug eyes and sloping forehead. But I would hate to die without having at least tried champagne."

Langdon looked at the three and sighed, knowing he was outnumbered yet again. "One glass and no more."

"Huzzah!" the three cheered, belatedly clamping

their hands over their mouths when Langdon shushed them.

"One glass, no more, and then to bed," Langdon instructed sternly. "Otherwise, I won't do it, I swear."

All three nodded this time, but Langdon wasn't going to fall for their tricks. "Say it. Out loud."

"I have heard champagne can have strange effects on some, including sleeplessness," Nicholas offered. "It would be impossible to make any promises *before* even setting our lips to the glass."

"Out. Loud."

"One glass, no more, and then to bed," the three children recited in near perfect unison, Nicholas's voice lagging just a touch behind the others.

"Very well," Langdon said, picking himself up off the floor and walking toward his room.

"But the stairs are *that* way, Langdon," Nicholas said, pointing in the opposite direction.

"Yes," Langdon acknowledged patiently. "But the stairs would lead me straight to the heart of our parents' party. Which is why I'm going to climb out the window to the tree, down the tree to Mother's cutting garden, and around to the library window."

Nicholas whistled in obvious appreciation. "I'm glad you are on my side, brother."

"But how will you climb back up the tree with a glass of champagne in your hand?" Sophia asked skeptically.

"Very carefully," Dash answered on his behalf. "If you break your arm, Lady Stonecliffe will have our heads. Come to think of it, Lord Stonecliffe will, too."

Nicholas bravely waved the warning off on his

brother's behalf. "The whole point is to *not* be careful. See what it is like to stray from the path of perfection, Langdon. You might even come to enjoy being bad."

Yes, Langdon realized, he was more than likely the only one of the four who'd given any thought to the future. And that was fine by him.

1

"You blackguard, I do not have to entertain your vile, hollow threats. I will go directly to the King and tell him of your actions. Entering my home by force and making demands of me? He will not look kindly on such behavior, I can tell you that much."

Dr. Rupert Crowther's furious words were clearly audible behind the false drawing room wall where Grace Crowther huddled with Mrs. Templeton, the Crowther household cook. The sheet of foolscap with the menu and market notes they'd been discussing only moments before was now crumpled, forgotten in Grace's clenched fist. The two women had hastily ducked into the hiding place when they'd heard Rupert responding to a pounding on the front door, not wanting to be found using his plume pen and ink.

But now it appeared they had much more important reasons to be hidden. Any mention of the King, the notorious leader of London's most feared gang, the Kingsmen, was truly cause for concern.

"Oh, will you?" The rough male voice that replied to Rupert held amusement and an unearthly, grating tone, as if the speaker were forcing the words out over gravel or broken glass. "And just who do you think ordered me to pay you a visit, eh?"

"I do not believe you." Panic leached through Rupert's words. "He would never hurt me or my wife. We have an agreement, the King and I. You are lying."

"Ah, now ain't this a shame." A labored sigh followed the words. "I am right disappointed, Doc. There you go, making assumptions. And you an educated man what's connected to the gentry, and all."

"What do you mean, assumptions?" Rupert's voice now held less terror and more hope.

"I am here for the woman, not you." Contempt laced the man's unnerving voice.

"As I said before," Rupert countered in a high, shrill tone, "the King and I have an agreement. My wife is not to be harmed."

"Should I kill you instead, hmm?" the man asked sarcastically.

"No," Rupert pathetically begged. "Not me."

Inside the hidey-hole, Grace covered her mouth to stifle a quick, disbelieving gasp, her palm faintly salty against her lips. A gift for cruelty came to Rupert with ease. Belittling and badgering counted amongst his favorite sports. And control . . . Grace gritted her teeth against the wash of scalding hate that instantly heated her cheeks. He had wanted to control her every move, every emotion—her very life. And when

Grace had failed to bend to his ways? The doctor's desire had only turned to deep-rooted loathing and contempt. Although she would never have planned to murder Rupert, she certainly wouldn't grieve his passing.

Beside her, Mrs. Templeton slid one arm around Grace's waist and pulled her protectively against her plump side.

Beyond the wall, the thud of heavy footfalls was accompanied by a string of filthy curse words. "The wife ain't here."

"She has to be. Everyone knows Mrs. Crowther never leaves this house," the first man replied, irritation making his rough voice even more of a growl. "Where is she, Doc? There's talk you tie the woman up for safekeeping."

"That is absurd and utterly false," Rupert replied with anger. "The minx has a gift for disappearing, is all."

Grace heard the meaty crack of a fist hitting flesh and Rupert cried out, groaning loudly.

"Perhaps she's in the kitchen below stairs. Spare me and I'll help you find her." Rupert's voice was filled with desperation, his breathing loud, coming in audible gasps. "As you said, it's Mrs. Crowther you want, not me. I'm no good to you dead."

Shock and outrage dragged a sharp breath from Grace and she closed her hand tighter over her lips to prevent any sound from escaping. Surely even a man as devoid of conscience as the doctor would recognize the need for atonement at such an hour. Would perhaps, even, welcome such a chance?

"You're no good to me alive, neither."

"No, no! You need me. I can find her, just give me some time. And you will be searching for the Queen's neck—"

Rupert's terrified words halted suddenly, dissolving into wet, gurgling sounds. The thud of something heavy hitting the carpet carried plainly through the wall separating Grace and Mrs. Templeton from the drawing room.

Grace bit her lip to keep from screaming, concentrating on the anger and hatred in her heart rather than the fear looming ever larger in her normally pragmatic mind.

"You did not need to do that, did you?" the second male voice commented.

"Useless, that one." The odd, gravelly voice of the first man was offhand, casual. "Forget about the doctor. Come help me with this desk drawer. It won't budge."

Both women jerked, startled by the loud screech of wood against wood. Grace's gaze flew to meet Mrs. Templeton's but the older woman appeared just as confused as she herself was.

"Not here." The man's voice held irritation. "Tear the house apart. Then we will go find the missus."

"I got no idea where to look for 'er," the second man complained. "You s'pose she got word we was comin'?"

Quick footsteps sounded on the servants' stairway.

"Let's ask whoever is coming up those stairs, shall we?"

Grace lunged for the lever to release the hidden panel, desperate to stop the unseen men from hurting a member of her staff. Mrs. Templeton grabbed her.

She wedged her body against the wood, holding Grace in a determined grip and blocking access to the entry.

Grace twisted, savagely pushing against the woman in an attempt to free herself. "That might be Mr. Templeton, or Timothy!" Grace barely breathed the words, frantic to protect her butler and errand boy.

Mrs. Templeton's arms remained wrapped tightly around Grace, pinning her hands against her sides. Her voice, barely audible even to Grace, quivered with fear. "I cannot let you do this, my lady. I won't willingly put you in the path of those jackals out there. I cannot. So stop your fighting. Mr. Templeton wouldn't hear of it. Neither would Timothy."

"Who the hell are you? And what are you doing in my mistress's house?"

Grace pushed Mrs. Templeton forward as she strained to reach the door.

"You will only make things worse, my lady." Mrs. Templeton's hushed words had become as implacable as her grip.

"I do not like your tone, boy."

Grace froze at the sound of the thug's reply, jerking in silent protest when once again, the sound of a fist hitting a body reached her ears. Timothy cried out.

"Tell me where your mistress is."

"I will not." Timothy's voice was defiant. "My lady always warned me that bargaining with the Kingsmen is the work of a fool. And I'm no fool."

Again, the thud of a fist meeting soft flesh was followed by a loud grunt of pain that carried clearly through the wall.

"We are not in the business of making bargains, boy," the coarse voice rasped. "Tell me where she is or I'll slit your throat just like I did the doctor's."

"I already gave you my answer," Timothy replied, still grimly defiant.

"Is that right?" the thug asked, his words holding only mild indifference. "You ought not to have used up all my patience, boy."

Grace made to scream, her violent cry for mercy cut short by Mrs. Templeton's plump fingers clamping across her mouth.

"I am not afraid of . . ."

Timothy's sentence dissolved into a sickening gurgle.

Grace gripped Mrs. Templeton's arm, barely feeling the pinch of the older woman's fingers as she did the same in reaction to the events outside their hiding place.

"I gave you fair warning, boy. Not my fault if you were too stupid to oblige."

The thud of Timothy's body as it fell to the carpet was loud in the otherwise silent passageway.

Grace's heart slammed, pounding in her ears as she strained to hear.

"The King won't like this at all—nor will the Queen, I am thinkin'." The second man's voice held unvarnished fear.

"Couldn't be helped. We'll find the valuables, then the wife. She can't have gone far."

Heavy footsteps sounded, the echo of the men leaving fading as they moved out of the room and down the hallway beyond.

Within the hidden passage, the two women remained motionless. It was a good while later when they heard the solid slam of the back door that led to the gardens and the mews beyond that they each drew a deep, shaken breath. Even then, they stood immobile, waiting several cautious moments more before truly believing the thugs had gone.

Then their grip on each other eased, and Mrs. Templeton removed her hand from Grace's mouth.

Without the support of Mrs. Templeton, Grace's cramped fingers and stiff limbs gave out and she sank to the floor. The rough planks were cold beneath her palms and fingers, echoing the icy chill of the blood moving sluggishly through her veins and freezing her tears.

Mrs. Templeton dropped to her knees beside Grace, her hands trembling as she reached out to offer comfort.

Grace squeezed the older woman's shaking hand in hers as she stared unseeing at the rough floor. The sound of Mrs. Templeton's quiet sobbing filled Grace's head. She could not understand what had just happened. Timothy was a big, strong lad of twelve, smart as he could be, and just as kind. Four years before, when Mrs. Templeton had discovered him boldly attempting to steal a pie cooling on a table near the kitchen door, she'd boxed his ears then asked Grace what should be done with the rascal.

Timothy had cried. Then Grace had cried. And Mrs. Templeton had followed right along. The boy was hired; one potential criminal saved from the streets, and a family was knit together out of odd scraps and old thread.

Family.

Grace lifted her skirt and reached for the knife she kept strapped to her thigh. She stood with the blade in her hand, bracing herself. "Come, Mrs. Templeton. We must hurry."

"My lady?" the cook asked, tears spilling down her cheeks as she looked up at her. "I can't go out there. Not with our dear Timothy . . ."

Grace swallowed hard. She dreaded the scene that she knew with deep certainty awaited them in the drawing room beyond the hidden panel. But she also recognized they had no time to waste. The killers would be back. She could not risk Mrs. Templeton's safety.

She tugged, urging the woman to her feet.

"You've no choice. Stay here and we will be found, as will Mr. Templeton. I need you to be strong. Can you do that for me?"

Mrs. Templeton nodded, her chin firming with purpose, and tightened her hold on Grace's hand.

"Good." Grace reached for the lever that would allow the panel to swing open. "Now, close your eyes. I will guide you. There's no need for you to see Timothy as he is now. Remember the lovely boy as he was."

She grasped the wooden handle and turned it, wishing she could also close her eyes.

Grace steeled herself, breathed a silent, fervent prayer, and pushed the door panel outward.

Langdon Bourne, the Earl of Stonecliffe, rubbed his tired eyes and then examined the deep wrinkles that crisscrossed his clothing. He attempted to stir some disgust within himself. Linen shirt, silk waistcoat, even his buff breeches looked as though the earl had recently slept in them—which he had. He could not remember when he'd last changed. Nor eaten a decent meal, for that matter. Or left the room he inhabited at present. And he did not particularly care.

Some would say his indifference was due to the urgent nature of the business at hand. As an agent for the Young Corinthians, a covert spy organization in service to the crown, Langdon had spent a long, grueling three days interrogating members of the Kingsmen.

Others would wonder if the recent marriage of Langdon's fiancée, Lady Sophia Afton, to his brother might have something to do with his detachment.

Both would be correct.

His entire life had been spent in the pursuit of what was right, honest, and true. Goodness was the ultimate goal. A true gentleman, who put family and honor first, the only role he ever possessed any desire to play. And where had all of his effort, his restraint, his sacrifice, his bloody goodness gotten him?

Langdon shrugged his wide shoulders as he considered the question. Nowhere. Or worse than nowhere—lost. He absentmindedly took in his surroundings for the hundredth time. The office supposedly occupied by the solidly respectable firm of Manx & Chisom was a fraud, though one would never suspect it to be so. Created by the Young Corinthians as a place for interrogation, the room's unadorned white walls, solid wood desk and chairs, and neat stacks of documents placed about the rooms proclaimed the resident to be a man who practiced law, not espionage.

What the spy organization set out to accomplish they did with single-minded determination, be it the minute details of the false office where Langdon now sat or the overthrowing of criminal gangs, duchies, and even countries. Formed during the reign of Queen Elizabeth, the Young Corinthians would have pleased Socrates, who so famously touted that necessity was indeed the mother of invention. Elizabeth's Golden Age had been a highly creative period in England's history, as well as a time of prosperity and peace—or so it looked on the surface. The Queen's father's reign had proven to be one of the bloodiest England had ever seen. As for the Virgin Queen? She had intended to end the Tudor dynasty on a high note and had ruled with a more moderate hand and forgiving heart.

But beneath the Virgin Queen's seemingly perfect empire? Plots, intrigue, and conspiracies brewed.

Queen Elizabeth was the target of many assassination attempts and conspiracies against her rule—a fact that did not please her particular friend and spymaster, Francis Walsingham.

In order to safeguard the Queen and her crown, Walsingham had formed the Young Corinthians and hidden the organization deep within the British government. The year was 1570. Though Walsingham had successfully defended the Queen countless times before, the infamous Ridolfi plot shook the spymaster to his core. An early supporter of the Northern rebellion, Florentine banker and ardent Catholic Roberto Ridolfi conceived of a plan that included support from abroad in a bid to bring Mary, Queen of Scots, to the throne.

The plot was foiled, the Queen saved. And the Young Corinthians were born.

Walsingham engaged those men whom he felt he could trust—in other words, nobles with a stake in the success of the Queen's empire. The spymaster recruited heavily from the ranks of dukes and earls, viscounts and barons. He funded the undertaking with his own coin and taught his recruits all that he knew about operating within the deep and murky world that lay beneath the shimmering façade of Elizabeth's Golden Age.

Now, nearly 250 years after Walsingham established his original band of noble spies, Langdon had already spent over a decade as a member of the Corinthians, their history as real to him as his own. He'd been but a boy of twelve when he'd first learned of the spy organization's existence. He, Sophia, Nicholas, and their friend Dash had found the lifeless body of Sophia's mother in the Aftons' country manor. The crime was somehow connected to the Young Corinthians and after the children had been inadvertently told of the organization's existence, they were sworn to secrecy. They were also assured that the agency would capture the killer, a task not one agent had managed to accomplish in the years that followed. Even as a boy, Langdon had known he was meant to find the man responsible and bring him to justice—as much for Sophia as for the boys.

Shortly after finishing his education at Eton, he'd joined the ranks of the Young Corinthians, just as he'd always planned.

His life goals had been determined and immutable. He would find the murderer and bring him to justice, marry Sophia, father an heir, and live the life he'd always known was his destiny as the Earl of Stone-cliffe.

Only resolution never came. The Corinthians' file contained clues to the Afton case but they were few and of little use. Henry Prescott, Viscount Carmichael, Langdon's superior, forbade him from officially pursuing any leads, convinced such activity would only further torment Langdon without purpose.

But Langdon did not agree. Apprehending the killer was Langdon's duty. His responsibility. And so he'd read through the case information until he could recite each line from memory.

Not that it had done much, if any, good.

Until recently, when a journal found hidden in the home of Dash's father—himself a retired Corinthian agent—had produced a lead. All three of Langdon's friends had pursued the new clues, discovering a link to the Kingsmen and one of their leaders, the Bishop. They had kept the existence of the journal a secret, convinced that Langdon would have insisted on involving the Young Corinthians.

Which he most surely would have, he thought grimly. Still, that was hardly the point. The three had called in the Corinthians to capture the Bishop and Langdon had learned the truth of their deception.

They'd betrayed him and endangered their lives when it was Langdon's case to solve. Even now, with Sophia married to Nicholas and no longer Langdon's fiancée, capturing the criminal remained Langdon's duty. Nothing else in his life had gone according to plan. He'd done as he should and forgiven Nicholas and Sophia when they'd revealed their relationship, and then insisted they leave the case in the capable hands of the Corinthians. Justice would be his. Something inside of Langdon felt altered—his neat, normally tidy interior had been ransacked and the contents of his mind and heart were out of place. A few bits and bobs had gone missing altogether. The only tie to his life before losing Sophia was his devotion to apprehending the killer. Solving the case would bring him back around to the man he'd once been and the only life he'd ever known.

Veni, vixi, vici.

I came, I lived, I conquered. The words—the Young Corinthians motto—were a faint murmur from Langdon's lips just as the heavy door opened and a fellow Corinthian ushered in yet another member of the Kingsmen, London's most powerful gang.

Langdon critically assessed the man as he took a seat in the only other chair, directly across the wide oak desk. He was tall and thin, dressed in a threadbare brown coat with pants that were a shade darker. His red vest and the once-white shirt that he wore beneath were stained, no doubt from food, and his square jaw and ruddy cheeks bristled with ginger beard stubble.

"Your name?" Langdon asked brusquely.

"Topper," the man answered with a grin that revealed yellow teeth, tipping his dirty, battered, and scarred high-crowned beaver hat.

Langdon folded his arms across his chest. "As I am sure you are aware, Topper, we've interviewed many of your fellow Kingsmen—nearly fifty of you, in fact, in relation to the untimely death of a man known as the Bishop. So you will forgive me if I forgo the niceties and get to the point: I want your legal, given name. The government requires such things, you see."

Topper nodded and raised one thick red-gold eyebrow in approval. "The guv'ment likes things neat and tidy like, right enough. I can see the sense in that. My name is Eugene Marks. Everyone calls me Topper, though, on account of—"

"Yes, the hat," Langdon interrupted, his voice gruff with irritation. Usually, he would find pleasure in the orderly nature of the required Corinthian paperwork. Name, age, known affiliations. Beginning with the basic necessities of an individual's life made sense to him. Much like the alphabet starting with A or one plus one equaling two, facts were reliable. Or they had been once.

Before Sophia and Nicholas . . .

Before the world as he'd known it, believed it to be, had been turned on its side.

Now, fact and fiction occupied the same space in Langdon's mind, each open to interpretation. He no longer had faith in any version.

Langdon stared hard at Topper and focused what

little energy remained in his exhausted brain on the criminal.

"I apologize, Mr. Mar—er, Topper," Langdon said, switching to the man's sobriquet when his bushy brows lowered with annoyance and he appeared about to object. Langdon had little time or patience to accommodate the other man. But he needed his cooperation, not his ire. Besides, a more sinister thought ghosted across his mind as he examined his actions. Impatient. Unprofessional. Neither word would have been used to describe Langdon in the past. He had to hold on to himself, before much more than Sophia slipped away. "As I said, we have spoken with many of your fellow Kingsmen. None have seen fit to share any information concerning the Bishop's death or who ordered it, despite the distinct advantages we've offered in exchange. I am sure you can understand how frustrating such a process can become—especially when no progress is made."

Langdon knew it was in his best interest to hold his temper with the man. But manipulation was an entirely different tool from anger. Topper had been bribed once in the past and had given up his immediate boss, the Bishop, in exchange for a sizable amount of coin. Langdon wondered whether the man's greed would sway him a second time.

Topper's beady eyes glinted from beneath his heavy brows. "Advantages, you say. And what kind of advantages might we be talkin' 'bout?"

Langdon was almost sure the man was salivating like a mangy dog peering into the butcher shop's window. His visceral distaste for Topper unnerved Langdon, but he focused on baiting the criminal.

"That depends on the quality of the information," Langdon answered, easing back in his chair. Despite tiredness, he watched Topper with wary eyes, analyzing his calculating expression.

Topper inhaled, his breath whistling through the gap separating his two front teeth. "I'll want passage to America and enough coin to get me settled in a new life."

"Afraid what you know will get you killed, eh?" Langdon said mildly. "That must be quality information, indeed."

"I am not afraid of anything, guv," Topper replied plainly. "But it is true enough I'd prefer to avoid a knife to the gut for a while longer. And what I have to tell you will take you to the King."

Langdon schooled his features into polite interest. "The mention of a king is hardly grounds for reward, Topper." Bile rose in his throat at the man's willingness to betray his boss. Clearly, honor was not a concept the man knew anything about.

"You can't go straightaway to the King—you ought to know that by now," Topper said, arching his thick brow with smug enjoyment. "Take notice of everything—that's what the Bishop told me. Even those things that do not seem important at all."

Langdon fought the urge to tell Topper he'd done nothing more than that for the last two weeks. Every incident within the Seven Dials district, where the Kingsmen were based, had been thoroughly investigated. And nothing had revealed a link to the man known as the Bishop.

"A man was found dead in Bedford Square recently,

ain't that right?" Topper asked, crossing one long leg over the other.

God, Langdon was tired of the man's face. Still, Topper had delivered on his promise once. He might do so again. "That is correct. He did not bear the Kingsmen tattoo, if that's what you are getting at."

"And who told you we've all been marked?"

No one had. Langdon, like his fellow Corinthians, had simply assumed all members of the Kingsmen were required to bear the tattoo of a chess piece on their right shoulder, just as all of the gang members they'd captured or interrogated had.

"Are you telling me differently?" Langdon countered, his interest sharpening, the scent and heat of a rekindled trail stirring in his belly.

Topper's scarred leather boot bumped the desk, the quick, rhythmic tapping giving away his nervous tension and belying his easy expression. "Soldiers carry the mark. Makes it easy to identify a body that's been maimed. But the generals and higher-ups aren't interested in being identified, you see. Quite the opposite for some of them."

"Even if you are telling the truth, what would one dead man have to offer me?" Langdon asked, disguising his piqued interest with subtle annoyance. "Nothing of note was found on the body. And he is far past talking."

"If you know what to ask, he has a message." Topper's boot stopped moving and the room grew eerily quiet. "Do we have a deal?"

"You will have to do better than a dead man, Topper." Langdon wasn't a man prone to lying. He'd ride the conversation out and if Topper had something useful to say he'd see to his request. But a rather large "if" stood between the ginger-haired man and freedom in America.

Topper's smile widened, indicating he was pleased with his progress. He leaned forward, his gleaming gaze fixed on Langdon. "That man? He was killed because of what you and your friends are up to."

2

"What would the King want with you?" Mrs. Templeton asked as she bustled back and forth across the length of Grace's room, grabbing up anything she could lay her hands on.

Grace stood in the center of her bedroom and stared at a painting that hung on the wall directly across from her bed. It was a landscape of minimal skill and featured a bucolic wave of rolling hills and green glens. When she'd first arrived at 3 Bedford Street, Grace assumed she disliked the work because it was homely.

Eventually, she realized there was every reason to loathe the picture. As she'd noted immediately, the artist lacked any real talent. And when one considered it hung on the wall of her prison cell? If not for her father's betrayal, she would never have come to reside at 3 Bedford Street. Lord Danvers had been a poor father, true enough. His constant state of inebriation had made any sort of meaningful connection with the man impossible. Grace could have lived with that. But when he'd gambled her away to Dr. Crowther in a game of chance? Grace's father ceased to exist altogether.

If not for Lord Danvers' betrayal, she never would

have darkened the door of the doctor's home, and Grace would have been spared the sight of the poorly executed painting.

"Honestly? I have no idea what he might want with me," Grace finally replied, fear shadowing her soul momentarily.

Mrs. Templeton flew past her en route to the wardrobe. Grace reached out and grasped the dear woman's elbow.

"And I've no intention of ever finding out," she added, forcing the woman to stand still. "Now, we need take only the essentials, Mrs. Templeton. Leave everything else."

Two days had passed since the doctor's and Timothy's brutal killings. Grace had ushered Mrs. Templeton out of the house and directly to the Dolphin Pub, where they had located Mr. Templeton. They'd been moving about the city for forty-eight hours, only now daring to return to the townhouse.

Mrs. Templeton gave Grace a pained look. "You cannot leave with only the clothes on your back, my lady. It isn't proper."

"Isn't it?" Grace asked, pulling the woman toward the window. "Then it is in keeping with the entirety of my tenure here. Besides, I want nothing that will remind me of my time with the doctor."

She unlocked the window and pushed up on its painted frame until the edge came level with her eyes. "Help me, will you?"

Grace turned and sat down on the narrow ledge, then leaned back and reached out with her right hand for a brick mortared in place in the far right corner.

Mrs. Templeton held on to Grace's left hand, her

strong, stocky body acting as an anchor. "No matter where we hide, you will require at least one change of clothing, my lady. And you cannot be expected to sleep on the coarse linens you find in a roadside inn. And what about your special tea? Hmmm? We will not be able to visit Master Chow's shop and you are nearly out of leaves."

Grace picked at the failing mortar around the brick with her index finger, closing her eyes as the chalky material flew from her efforts and dusted her face. "We will not require extra clothing, Mrs. Templeton. I plan on hiding us within the 9th Street's territory and I assure you one does not change for dinner in that section of London."

"Ninth Street?" her friend repeated with disbelief. "You could not find a more dangerous part of London, my lady—outside of St. Giles, that is. Bit like going from the frying pan into the fire, wouldn't you agree?"

Grace finished with the deteriorating mortar and brushed off her face. Opening her eyes, she grasped the brick with her fingers and pulled hard. "Which is precisely the point. If we've any luck at all, they will not think to look for me there."

The brick scraped along its neighbors and finally came free. Grace set it down on the sill then placed her hand in the space left behind. Her fingers grasped a coarse sack first. She tightened her hold and yanked. "In this bag is nearly enough coin for all three of us to leave London. Is your niece Rosie still employed by Huntleys in Bond Street?"

Mrs. Templeton nodded and took the bag with her free hand.

"We will take piece work from her as it becomes available," Grace explained, leaning out the open window once more. "And if my calculations are correct, we shall be in Devon before the new year."

She reached up once more and searched the hiding place, her fingers coming to rest on a second sack. This one was quite a bit smaller than the first. Made of the finest silk, with embroidered doves encircling the top, the bag was as familiar to Grace as her own face.

"And, if necessary, we shall sell this."

She grasped the bag and easily removed it from the hole. "Here," she prompted Mrs. Templeton, handing the silk bag to her friend then picking up the brick and returning it to its place.

"Never say such a thing," Mrs. Templeton breathed, pulling Grace back into the room. "It was your mother's, my lady."

The cook released Grace's hand and stood back, loosening the cords of the pouch and lifting a silver necklace from it. "When we first met, you wore this every day."

Grace had done many things differently when she first came to 3 Bedford Street. She'd still been nothing more than an optimistic, foolish girl, full of hope for her future despite all that had transpired. Yes, hers had been a childhood filled with the unpleasant effects of a father too fond of drink and gambling. And it was true he'd offered her up in a game of cards after spending every last coin he had, only to lose.

Still, Grace had held tight to her hope, believing the doctor could be a kind, caring man underneath his cold, leering facade.

She'd been proven wrong, of course, many times. The worst of which was when the doctor had stolen her mother's necklace and lost it gambling. He'd known what the keepsake had meant to her. It had been a gift given to her mother the year she'd come out. Each girl who'd attended Mrs. Van Allen's charm and grace classes had received one, all twelve of the necklaces alike save for the initials engraved upon the back of the heart-shaped pendant. Grace could see the empty spot on the dresser in her mind's eye—the one where she'd laid the necklace every night as she readied for bed.

The doctor had not even bothered to lie about stealing it. And that was when Grace had lost all hope for what her life *should* be and embraced the reality of what it was. She'd built a makeshift family with the Templetons and young Timothy and bided her time, saving every last coin she could get her hands on and waiting for the day there was enough to fund their escape to Devon.

After the theft, when Grace refused to accompany her husband to any social engagements or even leave the house with him, the doctor attempted to convince Grace of the depth of his regret by winning the necklace back. But he had been too late. Grace could not even look at the memento once it had been tainted by deceit.

And that was when the doctor had revealed who he really was. Grace had outlived her usefulness as his exquisite accessory. The verbal barrage of insults and slights that had intermittently tainted their marriage then began in earnest, leaving Grace no choice but to hide from her husband within their home.

She was a different person now. Much more strong and capable. Able to see situations and people for what they truly were. The world was a cold place. And so was Grace's heart.

Grace stood up and turned to push the window shut. "We are moving forward, Mrs. Templeton. Not looking back—never looking back." She latched the lock and looked out the window, realizing it would be the final time she took in the view from 3 Bedford Street.

"If you will not agree to bring anything else, then let us be gone from this wicked place," the cook urged, gently placing the delicate silk purse inside the larger sack and tying a knot.

Grace turned back and nodded, catching the homely painting from the corner of her eye. She walked to it and took it down from the wall.

"You cannot mean to take that painting?" Mrs. Templeton asked. "Truth be told, I never did care for it."

Grace held the picture low then put her foot through the canvas, satisfaction blooming in her chest at the sound of the hills and glens ripping beyond repair.

She was scared—more so than she'd ever been before. Grace decided fear was a good thing, at least for now. It would keep her running, and hopefully out of the Kingsmen's reach. "I never cared for it, either."

※ ※

"And you believe he is telling the truth?"

Langdon contemplated Henry Prescott, Viscount Carmichael's question as he surveyed the comfortable furnishings of the library in the Young Corinthians Club. He and Carmichael occupied two leather chairs set against the west wall. Ribbons of fragrant cigar smoke hung heavily in the air, enwreathing pairs and small groups of men as they discussed the day's news or, more likely, Corinthian business.

The club was comprised of agents and non-agents alike, but all men valued their privacy, making the premises ideal for such conversation.

"I do not have a choice, do I?" Langdon finally replied, all too aware of the frustration revealed in his tone. "I apologize, Carmichael. I am not myself these days."

Lord Carmichael took a slow sip of his brandy and swallowed, his keen gaze fixed on Langdon. "I would have to agree with you. But tell me, is it the Kingsmen, Stonecliffe? Or are other concerns troubling you?"

Lord Carmichael had known Langdon since he was a boy. He and Langdon's father had been dear friends and part of a closely knit group of families that included Sophia's parents. There was not a chance Carmichael misunderstood Langdon's statement, which meant he'd purposefully brought up the topic of Sophia.

"The Kingsmen, of course," Langdon said shortly, tamping down his frustration. "Surely you are as anxious as I am to move forward with the case. And Topper's information is all we have."

"I do wonder, though, if it is possible to separate the two—that is, the Kingsmen from Sophia." Carmichael took a second measured sip of the amber-colored liquid. His sharp gaze pinned Langdon.

Langdon stared at the man. He blinked, his mind racing to adjust. He couldn't quite believe what he was hearing. Carmichael's careful and painfully precise lectures to the men he led were the stuff of legend.

A legend Langdon could never have dreamt he would be written into. He'd always had the ability to spot those agents who'd one day find themselves staring across a desk at Carmichael. Their transgressions were varied and too many to count. Arrogance. Impatience. An inability to listen. A refusal to follow certain rules. What the sins all had in common was their ability to endanger both the men committing them and their fellow agents.

And Langdon fell prey to not one. It was not bravado nor competitiveness that drove him. But honor. And a strict moral code. The other men had often referred to him as the model Corinthian.

And now? he wondered, as he struggled to look his mentor in the eyes. *What drives you? Now that you've reaped the bleak rewards of an honorable life?*

He knew he should appreciate the older man's interest, but he could muster nothing more than embarrassment. "I promise you, Carmichael, I am as committed as ever—no, that is wrong," he amended grimly. "I am *more* committed than ever to finding Lady Afton's killer. Of that you can be sure."

"Is that the wisest course of action, Stonecliffe?" Carmichael asked, finishing his drink. "Even if Sophia was not the love of your life—"

"With all due respect, Carmichael, I do not think you are in any position to suggest that I did not love

Sophia," Langdon interrupted, his clipped words revealing more than he would have preferred.

Carmichael held his glass aloft to signal a waiting servant. "You are absolutely correct, Stonecliffe." He paused while the liveried footman took the glass from his hand and departed. "Though I did not say you did not love Sophia. What I suggested was that you were not *in* love with her. Two very different things."

"Is there a difference?" Langdon challenged, straightening his blasted cravat, which refused to lay as it should. "And even if there is, what is done is done. There is no denying . . ."

Carmichael's questions had laid open feelings that were still raw—and made Langdon further aware of the subtle, sneaking changes in himself. A rumpled appearance was out of character for him, but it was easily remedied. What Carmichael hinted at—that Langdon's ability to do his job may have been compromised? That would be the end of him.

"There is no denying that the two are *in* love," Carmichael finished for him.

"This conversation is not necessary," Langdon assured his superior, tugging at his too-tight cravat one more time. "It is work that will set me right. I am sure of it."

Carmichael methodically twisted the gold signet ring on his left hand. "You are rattled—and rightly so. Any man in your position would be. But you are a Corinthian and this case is important to many people."

Langdon's fingers tightened around his glass. "It is all I have left, Carmichael," he answered with brutal truthfulness. He flicked a quick glance around the room, relieved when no one appeared to be paying any attention to their quiet conversation. "You cannot assign me elsewhere. Lady Afton's murderer has always been mine to find. Even though Sophia married Nicholas, not me, that has not changed."

Carmichael studied Langdon, his gaze somber as he clearly considered his words. "And if, for whatever reason, you are unable to continue with the investigation," he asked, "I have your word you will willingly give the case over to another agent?"

"You have my word."

Langdon was not lying. But he knew in his bones he would be the one to solve the case—or die in the attempt.

"Very well," Carmichael replied, releasing the ring. "Tell me exactly what Topper revealed."

Langdon mentally lowered his hackles and cleared his throat. "According to Topper, the Kingsmen are nervous. The Bishop's capture forced the gang to realize they are vulnerable. So they've sent a message to all who would consider betraying them by eliminating a key advisor to the King. Oddly enough, the man is not anyone we are familiar with, nor is he a high-ranking member of the gang. He is a doctor."

"A doctor?" Carmichael asked, puzzled.

"Yes, one Robert Crowther. Apparently a distant relative to someone within the peerage."

"And husband to Lady Grace Audley," Carmichael added, disapproval coloring his tone and pinching his features.

"Audley?" Langdon repeated, letting the name linger on his tongue as he waited for some spark of recognition. "Yes, now I remember. Lord Danvers's child, correct? I remember hearing rumors about the wastrel gambling his daughter away in a game of cards while I was on the Continent. Are you telling me Crowther was the very man Danvers wagered?"

Carmichael nodded. "I am. The shame and sorrow killed her mother. And Lord Danvers perished in a riding accident no more than six months after. No one within the ton has seen nor heard from Lady Grace since."

"Something we have in common with the London underbelly, apparently," Langdon replied, searching his mind for a mental image of Lady Grace but drawing a blank. "According to Topper, Lady Grace vanished from Crowther's house at the time of the doctor's death. The Kingsmen are intent on finding her."

"Then we must find her first," Carmichael said with deadly certainty.

"Precisely."

3

Langdon reclined back onto the silk-draped bed and rested against the massive mahogany headboard. Waiting for Serena to appear was always interesting and this visit promised to be no exception. Madame Frie's girls attracted men from all over the city of London, the brothel infamous for catering to the most exotic of tastes. The sounds that seeped through the walls were often recognizable grunts of pleasure and ecstasy. And then there were times when Langdon could not figure out just what sort of act could produce the noises he'd heard.

Presently, a gong featured prominently in Natasha's room next door. An Asian motif, perhaps?

The door slowly opened and Serena appeared in the doorway. She struck a dramatic pose, her seductive stare stirring Langdon's senses. "It is not polite to listen, Dorogoi."

"Is that so?" Langdon asked, beckoning for her to come in.

Serena stepped across the threshold, her scarlet silk chemise and matching nightrail whispering with each step. She closed the door and padded across the thick Aubusson carpet. "Very impolite," she assured him as she climbed up onto the bed. "You look tired—and troubled. This is not the man I know. Let me ease your mind." She winked at him wickedly then reached for his cravat.

Langdon gently refused her offer, Serena's observations pricking his worn patience. "That is not the nature of our relationship, but thank you for your concern."

"You do know what Serena was trained for, yes?" she asked, her sarcasm only made more adorable by her thick accent.

Langdon smiled at his friend. Serena had supplied him with information for the past five years—and nothing more. They had never made love and they never would. "I respect you too much to ask such a thing of you. Besides, you might find me lacking and decide to never see me again."

"Impossible," she muttered, her gaze languishing on his nether regions.

Langdon reached inside the hidden pocket in his coat and produced a velvet pouch. "I believe this will cheer you up."

Jewels made Serena happy. And Langdon liked to see her happy. She'd never spoken of her life before the brothel, but in his experience, one did not end up a prostitute unless something in their past had gone terribly wrong.

"You should not have," Serena cooed as she took the offered gift and opened it. "But I am very glad you did!" She scooped up the emerald earrings and examined them in her hand. "They are my favorite, Dorogoi. Of course, this is not new information to you. And new information is what you need, is it not? Tell me, what can I give you?"

Langdon watched her clip one of the earrings to her right ear, the candlelight catching the jewel's brilliance in fiery fashion. "Dr. Rupert Crowther. Do you know of him?"

"The King's man, yes?" Serena asked, clipping the second earring on. "I do not think the doctor will be of much use to you, Dorogoi. He is dead." She crawled across his legs and reached out for a handheld mirror that rested on the table next to the bed.

"I know. It is not the doctor that I want. It is his wife, Grace."

Serena scooted back to her original position and held the mirror up to her face. "What would you want with a dead man's wife?"

Langdon watched Serena as she admired the new baubles. "I want to get to her before the Kingsmen do. I want to save her life."

Serena continued to look in the mirror, but her mind was clearly working. She held the weight of one of the dropped emeralds between two fingers as though trying to decide if the doctor's wife for a pair of earrings was a fair trade.

"You will not harm her, Dorogoi? Give me your word."

Langdon reached out and took the mirror from Serena, then held her tiny hand in his. "I give you my word. She will be safe, Serena."

"No woman is safe in London," she replied with wisdom that outmatched her years.

Langdon's heart pinched at the sound of her voice. On several occasions in the past he'd offered to pay Serena's way out of the city and set her up with a cottage on one of his properties. But she had refused and would never tell Langdon why, only that jewels were harder to come by in the country.

"Mrs. Crowther will be safe, Serena," Langdon assured her. "If I get to her first."

Serena fiddled with the earring as she thought, finally releasing the jewel and letting it slowly swing. "Do you know, I believe you should buy me another gift, my Dorogoi. There is a shop, Huntleys, on Bond Street. Give them my name—but do be discreet. Mrs. Crowther does not boast many friends, yet those she has are very loyal to her."

"Thank you, Serena," Langdon said, then released her hand and made to leave.

Serena put it on his chest and smiled. "Must you go? I think Natasha will be finished with the gong soon."

"You are persistent," Langdon praised her, then placed his feet on the floor and stood.

Serena rose up on her knees and placed her arms about Langdon's neck. "Then be safe, Dorogoi. The Kingsmen are not to be trifled with."

※ ❧

Grace watched Mrs. Templeton stoke the pitifully small fire. "I promise you, the moment we are able, we will leave this place."

Mrs. Templeton attempted to hide her shivering with an exaggerated shrug of her shoulders. "We've a roof over our heads, my lady. That is all we need."

The steady plunk-plunk of raindrops as they fell into the bucket from the leak in the dismal building's roof tempted Grace to argue. Instead, she turned her attention to the delicate silk shift on her lap. "Thank heavens for Rosie," she said, holding up the sewing project to inspect the tiny, perfectly set row of stitches. "Two more months of seamstress work and we will have saved sufficient funds to leave London."

And disappear. Grace had dreamt of little else since her forced marriage to Rupert Crowther. And why wouldn't she? Her lackluster upbringing had been eclipsed in sadness by her marriage to the doctor. With each year her life had become more difficult and dangerous.

At the time of her marriage, some whispered she'd deserved what she had received. Grace knew she'd been a foolish girl, taking for granted all that she had in comparison to so many others. When her father had gambled her away to the doctor, she'd felt anger, even rage.

And fear. No one, no matter how foolish they'd been, deserved to be wagered in a card game.

No one deserved to be lost.

The quick stab of pain from the prick of her needle roused Grace from her pointless contemplation. She squinted as the candle's dim flame quivered in the night air that seeped through the ill-fitting window frame. Finding no blood, she continued her sewing, her stitches fine and detailed, creating delicate embroidered flowers on the white silk.

Ten years had passed. Grace no longer actively hated her father for what he'd done. Such an intense emotion required too much of her. And even worse, contemplation insisted that she accept her plight as something never-ending. Unchangeable. Doomed.

Grace would be damned to perdition before she

ever again allowed another person to decide her fate. She'd bided her time, hiding household funds from the doctor, and planning for the moment she could escape from London for the countryside, the Templetons and young Timothy in tow.

Grace pricked her finger again and swore indelicately under her breath. She could not think about Timothy. Not now that the Kingsmen had changed the game. That they'd killed the doctor did not surprise her. It had been bound to happen. But what possible reason did they have for wanting to kill an innocent boy? And in pursuit of her? Why?

A low, soft knock sounded at the door.

The two women froze in alarm.

"Should I wake Mr. Templeton?" Mrs. Templeton asked, her voice tense.

Grace set aside the sewing and rose from her chair, giving her companion what she hoped was a look of reassurance. "I know he stays awake all night and keeps watch over us. Let him sleep now. It is only Rosie at the door, I am sure of it. She forgot to take the finished work with her when she dropped off the new batch earlier."

"It is just the two of us, then." Mrs. Templeton used the fireplace poker to help her stand.

"I'll let Rosie in. You must rest," Grace instructed gently, gesturing for the older woman to reclaim her seat.

Mrs. Templeton bent to lean the poker against the chipped stone fireplace before wrapping her woolen shawl more tightly about her shoulders. "I've already made the effort and am up now. Let me see if we've any tea for the dear girl."

Grace stood aside and allowed Mrs. Templeton to leave the drawing room first, then followed, turning right toward the entry while the cook turned left and disappeared down the short hall. She picked up the completed sewing repairs from a scarred table and reached for the door handle, the brown-paper-wrapped parcel, neatly tied with a string, in her free hand.

"I am sorry you had to return, Rosie," Grace began as she pulled the thin wooden door open. "I am sure I do not know what I was thinking when I forgot to—" She broke off, eyes widening in shock and surprise.

A large man, a stranger, stood on the threshold, his broad physique outlined by the poorly lit hallway that cast his face in shadow.

"Mrs. Grace Crowther?"

His deep voice was refined and polite, deferential, even. No one had spoken to her in such a manner, with just that touch of respect and inquiry, for a very long time. Grace nearly let herself ignore the peal of alarm bells sounding in her head.

"You must have the wrong residence, sir," Grace replied, her senses returning. She moved to shut the door but the man placed his boot in the way and pushed solidly on the wood.

Instantly, fear raced through her and Grace kicked him in the knee and threw her weight against the door, widening her stance to push with all her strength.

He bit off a curse at the solid contact with his knee and pushed back, inexorably gaining ground.

Grace slid across the scarred wood floor, staggering backward, off balance.

"I apologize, Lady Grace." The stranger stepped fully into the entryway, closing the door behind him. "That was not how I wished for us to meet."

Grace batted his large hand away and opened her mouth to scream.

He hauled her up by her shoulders and clamped his fingers over her mouth, muffling her shriek. "You are making it quite difficult for me to remain a gentleman, my lady."

Grace needed for him to stop calling her a lady. Her heart pounded frantically, her breath catching as she struggled to pull in air. She planted her palms against his chest and shoved, desperate to gain some distance from his imposing build. The expensive wool superfine of his coat and the rough silk of his waistcoat were barely remembered textures under her fingertips. The heavy male muscles beneath the elegant gentleman's clothing went rock hard and he froze. The air surrounding Grace was suddenly fraught with tension, heated and dangerous. She focused her attention on his expertly tied cravat, wondering frantically if it would be suitable for choking.

Unable to free herself, she bit down on his middle finger until she tasted the faint copper flavor of blood.

The man grunted with surprise, but his hand remained. "I have no interest in harming you, but you must promise me you will not scream if I remove my hand," he ordered implacably, adding, "and never bite me again."

Grace's cheeks flushed at his words. In her world, biting a man was nothing more than one of many weapons in a woman's arsenal. Even a doctor's wife could not rely on the decency of the male sex—in fact, assuming every last man had dishonorable intentions made for a far less surprising life.

This man, though ... This man ... Grace's gaze moved higher, until her eyes met his. They were beautiful eyes. Fringed with thick lashes, they were a warm, deep umber that soothed her frantic nerves. His gaze was intent, focused on hers with an alert awareness that reflected sharp intelligence. But she sensed no corruption of character there and she abruptly realized that while his hold was immovable, it was also careful, as if he didn't want to hurt her.

This man was not with the Kingsmen. The sudden conviction flooded Grace.

He did not have to be a Kingsmen to be dangerous, her head replied, flattening any hope that might have been building in her chest.

Nevertheless, Grace nodded in reply to his earlier statement, signaling her agreement to not scream.

The man studied her face, his dark brows lowering as he did so. "I hope you are not lying to me. I cannot abide lying."

He slowly lifted his hand from her mouth and released her, stepping back until there was a respectable distance between them.

"Your name, sir?" Grace pressed her fingertips to her lips in an attempt to erase the feel of his hand against her mouth. She could still taste him, a not unpleasant combination of soap and a hint of salt.

He took a handkerchief from an interior pocket of his unbuttoned, caped greatcoat and offered it to Grace. "Clark."

No one within St. Giles was stupid enough to answer such a question honestly. "And now, your true name?" Grace accepted the pristine white cloth and blotted her lips. The cloth held the scent of his cologne and she breathed in the faint odor of citrus and sandalwood.

"That *is* my real name."

Mrs. Templeton appeared at the end of the hall, hidden from the stranger's view, a heavy pan clutched in her hands. Grace waved the hanky, her gaze fastened on the man before her even as she signaled the older woman to stay where she was.

"I do not believe you, but I'll not allow you to waste one minute more of my time than is absolutely necessary," Grace answered, frowning at him. "Now, tell me what you have come for, Mr. *Clark*."

He conceded their uncomfortable situation with a lifting of his chin. "Sadly, most of what I propose will not be to your liking. Still, in return I offer you your freedom—and your companions' as well," he said, turning to look down the hall, his gaze fixed unerringly at the place where Mrs. Templeton hid. "Do come out of the dark, woman. I have business with your mistress, but it concerns you, too."

Mrs. Templeton captured the man with a cold stare as she walked toward him. "Is that right? Perhaps I will wake my husband. You can tell the three of us why we should listen to what you have to say rather than braining you with this pan," she replied, raising the heavy cast-iron weapon with obvious intent.

"I understand your trepidation. But before you do away with me, first hear what I have to say, please.

Then decide." The stranger gestured toward the drab sitting room. "Shall we sit?"

Mrs. Templeton lowered the pan as she moved to Grace's side. "He seems polite enough," she proclaimed, rolling her shoulders back with false confidence.

Grace knew they had no choice in the matter, but she grudgingly appreciated the intimidating man's sensitivity in dealing with her companion. "I agree," she said, taking Mrs. Templeton's arm and leading her toward the warmth of the fire. "We will listen to your proposal, sir."

Grace took the heavy pan from Mrs. Templeton and waited while the older woman carefully lowered herself to the chair.

"Now, Mr. . . ." Grace paused, eyeing the stranger as he surveyed the room. "Clark."

The pan was heavy in Grace's hand. Still, she held on to the makeshift weapon, though she suspected it would be of little use against Mr. Clark. He wore the clothes of a gentleman, but the muscles that flexed beneath his breeches and linen shirt must surely belong to a man who undertook some sort of physical labor.

He removed his greatcoat and crossed the room to Mrs. Templeton. "If I may?" he asked, and then proceeded to tuck the warm wool about her without waiting for her answer.

As he bent to his work, Grace cast a critical eye across his wide shoulders and lean back, looking lower to where his waist tapered then gave way to a finely formed backside.

Grace gripped the pan tighter, her knuckles aching

from the effort. "Now, Mr. Clark," she said firmly, watching as he stood upright and turned around. "If you will have a seat?"

"Once you are seated, my lady," he replied, and waited.

"I am no longer a lady, Mr. Clark," Grace told him. "And I will stand."

4

Langdon fought the urge to pull her back into his arms. Ever since she'd planted her small hands against his chest and pushed him earlier, his already shaky hold on what was once legendary control had threatened to dissipate like smoke. Every muscle in his body had strained against releasing her. He had barely managed to remain still while he fought down a nearly overwhelming urge to haul her in tight. He'd never reacted to a woman with such gut-deep possessiveness before. He'd lusted after women, of course—with varying degrees of intensity. But this. Good God, this was not just lust. He'd actually heard the word "mine" roaring inside his head.

Carmichael would never let it go if he knew.

The image of his superior's disappointment grounded Langdon and he drew a deep breath.

"As you wish," he managed to say evenly, claiming a battered chair directly opposite Mrs. Templeton.

If he squinted at Lady Grace, Langdon could still see a remote glimmer of a lady of the ton, but only faintly. The woman's hands bore the telltale signs of a seamstress. She was far too slender and slight for good health, and there were dark shadows beneath her eyes.

Still, her fragile bone structure, iridescent skin, and diminutive stature were deceptive outer trappings for the strength of her character and resolve, which shone like burnished gold through her intelligence and spirit. This was a woman who had suffered and miraculously not been broken by her torment, but instead grown stronger. She held herself with an innate dignity that humbled him.

And it occurred to Langdon with sudden insight that she'd come through the trials forced on her with far more grace than he had. He'd been betrayed by fiancée and brother, but Grace had been betrayed by father and husband. Yet he saw no lines of bitterness carved on her face or bracketing her soft, full mouth. Even beneath the sadness that clung to her like a voluminous cloak, she was strikingly, incandescently beautiful.

"Now, Mr. Clark, I will hear your proposition."

Lady Grace's directive was undercut by the weary note that lay beneath her refined tones. According to Topper, she'd been on the run for three days—holed up in rented rooms and abandoned buildings. Clearly, the dangerous game of hide-and-seek that she was playing with the Kingsmen was taking its toll on her physical strength. Langdon was tempted to insist she sit down and rest, but suspected the pan would be put to good use if he tried.

"What I propose will be mutually beneficial," Langdon said, assuring Lady Grace, and himself, that what he offered her was of value. "I need your help to put an end to the Kingsmen once and for all. In return, I will pay you the amount needed to see you safely out of London and settled in a place of your choosing."

"What makes you think I am able to offer such a service?" Lady Grace asked, frowning as she began to pace slowly back and forth across the cheap, faded rug.

Langdon watched her walk. He could not look away. Everything about her fascinated him, drew his attention, and demanded his complete focus. He knew fighting the compulsion was the right thing to do. But for the moment, he gave in to the lure and enchantment of eyeing her slender figure as she moved. Despite her obvious exhaustion, her carriage remained strong, even regal, as she awaited his answer. It took a moment for him to realize she'd asked a question and was awaiting a reply.

"The Kingsmen believe you can, and that is good enough for me."

"I rarely left my home over the last ten years, Mr. Clark. How would I have managed to collect any information that would be useful to you?"

Langdon knew of the secret rooms in the home she shared with the doctor. Used by Catholic priests during the Reformation, many lambs of God had been saved from slaughter within the walls of the Bedford Square residence. He'd also done enough digging to learn Lady Grace had friends in the Dials. "Come, Lady Grace, do not lie to me. I know of your hiding places, the friendships you secretly constructed—Rosie, for one. You have not spent the last ten years locked away, of that I am sure."

Lady Grace did not so much as flinch at Langdon's words. She merely continued to pace with the ridiculous pan clutched in her hands. "That may be true. But I promise you, I am not lying. I am unaware of any specific information or connection that would lead to the Kingsmen's destruction. Trust me, Mr. Clark. If I knew of such a weapon I would have employed it long ago."

"It is entirely possible that you do hold the key but are not consciously aware of its existence," Langdon replied, satisfied that she was indeed telling the truth. "An overheard conversation, perhaps, or an intercepted letter concerning the gang—something you were not meant to hear or see. The most important of clues can go undetected if you are not looking for them."

Lady Grace eyed Langdon with consideration. "As you so astutely pointed out, I have not been biding my time the last ten years. How could I have missed something so important? It seems nonsensical."

"You were searching for the obvious—proof that tied the Kingsmen to illegal activities, yes?" Langdon asked, though he already knew the answer. "Perhaps there was a piece of information, or a person out of place, that may have given you pause for a moment—but only just."

Lady Grace grimaced as she thought on his words. "I have been over and over the conversation between my husband and his murderer—and I cannot think of what this information might be."

"Conversation?" Langdon said, sitting forward in his chair.

Lady Grace fidgeted for a moment with the handle of the pan. "I could not see him. Mrs. Templeton and

I were tucked away in the hidden room. But I heard him—heard everything that transpired."

"Your husband's death, you mean?" Langdon asked, such poking about in her privacy leaving him cold.

"And Timothy's," she answered, then looked at Mrs. Templeton. "Our errand boy. The man killed our Timothy."

The stark pain reflected in her eyes cut at Langdon. "The name of the killer?" he asked.

"No name was revealed. Only the fact that it was me they were after, not my husband."

"Are you certain?" Langdon asked as he thought back on Topper's words. The man had implied it was the doctor who was of importance. *Not* Lady Grace.

She tucked a piece of stray hair behind her ear and addressed Langdon with businesslike indifference, the emotions disturbed by the talk of Timothy apparently stacked and put away. "Absolutely. The man told Rupert as much. So there you have it, Mr. Clark. Now, if I agree to help you, how would we proceed?"

The answer to Lady Grace's question was of his and Carmichael's careful making. The Corinthians could no longer expect to bring down the Kingsmen without a bargaining chip.

Lady Grace was in need of money. The Corinthians were in need of information. An exchange of goods, nothing more.

As he and Carmichael had discussed it, the plan had seemed sound and well conceived. Relatively simple, even.

But that was before he had met Lady Grace. Now he wished he had an alternative to offer her. Any option would be preferable to what he had to say next. She didn't deserve this. But he had no choice. He knew it. Acknowledged it. Yet it did not help the guilt that ate at him.

He pinched the bridge of his nose, the pressure focusing him on the task—on his duty.

"Now you become my mistress."

Mrs. Templeton squeaked with outrage, fairly quivering with offense. "Leave my lady's home this instant, you, you . . ."

She sputtered, clearly searching for an appropriate insult as she pointed to the door.

Langdon took advantage of her loss for words and stood, raising his hands in a show of caution. "I must offer the Kingsmen something they cannot refuse. She would be my mistress in name alone. I give you my word."

Lady Grace showed neither disgust nor disinterest as she considered his proposal. "I am to be bait, then?"

"You would be under my protection, my lady," Langdon answered, hoping his reassurance was enough to lessen the insult of the proposal. "I would give my life before any of the Kingsmen came near enough to harm you or your friends."

Mrs. Templeton struggled to her feet, anger radiating from her stout frame. "My lady, surely you are not considering what he asks? This venture is certain to be dangerous, and no money is worth your life. And what of your good name? It has been sullied enough by the doctor, wouldn't you agree?"

"I do not make promises lightly, Mrs. Templeton," Langdon told the companion. "Lady Grace would be under my watch, or that of my men, every moment of the day and night. Five of them stand outside the building as we speak. She would never be without protection."

Lady Grace walked to Mrs. Templeton and took the woman's hand in hers. Her finely cut features were pale, and when she spoke, her voice throbbed with emotion, a faint echo of raw pain audible beneath the determinedly practical words. "My name was ruined long ago—by my father's heartless act, not the doctor's." She turned so that her face was hidden from Langdon's view.

"As for my life?" she continued in a hushed tone. "This man's offer is no more dangerous than the Kingsmen's presence in my husband's life, and thus in mine, for the last ten years—only he is willing to pay for the privilege. It is a chance, Mrs. Templeton. One that will surely not come again. I must see you and Mr. Templeton safe, you know I must," she pleaded. "If I am able to, our dearest Timothy will not have died in vain."

"And if we lose you, too?" the older woman asked anxiously. "I could not bear it, my lady."

Langdon looked on as Lady Grace reassuringly patted the woman's arm, such tender care serving to remind him of his own uncomfortable role in the situation.

"Am I really in a position to refuse?"

"My lady, surely there are other ways than this . . ." Mrs. Templeton countered weakly.

Langdon bowed his head. Mrs. Templeton knew it was a lie, as did Lady Grace. But no one was more aware of it than he. He wanted to tell Lady Grace that she didn't have to play the part—that he'd take her away from here and keep her safe. He and Carmichael were damn near blackmailing her. The knowledge that he had to use her grated on his already raw nerves. Still, it couldn't be helped; he had no choice.

"Now, who are you, Mr. Clark?" Lady Grace stepped away from her friend and turned to Langdon, stopping in front of him. Her direct gaze probed his as if testing for truth. "I will know who I am speaking to before I give you my answer."

Her eyes were rimmed in tears. Lady Grace was strong—fierce, even. Still, such a decision would cut clean through the heart of a woman who held strong moral principles and who had once dreamed of a much different life.

Langdon wanted to tell her that he understood. That he, himself, had mourned the loss of the future he had been assured was his when he'd been forced to let the woman he loved marry another.

He thought over the conversation with Carmichael. They had failed to take into account *who* Lady Grace was. She'd only been considered in terms of *what* she was able to provide.

Standard protocol, you imbecile, Langdon told himself. Emotions had no place in the plan. They could not. Not if he wanted to find Lady Afton's killer.

"Langdon Clark," Langdon answered, cursing himself for such softness. "Of the Hills Crossing gang, out of Liverpool."

"No gentleman, indeed," Mrs. Templeton hissed, eyes narrowed in anger. "Come away, my lady. Please.

You've just rid yourself of Dr. Crowther and this man is no better."

"But that is just it, Mrs. Templeton," Lady Grace answered the woman, continuing to stare at Langdon. "As long as I stay in London, I will be a wanted woman. Would I prefer Mr. Clark to be a reputable, honest businessman? Of course. But if it takes a more powerful gang to free me of the Kingsmen, then so be it."

She held out her hand and waited for Langdon to take it. "I agree to your terms, Mr. Clark. I will help you destroy the Kingsmen. And in return, you will provide me with funds, a home in the country, safe passage, and a guarantee that I will never again have to set eyes on this cursed city."

Langdon should have been relieved. Instead, there was a sense of loss, as if he was about to bargain away a piece of his decency. He took Lady Grace's hand in his, her delicate fingers fitting perfectly in his as they shook to seal the agreement. "We have a deal."

❦

"Who is he, this Mr. Clark?"

Adolphus Beaufort looked toward the carriage window and was able to make out a sliver of sky between the gap in the dark curtains. He preferred to meet the Queen after dark near the Serpentine rather than within the confines of her coach. He did not need to know what she looked like in order to understand it was dangerous to be in a confined space with the woman.

She'd been unnerving since their first meeting. And once the Bishop, her second in command, had been captured and the entire organization compromised? The Queen was unraveling right before Beaufort's eyes.

"Word has it he is up from Liverpool, my Queen," Beaufort replied, focusing on brief glimpses of the billowy blue wisps. "He's diversified—has his hands in smuggling, burglary, prostitution, guns for hire."

A letter had arrived only yesterday, passed from one grubby gang member's hand to the next, addressed to the King. In it, Langdon Clark explained he was coming to London for pleasure, purportedly. He had requested an audience with the King and cited their shared interest in enterprise. No mention was made of specific issues to be addressed, but the message was there, hidden between the lines of the man's precise handwriting.

Beaufort found the threat a welcome one. Years of playing the puppet King to the Queen's iron fist had worn him down. He wanted out—away from the Kingsmen. Away from her, before she went completely mad.

"Do you consider him a credible threat?" she asked, her throaty voice faintly muffled by the veil she wore.

Beaufort weighed his words. The Queen only came out of hiding to meet with him in person when she was nervous. She was unpredictable at the best of times, unstable at the worst.

Did she want him to say that, yes, the Kingsmen were susceptible to a rival gang's threat? Or did she want him to lie?

Beaufort rued the day he'd agreed to her terms to

act as the leader of the Kingsmen. Yes, he was now a very wealthy man with an entire criminal organization devoted to him—or to the idea of him, as it were. No one save the recently deceased Dr. Crowther knew of the Queen's real role within the Kingsmen. She, and she alone, controlled the gang from a distance. Not once had she told Beaufort why her identity must be kept secret, and he'd never asked. The more he learned of her, the less he liked her. She had a head for business, but she also had a ruthless dark side that outmatched any criminal he'd ever encountered.

Crowther's death had been carried out on direct order from the Queen.

Beaufort was far more valuable than the doctor had been, of course—at least for now. But one could never be too careful when it came to the Queen. She was as coldly calculating as any man he'd worked for in his checkered past and twice as driven.

"Well, I do not know that I would call him a 'threat,' my Queen," Beaufort answered, attempting to lighten the discussion. "He'll be in town for the Pimfield auction and thought it wise to introduce himself."

The Queen huffed lightly. "Some sort of criminals' code, I suppose he wants us to believe?"

"More likely an attempt on his part to make himself seem more important than he is," Beaufort replied, relieved by her lack of tyrannical response. "Everyone knows the Kingsmen run London. Seems only fitting the underlings would come to pledge their fealty. At least to my way of thinking."

Beaufort hazarded a glance at the woman, the scant

light in the coach illuminating a thin-lipped smile of satisfaction behind her veil.

"You know I loathe false flattery, Beaufort," the Queen warned, her distaste for his attempt lacing her tone. "But I see no reason to deny the man his request. It will give us the opportunity to see what we are dealing with in the south. One can never have enough information when it comes to an opponent."

Opponent. So the Queen was concerned. Beaufort would need to tread lightly.

"Agreed," he said, returning his gaze to the curtained window. "I'll ask Rufus to make the arrangements."

"I'll not allow an imbecile such as Rufus to handle the matter," she ordered, reaching out to grip the cushion as the carriage swung wide. "The Kingsmen are the most powerful organization in London—in all of England, according to those who have knowledge of such things. It will not do to give this Mr. Clark the impression that we are anything less. Send Mitchell."

Marcus Mitchell was a tall, handsome man with a keen mind and an even keener eye when it came to shooting a pistol. He had been a promising young lawyer when the Kingsmen had come across him. He'd run up a gambling debt at the Four Horsemen, operated by the Kingsmen. He'd pledged his gun to the gang in exchange for the money to pay off his debt—intent, Beaufort had heard tell, on leaving as soon as he could.

But the Queen had found him too valuable to set free.

There was never a way to win with her. In favor,

you were doomed to a life of service. Out of favor, you were demoted to death.

Mitchell was smart, a skilled speaker, and a killer. The Queen wanted to impress Clark, that much was clear.

"And do you want me to meet with Clark?" Beaufort asked, hopeful she'd find him too imbecilic for the errand as well.

The coach rolled to a slow stop and the Queen released the cushion, gesturing imperiously for Beaufort to get out. "I do not think it will be necessary, no. We would not want him to believe you'd stoop so low as to accept his last-minute request."

Beaufort did not wait for the driver to open the carriage door. He lowered the carriage window, reached out, and depressed the latch, his weight against the lacquered wood opening it easily. "Very well," he replied, keeping his tone even.

He stepped out and onto a deserted lane, pausing to bow. "I'll await further instruction, my lady."

"That goes without saying," the Queen answered haughtily. "Close the door."

Beaufort obliged then watched the carriage roll away. "Bitch."

5

A prostitute trudged up the narrow stairway of Lady Grace's apartment building and started down the dingy, dark hallway, catching sight of Langdon and Niles Spencer as they leaned against the wall. "Evenin', gentlemen," she drawled, winking garishly as she hiked up the hem of her bright blue gown.

Niles pushed off from the wall as if to address the woman.

"No," Langdon instructed sternly.

The prostitute offered the men a disappointed frown, then opened her apartment door and disappeared inside.

"You really are becoming a bore, Stonecliffe."

Langdon elbowed Niles in the rib cage. "We are here to see to the safety of Lady Grace and the Templetons. That is all."

"I'll see to their safety if you will stop staring at that knife of yours," Niles answered, looking at Lady Grace's closed door. "Honestly, if you are going to kill yourself, just do it already. I am quite sure I could manage your part in this assignment."

Langdon returned the knife to its hiding place within his boot. "Are you not going to play the sympathetic friend to my jilted fiancé?"

"Please," Niles said, rolling his eyes at Langdon's question. "What have I always told you? Hmm? Marriage is for penniless lords and love-struck fools. Neither of which category you fall into, by the way."

Langdon chuckled at his friend and fellow agent's words, though one phrase in particular grated against his ears. "Is that right?"

"You tell me," Niles replied, casting a longing look toward the prostitute's door. "As far as I know you have managed to hold on to your family's money, correct?"

Langdon nodded in agreement.

"Then that leaves love-struck fool. You certainly possessed affection for Sophia, but you were not *in* love with her. In order to qualify as a fool one must pine, need—nay, require—the woman in a wholly irrational and idiotic manner."

"Do you know, Carmichael told me the same thing," Langdon said, frustrated by the coincidence.

"Is that so? Even the bit about pining? Does not sound like Carmichael."

"No, not the bit about pining, Niles," Langdon admitted reluctantly. "But the rest? Verbatim, if I am remembering the conversation correctly."

"Well, there is a first time for everything, I suppose."

Langdon looked up at the ceiling where a spider was busily constructing its web. "If I am not meant for marriage, then what?"

"How the bloody hell am I supposed to know?" Niles replied. "This is where a woman would suggest self-reflection—"

"Stop right there," Langdon commanded his friend.

He could not take any more thinking on his feelings. It had become a frustrating habit of late.

"Lucky for you, I am not a woman," Niles continued despite the directive. "I say forget everything that happened in the last three months—no, make it six, just to be safe. And if you cannot manage that on your own, drink until you can."

Lady Grace's door suddenly flew open and an ancient man appeared before them, the pan from earlier that evening gripped in his gnarled fingers.

"Mr. Clark, I presume," the man said as he stood on the threshold.

"Best wait on the drinking," Niles said quietly to Langdon. "At least until tomorrow."

"I never was a drinking man," Langdon answered his friend, then bowed to Mr. Templeton. "I am. And you must be Mr. Templeton. I apologize for the inconvenience, but I wanted to personally ensure Lady Grace's safety until the morning, when all three of you will be escorted to my home."

Mr. Templeton narrowed his eyes and screwed up his mouth as he considered Langdon.

"Mr. Templeton, do step away from the door."

Lady Grace joined the man, Mrs. Templeton close behind. "Here now, give me the pan. You should be in bed."

"I will be watching you, Mr. Clark," Mr. Templeton warned Langdon as Lady Grace pried the pan from his fingers. "One wrong move and you will be sorry for it."

Mrs. Templeton took her husband's arm in hers and steered him back inside, leaving Lady Grace. And the pan.

"As you can see, Mr. Templeton is brave beyond his capabilities," she explained, wearily glancing down the hallway of the derelict building.

"I rather hope I am just like him when I reach such an advanced age," Langdon answered, genuinely impressed by the man's actions.

"As do I," Lady Grace agreed, offering Langdon a small but sincere smile. She stared at the pan for a moment as if words failed her, then looked up again. "Good night, Mr. Clark."

"Lady Grace."

"I do not believe we have been—"

Niles's words were lost under the squeak of the warped wooden door meeting the frame.

"—introduced."

"Next time," Langdon assured his friend, then leaned back against the wall once more.

Niles looked at the door, then at Langdon. "Well, if you are not a drinking man, might I suggest Lady Grace? I suspect the woman could make a man forget a lifetime of regrets."

"What are you talking about?" Langdon asked, considering the spider's progress.

Niles sighed loudly. "I believe your exact words were, 'If I am not meant for marriage, then what?' Perhaps Lady Grace has some inkling as to how you might make it through these trying times."

"The woman's future was lost in a card game by her father," Langdon countered, offended by the suggestion. "She endured ten years of marriage to a degenerate member of the Kingsmen. I will not be the next man in line to use Lady Grace."

Niles playfully punched Langdon's arm. "I am a

bloody bastard, true enough. But you must know I did not mean for you to 'use' Lady Grace. You are a good man. She is a woman who deserves thoughtful, considered attention. The distraction may be mutually beneficial. That is all."

"She is key to this investigation," Langdon argued, Niles's explanation repeating in his head.

"Still playing by the rules, are we?" Niles asked, referring to the strict Corinthian code that forbade agents from involving themselves with any individual involved in a case.

Langdon grit his teeth. "Carmichael threatened to take the Afton case from me. He is concerned the situation with Sophia will inhibit my ability to focus. So, yes, I will be playing by the rules. Every last one."

"Pity, that," Niles replied, crossing one ankle over the other.

Langdon knew he should not ask Niles to explain himself, but he could not resist. "Why?"

"You've done so all your life and look where it has gotten you," Niles answered simply. "Just once, wouldn't you like to do what you *want* to do, rather than what you should? Aren't you the least bit curious to see where such thinking might take you?"

"And what if they are one and the same?" Langdon asked, irritated by his friend's question.

Niles sighed again. "Then you really are a bloody saint and there is no hope for the rest of us."

"I have waited over half my life to catch Lady Afton's killer," Langdon ground out.

"The same amount of time you spent thinking Sophia would be your wife. Plans change. Priorities shift. And people disappoint you. You asked me what was next for you. I think the sooner you accept life for the impressive wreck of contradictions it is, the sooner you will have your answer. Don't let anyone keep you down, Langdon. Not Sophia and Nicholas, nor Carmichael or even me. And for the love of all that is holy, do not use this fork in the road as an excuse. You are too brave a man to let life go."

Langdon pushed off from the wall and turned to face Niles, unsure of what to say. "Did all of that . . . insightfulness really just come out of your mouth?"

"Well, it didn't come from the prostitute down the hall, if that's what you are wondering," Niles replied sarcastically, uncrossing his ankles. "I'm off to check in with Jones downstairs. You stay here and think, why don't you?"

Langdon watched as his friend took the stairs two at a time.

Impressive wreck of contradictions. At least Langdon could agree with that.

❦

"I told you so," Mrs. Templeton whispered vehemently to Grace as they were quickly ushered through the servants' entrance of Mr. Clark's elegant London home. "And why would we not enter through the front door? Being treated like you are inferior and you've only just arrived. And disguised in such a costume, no less!"

Grace looked down at the voluminous folds of her black silk mourning gown through the thick netting of her bonnet. The ensemble had arrived with the carriage that very morning along with a letter from Mr.

Clark, who had been relieved by another of his men by the time Grace awoke. In it, he had explained his desire to keep her true identity a secret from any outside the Kingsmen and those associated with the gang. The Widow Crowther would be known to the King. Lady Grace Audley did not need to be revealed to anyone within the ton or those connected to the peerage, such as servants, deliverymen, or—God help them—an actual lord or lady.

"We must trust that Mr. Clark knows what he is doing," Grace urged Mrs. Templeton as a portly man appeared in the entryway.

"Welcome to Aylworth House. I am the butler, Yates," the man said, his round spectacles matching his frame.

Mr. Templeton cleared his throat and took a step forward. "Mr. Templeton, Yates. If you would show the ladies to their rooms, I will have a look about the facilities, if you do not mind?"

If Yates wondered at Mr. Templeton's unusual request, one could not tell from his placid demeanor. The butler simply nodded in understanding, then turned to the women. "Of course. Shall we?"

Mr. Templeton pointed his forefinger at a footman who sat at the servants' table polishing a silver candlestick. "You there, you are meant to stand when the lady of the house is in your presence, are you not?"

Startled, the young man shoved back his chair with alacrity and stood, the silver candleholder and cloth still in his hands.

Mrs. Templeton rolled her eyes and sniffed at the footman's impertinence.

Mr. Templeton grunted his approval of the lad's

change of attitude and patted his wife's arm. "Leave them to me. You go on up now and rest."

"Yes, Yates, please show us to our rooms." Grace smiled briefly at the butler, anxious for a few quiet moments to herself. She and Mrs. Templeton followed him up the stairs and onto the ground floor, where Grace involuntarily gaped at her surroundings.

She knew very little about a mistress's life, having only overheard whispered gossip between her mother and friends concerning Lord So-and-so's piece of muslin. A kept woman could expect jewels and dresses, even a cozy, well-afforded townhome, in exchange for her services.

But this was no cozy townhome. The carriage windows had been covered by curtains, so Grace could not say where, precisely, they were within the city. Still, from the interior she had to assume it was one of the best, if not the best, of locations.

The large entry hall boasted white and black tiling laid out in a chessboard fashion, every last square sparkling in the sunlight peeking through the mullioned windows that graced each side of the front door. A gilded mirror hung on the wall, accompanied by a handful of landscape paintings, artfully arranged. All, much to Grace's surprise, to her liking.

The highly polished oak staircase ascended to the first floor as if suspended, the intricate and expensive detailing on the rail consisting of scrollwork and Grecian-inspired motifs.

And at every doorway, one of Mr. Clark's men stood, staring straight ahead, his face devoid of emotion, his demeanor detached.

Grace forced her mouth to close and mounted the

second staircase. Clearly, Mr. Clark was a man of some importance in Liverpool—with the funds and men to make his London plans succeed. This should have soothed her. So why did her chest tighten with nervousness?

"Mr. Clark informed me that he will be joining us for dinner," the man told Grace in a quiet, kind tone.

She chose to put the information far from her mind for the time being and instead focused on the man's amiability. "Thank you, Yates."

"You are most welcome . . ." The man paused, his discomfort palpable.

The trio reached the landing and walked to the first door on the right, Yates indicating they had arrived at their destination.

"Grace, Yates," Grace offered, giving the man her name. "Call me Grace."

The butler cringed at the suggestion to use her first name only. To his credit, he merely nodded in reply. "Here is your room, *Grace*," he said, the effort turning his cheeks a soft red. "Mrs. Templeton, you and your husband are right across the hall. I will send Mr. Templeton up once he's finished below stairs."

Mrs. Templeton made to wave the man off, obviously planning to join Grace in her room.

"I am going to rest, Mrs. Templeton," Grace said before her friend could refuse the butler. "Would you wake me when it is time to dress for dinner?"

Mrs. Templeton eyed Grace with concern. "All right, my lady. Should I fetch your favorite tea?"

Grace felt a rush of emotion clog her throat. When she'd first employed Mrs. Templeton, the dear woman had insisted on having Jasmine tea in the house despite its being one of the most expensive teas to purchase. At first, Grace enjoyed the very fact that her husband would disapprove of the costly tea. Eventually, when her flash and fury of anger and betrayal burned down to steady embers of bitterness and patience, Grace worried the money spent on the restorative tea should have gone to her stash of coins—the very money that would one day take her away from the doctor.

But Mrs. Templeton would not hear of it. She knew without ever having to ask that Grace's nerves were soothed by the tea. And that alone was worth the price.

"Yes, Mrs. Templeton, that would be most welcome," Grace answered, smiling at her friend. "But let us both rest first. Perhaps an hour from now?"

Mrs. Templeton returned Grace's smile, the sheer pleasure of being useful showing in her eyes. "An hour it is."

Then she turned to Yates. "Now, go on, Yates. My lady needs to rest," she added with a firm nod before crossing the hall to her own room and disappearing within.

Yates looked lost. Being required to address the woman of the house by her first name had more than likely been enough to drive the man to drink, Grace imagined. And now Mrs. Templeton was giving him orders. Poor man.

"Will there be anything else, my lady?" he asked, a shaky recovery managed before Grace's eyes.

"It is Grace, Yates—I insist," she gently reminded

him. "And I believe I have everything I need. Thank you for your kindness."

The man cleared his throat. "I am only doing my job, *Grace*."

"No, that's not true," Grace replied, walking through the open door to her room. "Your job is to be a butler. Being kind and considerate to a woman in such a situation? That is not a man doing a job. That is a man being a decent human being. And men like you are hard to find, Yates."

The butler cleared his throat again, though Grace caught a quick glimpse of a smile as it curved his lips. "Perhaps you have been looking in the wrong places, my la—Grace."

"Perhaps I have been, Yates," Grace agreed, the knot in her stomach loosening a touch.

He bowed, then turned and walked down the hall.

Grace slowly closed the door before leaning against it, exhausted. She wouldn't let herself cry. She could not. She turned her attention to the heavy black bonnet atop her head, carefully unwinding the seemingly yards of netting that hid her face from the world.

Next, she saw to the hat pins, yanking them from her smooth chignon and poking them carefully through the bonnet's brim for safekeeping. And finally, she bowed her head and let the frothy, overdone accessory drop to the floor. She buried her face in her hands, blocking out the natural light pouring in from the mullioned windows. There was no other way to move forward than this.

"Leave the fretting to Mrs. Templeton," Grace whispered, removing her hands and willing her limbs to move. She walked the perimeter of the large, beautiful room, taking inventory of its contents while steeling her will. The walls were covered in a subtle silk fabric that matched the bed linens, the soothing violet shade quite to her liking. There was a lovely mahogany bed, a delicate writing desk in the far corner, and two inviting chairs positioned before the fireplace.

And there were flowers. Many, many flowers. Crystal vases held bouquets of spring flowers on every available surface. A large arrangement occupied the space between the two chairs near the fireplace. Even the writing desk sported a gathering of white and pale pink roses.

Grace attempted to focus her attention on Mr. Clark's thoughtfulness rather than the knot in her stomach as it tightened yet again, her breathing constricted by the weight of her conscience. She turned toward the bed and quickly walked to it, sitting down on the silk counterpane and bending to untie her kidskin boots.

She was a pawn yet again. First, she had been carelessly played away to her ruination by her father, every last hope and desire for her life forcibly taken from her. And now Mr. Clark held her reimagined future precariously in his hands. There would be no turning back from here.

Grace finished untying her left boot and dropped it on the thick Aubusson carpet, the thud as leather hit the floor underscoring the weight of the situation. The first tear trailed a damp path down her cheek, cutting across to her chin, where it hesitated before falling to land on the toe of her remaining boot.

Grace pulled it off and gently set it down next to its twin.

When yet another tear made its way down her cheek, Grace understood that a full-blown crying jag was unavoidable and lay back on the bed, turning her face into a pillow and quietly letting go. She had been such a fool. Her time spent married to the doctor had been an education, but had she learned enough to face the Kingsmen and walk away with her life? And if not, could Mr. Clark be relied upon to provide whatever it was Grace lacked? Was he a man she ought to trust? The threadbare scrap of softness in her soul that had survived the past wanted to believe in Mr. Clark's honor. While the rest of Grace feared she had only played directly into his hand.

She needed more than a stiff upper lip and the ability to willingly ignore the desperate hole growing in her heart. She needed a suit of armor to see her through. And a strong one at that.

※ ☀

"You cannot go into her room."

Langdon stared down his nose at Mrs. Templeton, attempting to intimidate the woman with his steely gaze. "Actually, I can."

Mrs. Templeton pursed her lips, the wrinkles around her prim mouth tightening, underscoring her frustration. "Well, that may be. Still, surely you wouldn't, would you? My lady is resting."

Langdon narrowed his eyes. He was unaccustomed to having his actions questioned by servants. "I would—I will." He took the silver tea tray from her sturdy, work-worn hands.

"Midge," he addressed the Corinthian standing guard outside Lady Grace's room. "Open the door."

God, but this was more work than it should be, he thought grimly. He could have postponed his meeting with Grace for a few hours, but knowing she was at Aylworth House was an irresistible draw. He'd left the Corinthian Club early, unable to ignore the lure of her presence. He only wanted to be sure that she was comfortable. Nothing more. And yet, here he stood, outside her door, arguing with a servant and holding her tea.

Thankfully, the steeliness seemed to work. Mrs. Templeton attempted one last pursing of her lips.

"Would you have me serve Lady Grace cold tea?" Langdon asked flatly.

"Very well," she said, grasping the doorknob and slowly turning it, adding, "But my lady won't like it."

"I come bearing tea, Mrs. Templeton. No woman of my acquaintance would be displeased with such service," Langdon answered, feeling satisfied with his win.

Midge opened the door, eyeing Mrs. Templeton as though at any moment she might throw herself over the threshold.

Mrs. Templeton stood back. "We shall see," she muttered just loud enough for Langdon to hear.

"Yes we will," he answered, irritated with the slight. And oddly irritated by his irritation. "Midge, close the door behind me."

He stepped into the room and waited until the agent did as he'd asked, then looked for Lady Grace.

She was lying on the bed, knees pulled to her chest and her face hidden by a pillow.

"Lady Grace," Langdon called out before taking a step toward her. "I have brought your tea."

With an abrupt, jerky movement, she shifted and sat up, her feet on the floor, her face turned to the wall. Her shoulders rose as she inhaled through her nose, the telltale catch of restorative oxygen as she exhaled pricking at Langdon's ears. "Mr. Clark, please do call me Grace."

She had been crying.

Langdon looked down at the tea service in his hands and fought the urge to care. All of his energy was needed for the case. Nothing could be spared, not for Carmichael's doubts, nor Niles's blasted insights. Not even for Lady Grace's tears.

He strode across the room and stopped before her, intent on ignoring anything to do with what troubled her.

Lady Grace stood, her back rigid with propriety. "In front of the fire, please."

He could not help but admire her strength. Even though her stunning violet eyes bore unshed tears, Lady Grace had instantly composed herself.

She did not wait for a response, but instead led the way, covertly brushing her fingertips over her damp cheeks and smoothing her blond hair into place.

He set the tray down upon a low table and waited for Lady Grace to take her seat.

"Will you join me?" she asked, gesturing at the two teacups laid upon the silver tray.

Langdon sat and inspected the tray, noting it held a plate of his favorite jam-filled biscuits. "No, thank you," he answered, as if depriving himself proved something.

"Very well," Lady Grace replied, reaching for the teapot. "But I must tell you, this is Jasmine tea—one of the most beautiful in the world."

Despite himself, Langdon leaned forward and watched as she poured the steaming water into the cup. Suddenly, what appeared to have been a small, dried flower lying at the bottom of the cup came to life, growing two, nearly three times its size into a magnificent, delicate bloom. "Good God," he breathed, ensnared by the beauty.

"Isn't it lovely?" Lady Grace asked, returning the pot to the tray. "Jasmine is as comforting to the nerves as it is stimulating to the eyes. It is terribly frivolous, but Mrs. Templeton insists we keep a supply on hand."

Her shoulders relaxed and she too leaned forward, until their foreheads nearly touched as they bent over the cup. "It reminds me to look for the miracles that surround us. Even in the most unexpected of places. They might be minute and short-lived, but they are there, waiting for us to find them."

The blossom grew heavy with liquid and slowly, almost tentatively, eased lower until it rested upon the cup's porcelain bottom.

Langdon sat back in his chair, purposely inserting distance between himself and Lady Grace. "Can something 'minute' really be a miracle?"

She picked up her cup and saucer in one dainty hand. "Very much so, Mr. Clark. A kind word from a stranger may take no more than ten seconds, but the sentiment stays with you for some time—is even capable of changing your life, some would say."

"Sounds a bit unnerving, if you ask me," Langdon replied, gazing at Lady Grace.

She lifted her fingers to her cheek and discreetly brushed the tips over the faintly reddened skin. "Why is that?"

Langdon abruptly realized he was staring. He swallowed hard and focused on the conversation. "What if you preferred your life the way it was? Change can be difficult, especially if you did not ask for it."

"You sound as if you believe we have control over these things." Lady Grace took a sip of her tea, clearly savoring the fragrant blend.

"Do I?" Langdon asked, pondering the notion. "Well, I suppose I do wonder if we have a certain measure of control. Through the choices we make and such."

Lady Grace considered his words carefully as she enjoyed another sip of tea. "By that way of thinking, I must have done something terribly wrong in my youth, then, correct? Otherwise, how would one explain me being married off to the doctor, then hunted down by the Kingsmen and having to pretend to be your mistress?"

"You did nothing to deserve such treatment," Langdon countered, cursing his insensitivity. "There are forces beyond our . . ."

"Control?" Lady Grace finished simply, her gentle tone demonstrating she took no pleasure in having proven her point. "Let me be clear, Mr. Clark. I believe striving to be an honorable person is one of the most estimable goals an individual may possess. But each of us must be realistic about these things. There is good in life. And there is bad. It is what you do, especially with the bad, that makes you who you are."

Langdon sat up and reached for a biscuit, then stuffed the entirety of it into his mouth. He chewed and chewed, unsure of how to respond. *The miracles that surround us.* Indeed. Small and minute, one was showing itself now, at a time when Langdon did not know if he had the strength to answer its call.

"And you," Langdon finally replied. "How do you deal with the bad—the very lowest points in life, the ones that cause you to cry?"

Lady Grace self-consciously touched her reddened cheek. "I was crying because I find myself in a difficult position. I can see where I want to be, but it will take everything I can manage to muster to get there. For as long as I can remember, I have dreamt of escaping this life—of securing the Templetons' happiness. And now the opportunity is at hand, not only for a new life but also to avenge Timothy's murder. And I find myself afraid. And resolute. And anxious. And determined. Such a mixture of extremes, which, you should know, is very foreign behavior for me. As for what I will do? I will move forward. That is the only way I will reach my dream."

Langdon pointedly looked around the room at the flowers, suddenly unable to gaze upon Lady Grace any longer. Niles had managed to get Langdon thinking. But Lady Grace had him believing—in life after Sophia. Possibly even love?

His fascination with her was unparalleled in his experience. Not even Sophia had elicited this level of unexpected emotion.

"And you, Mr. Clark. What will you do with the bad that life brings?" Lady Grace asked.

Langdon abruptly stood. He was too close. Too warm. Too—everything. Suddenly he felt desperately uncomfortable. And he was never uncomfortable. He moved away from the fire and walked to the writing desk, taking one of the pink roses from the vase situated there. "That is a very good question."

6

What is the man up to? More important, what are you up to? Grace stared into her china cup and pondered the surprising situation. It was true enough that she saw no point in disliking Mr. Clark. The sooner they engineered the Kingsmen's demise, the sooner she could escape from London and begin to build a new life for herself and the Templetons. Friction between them would only complicate their efforts—and, perhaps, even compromise the outcome.

Still, her role did not require that she reveal anything more than that which would help in their shared quest. Why had she so flagrantly sought out consoling?

Yet something within her grieved the need to deny the powerful tug of attraction he seemed to exert effortlessly with each glance, each smile, each moment she spent in his company. Despite the less than reputable basis of their alliance, she was drawn to him. Grace was no naïve debutante and had been a wife, yet the emotions that swept through her when she was with him were all new, disturbing and exciting. And potentially dangerous, she acknowledged with an inner sigh of regret.

She had gone too long without attention. That had to be the answer.

He's a criminal, Grace. More attractive and charming than the doctor, but a criminal just the same.

She studied Mr. Clark through the screen of her lashes, cataloguing his sensual features and steeling herself to remain unaffected. His hair was so black as to possess a bluish sheen in the right light. His umber eyes reflected a somberness that his full lips shared. His large, muscled frame overwhelmed Grace whenever he entered a room.

He was beautiful. A beautiful criminal.

But a criminal nonetheless. She'd best not forget who and what he was.

Grace exhaled and carefully returned her cup and saucer to the tray, watching as the man hovered near the writing desk. Was he anxious to leave? "Now, Mr. Clark, was there something you wanted to discuss with me?"

"Yes, actually." He returned the flower to the vase and came to stand behind his chair. "Though I have yet to hear back concerning my request to meet with the King, I think it best if we make an appearance."

Grace considered the man's words. Once she was seen on his arm, the Kingsmen would know exactly where she was, and with whom. Half of her felt relief at the prospect of not having to hide. And the other went cold with fear.

"I've gone to great lengths to secure your safety, Lady Grace," Mr. Clark reassured her.

He looked beyond confident. He sounded completely convinced.

Clearly, Grace did not radiate the same.

She wanted desperately to believe his efforts were enough. "I do not doubt you, Mr. Clark. But you yourself know what an organization such as the Kingsmen will do in order to protect their interests."

"Which is why I am the ideal man for the job of protecting you, Lady Grace," he pressed, his tone too low, too real for her comfort. "I know how the Kingsmen think."

"There are times when it is to one's advantage to have a criminal on your side," Grace replied, forcing a smile. "But I am afraid we have a more practical problem. The dress I wear is hardly suitable for an evening's entertainment."

He looked relieved, and then he frowned. "I took the liberty of ordering a wardrobe for you—as your protector, I assumed such an action was in my purview. But now, as I sit in the midst of an army of flowers, I wonder if I was too enthusiastic."

"But how?" Grace wondered aloud.

His frown deepened. "I made a guess at your measurements." His gaze held hers as he bluntly quoted numbers.

"Oh." Grace could think of nothing to say in response. The man had recited her exact measurements. A tingling of heat kissed the nape of her neck and she shivered. "Well, you absolutely had those correct; now let us see if you've any taste when it comes to fashion."

She slowly stood, heat prickling her skin beneath the concealment of her gown.

"I believe this is where I leave. Until dinner, then," Mr. Clark said before quickly walking from the room and closing the door behind him.

"Until dinner," Grace repeated to the closed door. He appeared. Disappeared. Asked questions. Changed topics.

Despite Mr. Clark's peculiar behavior, there was one constant: keeping up with the man would be a challenge.

⁂

"I feel rather exposed."

The main room of the Four Horsemen literally vibrated with raucous laughter, the clink of champagne glasses, and dozens of competing conversations. Langdon could not be sure that he had heard Lady Grace correctly.

He leaned in until his lips brushed the delicate outer curve of her ear. "I'm sorry?"

She jerked, clearly startled, and caught her breath, her eyes round with surprise as she looked up at him.

"Remember who you are and what I am to you," he warned softly, beginning to question Lady Grace's ability to follow through with the evening's objective. Despite having been married, she seemed to have no familiarity with being touched by a man, not even in the most casual, innocent of contacts. "You are playing a part, as am I."

Her almost imperceptible nod conveyed she understood his warning.

"I feel rather exposed," she murmured so only he could hear, her fingers fiercely gripping his arm and giving away her tension. "I have been hiding from the Kingsmen in one way or another for the last ten years.

And now here I am, presenting myself on a platter. And all but asking them to eat me alive."

Langdon covered her gloved hand with his and pulled her closer, tucking her protectively against his side. "You are safe with me," he assured her. "It is important that the Kingsmen see you, here in London, and under my protection."

A drunken man seated at the faro table suddenly laughed, releasing a seemingly endless string of brays. Lady Grace watched the man as she fidgeted with the swath of netting covering her face, the ridiculous display of laughter making her smile.

"Tell me, is the gown to your liking?" Langdon asked, relieved at her distraction and wanting to keep her from focusing on the danger inherent in their visit to this particular gaming den. He strolled forward, slowly drawing Lady Grace with him deeper into the club.

She peered down at the neckline of her deep green silk gown, its design constructed to blatantly cup her breasts and cling to her curves. "The fabric is sumptuous and I daresay it could not have fit any better even if the seamstress had taken my measurements herself. But the bodice will take some getting used to, I believe."

Langdon knew there was no possibility he would ever grow accustomed to seeing Grace in gowns as sensuous as the green silk. He glanced at the neckline and felt the urge to stroke his fingers over the soft fabric and farther, where gown met soft pale skin.

His voice was lower, rougher, when he replied. "I gave the dressmaker very little information, but I would be surprised if she did not deduce for herself the nature of our relationship. Such necklines—"

Lady Grace stifled a laugh, her nerves appearing to dissipate somewhat. "Mr. Clark, that was my weak attempt at humor. It is true that I am rather more exposed than I am accustomed to being. But that seems to be the theme of my life these days. Eyes on mine, Mr. Clark."

Langdon jerked his head up, realizing he'd been staring at her breasts and wondering if her nipples were pale pink or dusky rose. Grace was proving a dangerous distraction. "I apologize."

Lady Grace gripped his arm tightly and leaned in, affording him an even more intimate view. "Do stop apologizing, Mr. Clark. We have been spotted. Far right of the room, near the bar. He goes by the name of Moth. Lower rank than the doctor, but high enough to have the ear of someone who would be worth our time."

Her voice was soft; she seemed to barely breathe the words but they were laced with conviction and fear.

Langdon kissed the nape of Lady Grace's neck, noting the slight tremor running through her. "Remember, this is what we came here to do," he whispered in her ear. "Prove to me that I was not wrong to bring you here this evening. Remain calm. I have twelve men in the hall and another twelve outside."

The muscles in her jaw clenched momentarily, then all at once the tremors abated and her features assumed an unconcerned expression, even faintly bored. "Thank you," she murmured.

Langdon led Lady Grace to the vingt-et-un table and gestured for her to take a seat.

"My favorite game, Mr. Clark," she drawled, offering him a coquettish smile and fluttering her lashes. "You know me so well."

The table immediately took notice of the two, the men openly ogling Lady Grace's breasts. Langdon claimed the chair next to her and with slow deliberation gave each man a deadly, threatening glance, staking his claim. The men shifted, cleared their throats, and immediately looked away.

"My dear Widow Crowther," Langdon purposely spoke loud enough for the table's occupants to hear, "if I had to hazard a guess, one thousand days and nights in your company would no more tell me everything there is to know of you than an afternoon."

One of the men twitched when Langdon mentioned her name. He stared at her for a moment before he threw down his cards and informed the table he was in need of a drink. A moment later, Langdon saw him join Moth at the bar, where he stood chatting with another man.

The dealer began the round, the cards gliding across the felt surface with ease. Langdon watched Lady Grace pick hers up and neatly fan them out in her hand, stealing a glance at the three men talking at the bar.

"I do believe I am going to win," Lady Grace commented casually, offering Langdon a sly smile.

"Is that so?" he replied, retrieving his own hand from the table. He examined the cards and frowned with theatrical flair. "I do believe you are right."

The man seated farthest from Langdon dropped

two cards and waited for the dealer to take them, his free hand fumbling with a pile of coins.

It was obvious from his nervous fingering that he held nothing of note. Langdon never had the patience for such establishments. Most men gave themselves away to anyone willing to pay attention. And if they did not, then Langdon risked losing his own money. Might as well bury it in the ground for all the good such entertainment provided.

The three men had finished their discussion at the bar; the man who had left the table only moments before was now working his way around the perimeter of the room, stopping behind Langdon.

"If you will, it is my turn to bid," Langdon said over his shoulder. "I will be with you in a moment."

He carefully considered his hand, then lay all his cards facedown. "Not this round, I am afraid."

The man tapped him on the shoulder. Langdon held up his hand.

"Not until the Widow Crowther plays her hand."

Lady Grace's knee pressed against Langdon's under the table. "I have no need for new cards, dealer."

The man nodded, and then advised all to show their hands.

Lady Grace was the last to lay down her cards, revealing the winning hand. "I told you I was going to win," she said to Langdon, her laughter a melodious sound that underlined her satisfaction.

"You always do, dear Widow," Langdon replied, pushing his chair back and standing. "Will you join us?"

He held out his hand.

"Only you," the man commanded.

"I am afraid that is not how this works," Langdon said, taking Lady Grace's hand as she stood. He turned and looked the man up and down, then smiled. He knew the curve of his lips was not reflected in his eyes. "Apologize to the Widow for being rude. Then take us to your boss."

The man made no movement, just stared into Langdon's eyes.

It could go either way. But in Langdon's experience, it was always best to establish dominance. Made it far easier to maintain control as the case played out.

Of course, such behavior could also get you killed.

7

Grace squeezed Mr. Clark's hand and held her breath. She was not acquainted with this particular thug, but he looked to be very much like all the others. In other words, unpredictable.

The man grunted then turned, gesturing for them both to follow him.

Mr. Clark politely allowed Grace to go first, his warm hand settling possessively on the small of her back.

She shivered involuntarily at the intimate touch.

They approached Moth, and Grace recognized another of the three. Marcus Mitchell looked their way and saw her, surprise shadowing his eyes for a split second before he turned his attention once again to his companions.

Grace's heartbeat calmed slightly at the sight of Marcus. They were friends, or something of the sort. No one affiliated with the Kingsmen gang could claim a true friend. Trusting someone enough to build a lasting acquaintance was far too dangerous in the Seven Dials.

Still, outside of Mr. and Mrs. Templeton and Timothy, Marcus was as close to a friend as she'd had in

the last ten years. They'd first met when he had come
to the house in need of the doctor's services. Her husband had enlisted Grace in helping to stitch up a
nasty cut the man had received in a fight.

While Dr. Crowther had gone in search of supplies,
the two filled the awkward silence with conversation.
Grace learned that Marcus had not come to the
Kingsmen of his own accord. He was counting the
days until he had paid off a debt he owed to the gang
and then he would leave the city, bound for America,
where he would be able to practice law without the
threat of retaliation and a damaged reputation lingering in the air.

They were two of a kind. And when he'd told her
that the King would not let him go, Grace had cried
for him—and for herself, too. Could anyone ever be
truly free? She looked at the three Kingsmen standing
before her and realized she was about to find out.

Marcus pushed off from the bar he had been leaning against and stood tall, offering Grace a friendly, if
confused, smile. "Mrs. Crowther, I am surprised to
see you here. I always believed such activities were
not to your liking."

"So did I," Grace answered, glad Mr. Clark's powerful body supported hers as she halted in front of the
trio. "But a woman is allowed to change her mind, is
she not?"

Marcus was disappointed. She knew him well
enough to detect it in his posture, which was just as
rigid as his tone. He would have heard of her disappearance from Rupert's house and been happy for
her. There was no way for him to know why she had

come back. And even if there was, she could not completely trust him with the whole truth.

She could not completely trust anyone but herself and the Templetons.

"You, Mrs. Crowther, should be allowed to do *anything,* that much is true." Marcus's words were completely proper but his voice suggested something else.

"I wholeheartedly agree," Mr. Clark interrupted, his arm sliding about Grace's waist with ease. "As long as she does it with me."

Marcus looked at Langdon and offered a glacial smile in recognition. "Mr. Clark, I presume."

Grace forced herself to relax into the man's hold and attempted to ignore the uncomfortable edge of danger, almost hostility, that filled the air. A woman in her feigned position would be pleased by two men competing for her attention.

"That is correct," Mr. Clark answered, squeezing Grace's waist once before releasing her. He held out his hand. "And you are?"

"Marcus Mitchell. We were not expecting to see you this evening, Mr. Clark."

The two men shook hands, a brief clasp of palms and fingers.

"No, I do not imagine you were," Mr. Clark drawled, polite amusement layered over a voice that was lethal, cold steel. He released Marcus's hand. "If there's one thing you should know about me, Mr. Mitchell, it is that I am not a patient man."

Grace watched the two men as they openly took each other's measure. The doctor had threatened to kill every last member of the Kingsmen for the lack of respect they showed him. But the threats were always voiced when he was safely ensconced inside his home, with the doors locked and the windows shut.

This was the first time she had heard anyone threaten one of the King's representatives. It scared Grace. And thrilled her, too.

"That's a pity," Marcus finally replied, cracking the knuckles of his right hand. "Especially as the King does things in his own time. A visitor from Liverpool cannot expect an audience to be approved with undue haste."

Mr. Clark watched Marcus crack the knuckles on his left hand, then smiled. His low, sinister chuckle raised the hair on Grace's nape and she froze.

"You know my name, as do your men," he said beside her. "Clearly, I am more than just any visitor."

Grace held her breath. Her heart beat furiously, pounding in her chest. She had a nearly overwhelming urge to run.

Marcus tilted his head and pursed his lips. "That may be so. But the King operates on no one's schedule but his own. You will receive word from him when he is ready. And not a moment before."

Mr. Clark lifted Grace's hand to his lips, placing a soft, slow kiss on her palm. "I believe I crave more carnal delights than are offered here, my Wicked Widow." He produced a paste card from an inner vest pocket and held it out to Marcus. "Do let the King know I stopped by. I will not wait forever."

Marcus took the card and examined it, then handed it to one of his men. "Of course."

"Come, my love," Mr. Clark said, gently turning Grace away from the bar and toward the door.

Grace glanced over her shoulder at Marcus. He mouthed "Be well," concern evident in his eyes.

She tilted her head in understanding and moved away, shaken by the full realization that there was no going back. The crowd cleared a path for them, none-too-subtle whispers ricocheting from one man to another, to prostitute, to barkeep.

The sound and the stares, the garish hues of the women's gowns and the frantic pace of the gambling hell melted into one, assaulting Grace's senses as they pushed against her on each side. She gripped Mr. Clark's hand and kept her eyes on the door, counting every step toward her escape.

"Wicked Widow." Grace could not be sure if she'd heard someone within the crowd say what Mr. Clark had only just called her a mere five minutes past, or if her brain was repeating the title in an attempt to come to terms with what she now was.

Twenty. Twenty-one. Twenty-two. Grace focused on her careful steps, but the clamoring in her head would not cease.

A member of the Kingsmen held the door open just as Grace reached thirty.

Mr. Clark led her out into the blessedly cool air, pausing to whistle for their carriage. A number of the Hills Crossing gang appeared and formed a protective circle around them. The coachman immediately moved the horses toward them from where they waited, half a block down the dark street.

"Judging from your grip, Lady Grace, you are glad to be leaving."

"Take me home," Grace whispered, gritting her

teeth against the threatening tears. "Take me home now."

⁂

Langdon tapped the roof of the carriage to signal his driver, and the coach lurched into motion. He'd accomplished what he'd set out to do, he thought. The Kingsmen now knew he was not a man to be trifled with. The plan had been put into action exactly as Langdon wanted. He waited for the customary flush of satisfaction he always experienced in such situations.

It did not come.

Lady Grace sat next to him, her hand still tucked into his, her clasp just as strong, perhaps tighter, than moments before. Her eyes were downcast and he couldn't read her expression, but she was clearly upset.

Which was only to be expected, Langdon reminded himself. What woman would not be shaken after confronting and challenging one of England's most powerful gangs?

Her reaction was completely understandable and made perfect sense. Langdon's practical mind struggled to understand why he was stealing worried glances at her.

"Lady Grace?" he said rather more loudly than he'd intended.

She looked up from her lap as if he had awoken her from an unpleasant dream. "I must apologize, Mr. Clark." She pulled her hand from his and began to remove the pins from her bonnet. "I had rather hoped

I would not be affected by interacting with the Kingsmen again."

Langdon's hand felt oddly empty without her smaller, softer fingers and palm pressed closed within it. "Do not apologize, Lady Grace," he said with an attempt at light reassurance. *No, really. Please do not. It only makes me want to ease your unhappiness even more than I already do.*

Langdon cursed his seemingly unending need to play the protector. Was it a trait he'd been forced to own by the death of Lady Afton? Or had he been born with the bloody anchor about his neck?

"I was not expecting to see Marcus," Lady Grace continued.

He'd seen the male interest that lay beneath the concern on Marcus Mitchell's face. Mitchell wanted more from Grace than friendship. Langdon wasn't prepared to hear her talk about him. His control was already dangerously close to the breaking point. He needed her to stop talking. Now. Before he said—or did—something he should not. Like kiss her.

"I was surprised, to say the least. I would have told you everything I know about Marcus if I'd thought for a moment he would be at the Four Horsemen."

Langdon's arm itched to encircle Lady Grace's slim shoulders and pull her close. He swallowed hard. "There is no need to apologize," he ground out, regretting every last syllable as soon as they left his mouth.

"Are you angry with me?" Lady Grace asked, worry and, if Langdon was correct, hurt lacing her tone.

"Lord, no—you couldn't be more wrong," Langdon muttered, balling his hands into fists.

Lady Grace flinched as if he had hit her, the curve of her mouth trembling with vulnerability before she turned her face away and looked out the window.

Langdon did not need to see her to know that he had made her cry. Which only made matters worse.

"I am the one who should be apologizing." Langdon took a linen handkerchief from his coat pocket. "I work with men, not with women. Talk is limited to the job at hand, whereas with women . . ." He offered the pristine white square of fabric to Lady Grace. "Things are different. It will take some getting used to."

She accepted the handkerchief and blotted her eyes. "Yes, we ladies do tend to talk more than your sex."

Langdon smiled at her wryness. "And about far more complicated topics than brandy and guns."

He could not pretend that he did not care for her, he realized. For better or worse, and despite how much he would prefer to have no feelings about her whatsoever, he needed to protect Grace. "Now, tell me about Marcus. Who is he to you?"

"A friend," she answered, twisting the linen handkerchief between her fingers, her hands resting in her lap. "He was forced into the Kingsmen because of a debt. And now they refuse to let him go. He is a good man, but a Kingsmen nonetheless."

Langdon was thankful Grace had been able to count more than the Templetons as friends while married to the doctor. Still, Marcus Mitchell's reaction to her presence troubled him beyond his personal reasons. He needed to know if Mitchell's friendship with Grace could create problems for the Corinthians' plan. "He did not appear to be pleased with you."

"I am sure when he learned of my disappearance, Marcus assumed I'd finally escaped," Grace answered, turning her head to look at Langdon. "To see me willingly return to Kingsmen territory would be both a shock and a disappointment for him."

"Was he—*is* he more than a friend to you?" It was an indelicate question, but a necessary one.

Grace raised one slim brow. "Straying from the topic of 'brandy and guns,' are we?"

Langdon chuckled at her jab. "Your relationship with Mr. Mitchell could be a problem. I simply need to know how big of a problem."

"When I said he was a friend, that is exactly what I meant. Nothing more and nothing less."

"Such questions should not be put to a lady," Langdon said, painfully aware of the ambivalence Grace caused in him.

"Well, as I mentioned when we met, I am no longer a lady, Mr. Clark," she replied, her brow smoothing.

She was a puzzle, flashes of insight into who she was—what she was—appearing and just as quickly disappearing. Langdon knew it would be best to ignore his interest in her. The question was, could he?

The carriage slowed to a stop and Langdon broke eye contact with Grace in order to part the curtains and look out the window. The Corinthian agent posing as a footman stepped over the Aylworth House threshold and walked toward the coach. "Safely at home," Langdon said. "You did well this evening, Lady Grace. Midge will see you inside."

"Thank you," she said, tucking the handkerchief into her reticule and gathering up her skirts in preparation for exiting. "Your support this evening"—she hesitated as her eyes searched his— "made all the difference."

Midge opened the carriage door and waited. Langdon moved to the bench opposite so Lady Grace would not have to climb over him in order to disembark. "There is no need to thank me. I promised you protection, and I am a man who keeps his word."

"I see that now, Mr. Clark," she replied, allowing Midge to take her hand as she stepped down.

Langdon had an appointment with Carmichael at the club. First contact had been made with the Kingsmen, and the leader of the Corinthians would want to know the specifics. And Langdon was anxious to learn more about Mr. Marcus Mitchell. He could not recall the man's name in any of the Kingsmen documents he'd reviewed, but that did not mean the Corinthians lacked information concerning the lawyer.

All good reasons to leave.

Then why did he want to stay?

"I will see you tomorrow, then?" Langdon had meant to make a statement, not ask a question.

"Of course," Grace replied with surprise, frowning at Langdon in confusion.

Langdon believed he'd succeeded in establishing the upper hand with the Kingsmen. He could not be so sure with Lady Grace. He gestured for Midge to close the door. "Good night."

Though it was dark, his gaze followed Midge as he accompanied Grace's slender figure up the stairs, and inside the house. The large entry door closed and Langdon continued to stare, lost in thought.

"Blast," he muttered at length, realizing the carriage had yet to move. He pounded his fist on the ceiling, the noise frightening the horses. The carriage lurched as they surged into the traces and Langdon fell back against the cushions, thankful for the distraction.

8

Langdon slipped down the hallway that led to the club kitchens, looking behind him to verify he was alone before he triggered the hidden entryway to the Corinthian offices. The door slid open and he passed through, reaching to reverse the action and waiting to hear the click of the hinges.

Then he walked down the corridor toward the room where case information was stored.

"You are late."

Langdon stopped and backed up three steps, pushing open the door of Carmichael's office to step inside. "I am?"

"You are never late," his superior noted, straightening a sheaf of papers he'd been reviewing. "Trouble?"

Langdon chafed at the very thought. He needed Carmichael to believe in his ability and commitment to the case.

"Did we not agree on one o'clock?" he asked, looking at the large marble-based clock centered on a carved mahogany table against the far wall.

The brass hands pointed to half past one.

"Precisely," Carmichael confirmed, frowning. "News?"

Langdon nodded grimly. "We made contact," he said succinctly, wanting to waste no more of his superior's time.

"Were they expecting you?"

Langdon dropped into a chair facing Carmichael's desk and slumped slightly. "Yes—though I do not know that I would say 'expecting.' Perhaps 'prepared' is a better description."

"Either way, a good sign," Carmichael commented, resting his elbows on the broad oak desk. "Who received you?"

"A Mr. Marcus Mitchell. Mid-rank, I believe. And an acquaintance of Lady Grace's."

Carmichael tapped his fingers on the desktop in a rapid, absentminded tattoo. "An acquaintance, you say?"

"A lawyer," Langdon further explained. "Apparently, he got into a spot of trouble and found himself indebted to the Kingsmen. He has paid off the money, but proven himself too useful to be let go."

Carmichael continued to tap as he mulled over the information. "And his relationship with Lady Grace?"

"She assures me it is of a purely platonic nature," Langdon replied. "But from what I saw this evening, Mr. Mitchell would have preferred it to be otherwise."

"And continues to do so?"

"If I had to guess, yes."

Carmichael stopped tapping the desk. "If? Stonecliffe, it is your job to assess and make a calculated guess. Is something wrong?"

"Tell me, would we have so thoroughly manipulated Sophia, given the opportunity?" Langdon asked, barely sustaining a respectful tone. "The answer is, of course, no. How is Lady Grace any different from Sophia?"

His superior pushed back his chair and rose. "Rather off course, but I will answer your question regardless. You are correct," he began, walking around the desk to a side table. He unstopped a carafe of brandy and poured two glasses half-full. "Even if we had known of Sophia's involvement in the search for her mother's killer, we would not have used her in any capacity. We certainly would not have used her as bait to draw the guilty party out of hiding."

Carmichael handed Langdon a glass and reclaimed his seat. "Lady Grace, through no fault of her own, is not in the same position as Sophia. And she never will be again. The Corinthians cannot change the truth—you cannot alter the past. The most we can do for her is aid in her eventual escape from a life she never deserved."

Langdon took a long swallow of the mellow brandy, letting it slide down his throat as he considered Carmichael's words. "Cruel and heartless, but practical, I'll give you that."

"Practicality has always been your bread and butter, Stonecliffe," his superior replied.

"True enough," Langdon agreed, taking a second sip. "Perhaps it is Lady Grace's background? Paying prostitutes and washerwomen for their help seemed far more palatable compared to what I am asked to do now."

"So you find fault with our methods because she is of the nobility."

"Of course not," Langdon said automatically.

"Then it is because you find her faultless. Whereas, prostitutes and washerwomen are not?" Carmichael asked, setting his glass down with the contents barely tasted. "You opened Pandora's box, not me, Stonecliffe."

Langdon considered downing his own brandy and then claiming Carmichael's. "They are blameless as well—in many cases."

"I am afraid I do not understand."

Langdon emptied his glass with no time spent slowly savoring the excellent liquor, something he normally would not do, and stared into the cut crystal. "I will be honest with you, Carmichael. I do not know that I understand, either."

This was all new to him. If Langdon met Carmichael's gaze, he would see doubt. Not that he knew so firsthand, but because he had borne witness to such conversations, purposely been present to echo what Carmichael always told the agents who wavered.

Was that it, then? Was he questioning the methods used by the Young Corinthians? Even more, having doubts about his place within the organization? He knew that Carmichael was considering the same at that very moment.

What was happening to him?

"I trust you, Stonecliffe," Carmichael said. "I *want* to believe you are more than prepared to handle this case. But the man I see before me is not the same man—"

Langdon could not listen to any more. "I've never failed you before and I am not about to start now," he ground out, setting his glass down and standing. He forced himself to slow his breathing. Flexed his fingers on each hand, balled them into fists, then spread them open, laying them flat. "I will alert you when I hear from the Kingsmen."

"You are not yourself, Stonecliffe."

"Tell me something I do not already know," Langdon muttered under his breath.

⁂

As superiors went, Adolphus Beaufort could have been worse. Marcus Mitchell eyed the man through the doorway that presently separated them. The King looked to be threatening his guest, the telltale bulging veins at his temples almost glowing hot with anger. He did not yell, but spoke in a quiet, controlled tone that seemed to be tightening the guest's already tense frame.

Marcus was not afraid of the King. He probably should be—and most certainly had been back when the gang had seen to his debt and made him their own. But somewhere along the way Marcus had lost the ability to care what happened to him, or when. Until he had met Grace.

And then everything had changed.

The man with the King hastily pushed his chair back, the screech of wood grating over wood rousing Marcus from his thoughts.

"You'll have it by midnight tomorrow," he heard the man say to the King.

Marcus watched the man scuttle from the King's office into the room where he waited. He was careful to avoid eye contact with the poor bastard. The last thing Marcus needed was to feel pity for him. The first rule of the Kingsmen: feel nothing.

"Mitchell," the King called.

Marcus stood and brushed a speck of lint from his dark blue coat. Then he adjusted his cuffs until they lay just as they should.

"Do not keep the boss waitin'."

Marcus looked at Four Fingers, the man who'd addressed him so rudely, and offered him a charming smile. "Wouldn't want to go before the King with my suit out of sorts, now, would I?"

"I'll show you out of sorts if you do not haul your educated ass in there right now," Four Fingers growled, the severely deep wrinkles on his forehead extending back to his bald pate.

Marcus adjusted his cuffs once more then strolled toward the King's office. "It is true what they say, then; losing a digit has made you quite cross."

The squat thug lunged, a string of curses spilling from his thick lips as he narrowly missed wringing the life from Marcus's neck.

Marcus slammed the office door shut and crossed to the King's desk.

"He'll catch you one of these days," the man warned Marcus.

"I like my chances," he replied, waiting to sit until the King told him to.

There were times when the man instructed you to take your seat before beginning the conversation. And there were others when he made you stand for nearly the entire meeting.

Marcus noted, not for the first time, how appearing before Henry Tudor or William the Confessor must have been quite similar to what he endured each week. Only this king did not wear a ring, nor require his subjects to kiss it.

At least, not yet.

"Take your seat, Mitchell."

Ah, the sire speaks.

Marcus obeyed, sketching a half bow before sitting.

"Your talent is, at times, the only reason I keep you alive," the King said, frowning at the comical move. "You know that, don't you?"

"That and my natural charm, of course," Marcus replied, amused by the man's displeasure.

Marcus had considered cutting off one of his hands. The Kingsmen valued him for his skill and accuracy with a gun. And if he could no longer shoot?

"Careful," the King told him, his temples beginning to throb.

Marcus had ultimately decided not to maim himself. The gang had taken everything from him. Why give them his hand as well?

Marcus bowed in surrender. "Say no more."

"Well, get on with it," the King said impatiently. "Tell me about this Mr. Clark. Moth said he had the nerve to bring Crowther's widow with him?"

Marcus casually rested his elbows on the chair arms. "Ah, yes, Mr. Clark from Liverpool. Well, to begin with, the man has superior taste in clothing."

"The important bits, Mitchell."

The prominent veins in the King's temples visibly throbbed. Good, Marcus thought. Perhaps he'd erupt in a rage and throw Marcus out before the subject of Grace came up again.

"He came unarmed—rather daring, don't you think?"

"And his men?" the King asked impatiently.

Marcus shook his head. "Several inside the Four Horsemen. And several more on the street. Nothing showy, though."

"Ballsy bastard," the King swore.

"My sentiments exactly," Marcus agreed.

The King leaned back in his chair and crossed his arms. "Moth said he gave you a card of some sort."

Dammit, Marcus thought. He was not ready to share the address. Grace's predicament had him pondering the situation, considering possible alternative actions, and Marcus preferred to move forward only after deciding on the exact path he would take. Giving the King Mr. Clark's address might hinder his plan.

Or it might not.

"Really, I do not know why you are bothering to ask me anything. Moth seems to have already told you everything you need to know. Quite the accomplished young man, Moth."

The throbbing in the King's temples picked up speed. "The card, Mitchell."

Marcus had no choice. He reached into his vest pocket and produced the card, the address listed upon it already safely stored in his memory. "Rather nice address, that." He reached across the desk and set the paste card in front of the King.

"Have our boys take a look at the house," the man ordered, picking up the card and staring at it. "I want to know how many men he has with him. When they eat, sleep, relieve themselves. And keep an eye on our

Mr. Clark. Anything odd and you come straight to me, all right?"

Marcus had already done everything the King had listed, except, of course, for coming to him. Mr. Clark had brought an army with him to London. But he would not share this with the King. Sending the boys off to do the King's bidding would buy Marcus some time.

"Will do," Marcus said. "With pleasure."

"Go," the King commanded. "I am sick of the sight of you."

Marcus clutched at his heart, but was careful not to waste his opportunity to escape. He stood and turned to leave.

"And do not think I've forgotten about the Widow," the King added. "Now that we know where she is, it should be a simple enough task to kill her."

Marcus continued to stare at the door. "I have the feeling Mr. Clark would be rather displeased if the Widow Crowther was to turn up dead."

"Mr. Clark's presence in London does not change our plans."

We shall see.

9

Grace sat in the sunny back garden of Aylworth House. Her eyes were closed. There was a light breeze that occasionally carried snippets of sounds to her, of the servants inside the home and Mr. Clark's men standing watch on the grounds. She had no idea what time it was nor how long she'd been sitting on the stone bench. And she did not care.

The first step had been taken—and she was still alive. She breathed in deeply and exhaled, thankful for Mr. Clark's . . . Mr. Clark's . . .

Thankful for Mr. Clark, Grace thought. For his cleverness and ease at the Four Horsemen. For his reassuring words and comforting touch. For his strong arms and kind smile.

For him.

What was she going to do?

"Are you asleep?"

Grace's eyelids flew open and she peered at the brick garden wall that separated Mr. Clark's home from the one next door. A pair of hands gripped the wall, a woman's neck and head just visible above the gray stones.

"Are you dangling there? From the wall?" Grace called out. "Is that quite safe?"

"Of course I am dangling," the woman replied as if Grace had just asked the silliest question in the world. "And I've no idea if it is safe or not. Do come over here and help me."

Grace leapt from the stone bench and ran toward the wall, capturing the attention of Midge, the man Mr. Clark had ordered to stay with her. "There is a woman," she shouted at him. "On the wall."

"Oh dear, I believe my hands are slipping," the woman cried.

The guard reached the woman before Grace did and leapt up, placing one foot on the wall and capturing her hand in his.

Grace reached him and stopped, a faint burning in her lungs from the sudden exertion. "Oh, well done, Midge."

"Midge?" The woman's head appeared again. She looked at her hand in the guard's and laughed. "You are not the Wicked Widow."

Grace froze at the woman's words.

"*You* are," the woman continued, eyeing Grace with keen interest. "And I am afraid this was all a ridiculous plan to make your acquaintance."

The woman was clearly mad.

"Oh dear, you think I am mad, don't you?" she asked, reading Grace's mind. "First, my name: Imogen Smithers—awful, isn't it? That's precisely why I go by Mademoiselle Louise LaRue."

"Go by?" Grace repeated, knowing she should not encourage the insane, but unable to stop herself.

"Well, I'll admit it is nowhere near as fetching as the 'Wicked Widow.'"

"Oh," Grace said, putting the pieces together.

"Then you are a . . ." She wasn't sure what the polite term was, and she did not want to insult the woman, in case she actually was crazy and capable of violence.

"Companion? Bird of paradise? Bit of muslin? Cyprian?" Imogen offered, ticking off the terms. "Oh please, Midge, you are blushing."

Grace looked at the guard, who was indeed red in the face. She patted the man's arm reassuringly and attempted to not be amused. "Yes, to all."

"Well, of course 'yes to all,' otherwise I truly would be mad—which obviously I am not," Imogen said. "Now, will you come to tea? I simply must know more about the Wicked Widow. And I have grown weary of taking tea all by myself."

"I am afraid that won't be possible," Midge answered on Grace's behalf, his cheeks having returned to their normal color.

Imogen waved the man off with the flick of her long, delicate fingers. "Be quiet, Midge. The Widow and I may not be proper ladies, but that does not mean we will allow our protector's protector to dictate our schedule."

"Protector's protector?" Midge repeated.

"Are you hard of hearing, Midge?" Imogen yelled.

Midge cleared his throat. "No. What I meant is that the Widow is required to be at home on certain days and at certain times."

Imogen stared at the man as if she did not understand.

"At home—she cannot leave the property," Midge explained, pointing at the house and gardens. "At home."

Imogen's mouth formed a perfect O of understanding. "I see. In that case I will simply have to come to you."

She released his hand and disappeared behind the wall, the sound of slippered feet pattering quickly on a stone path prompting Grace and Midge to look at each other with the same surprised expression.

"Is she . . . ?" Grace began.

"She wouldn't," Midge replied. "Would she?"

Grace could no longer hear the footfalls—presumably because the woman was nearly at her front door. "There is only one way to find out."

Midge stepped aside and allowed Grace to go first. By the time she'd arrived in the entryway, Yates was arguing with Imogen on the front step, no less than four Hills Crossing men surrounding them.

"I do not have a calling card," Imogen told the butler. "But your mistress is expecting me."

Well, Grace thought to herself as she approached, *she isn't lying. Not exactly.*

Grace joined the butler at the open door. "I apologize, Yates. I should have informed you that I would be receiving a guest for tea. Imogen, do come in."

"I do not think it is right that you are apologizing to him," Imogen started, sashaying into the foyer in a silk morning gown—a sprig of ivy clinging to the hem.

Grace had only lived at Aylworth House for less than a week. But in that time she'd come to like Yates very much. Once he'd recovered from the shock of having to call her by her first name, the butler had proven himself to be practical, forthright, and quite kind.

Still, Grace worried that Imogen's sudden appearance on the doorstep, with no calling card nor formal invitation, might test the man beyond his means. Never mind the garden wall introduction.

As a well-bred lady, Grace had been trained to know when a situation called for a full-fledged assault and when it warranted diplomacy. If Grace remembered correctly, under her parents' roof the butler almost always won. And if he did not, copious amounts of soothing of the nerves were essential. Butlers—good butlers—were worth their weight in gold.

Imogen had a bit to learn.

Grace decided not to address the woman's comment. "Would you inform Cook that we will take tea in the green parlor? I would be ever so grateful."

"You would be grateful?" Imogen incredulously asked.

Grace could not bear to see the look on Yates's face. She took Imogen's arm in hers and steered her down the hall to the parlor.

"Well, I must—"

"No, not another word," Grace whispered, leading the woman into the parlor and depositing her on a pale green, silk brocade–covered chair near one of the tall bay windows that looked out onto the gardens.

Grace claimed the chair across from Imogen and arranged the skirt of her sprigged muslin gown. "You must treat your staff with respect—especially your butler. Without him the house falls to pieces. You need him on your side."

"But *he* works for *me*," Imogen replied, removing her gloves.

The woman's accent was almost perfect. Grace had

become quite adept at using speech patterns to discover where the Kingsmen she met came from.

"Welsh?"

"How did you know?" Imogen asked as she self-
consciously patted her meticulously curled and up-
swept hair.

"Beautiful country, Wales," Grace replied, remembering a trip she'd taken there as a girl. "Why did you
ever leave?"

Imogen waited.

"The lilting quality," Grace explained with a
friendly smile. "The Welsh tend to sing rather than
speak."

"Cyfrgoli," Imogen swore with exasperation. "I
left Wales for my man Thomas. He said we'd find our
fortune in London. And then he left me for a serving
girl. Not exactly the fortune I had in mind."

"And now you are a man's mistress," Grace said,
attempting to picture Imogen in her life before London.

Imogen smiled, tilting her chin, the tension in her
neck giving away her sensitivity to Grace's description. "I am. And I've worked hard to get here. Folks
back home wouldn't know me anymore. My face, my
clothes—the way I walk, talk. I changed everything
about myself. And now, as they say, I am reaping the
rewards."

A footman arrived with the tea and placed it on the
small parquet mahogany table between the two
women. He bowed to Grace and left.

"And you?" Imogen asked, removing her gloves
and dropping them on the cushion beside her. "What's

your story? I can tell already it is different from mine. There's no disguising you are a lady."

Grace moved to pour the tea. "Very astute, Imogen," she said, handing a delicate floral china cup and saucer to her. "I was the daughter of a nobleman until my father gambled me away to a doctor."

"Some father," Imogen remarked with disgust. "And the doctor?"

"Very much like my father," Grace replied, dropping two sugars into her tea and stirring. "Fond of gambling. Fond of drink. Old. And not particularly trustworthy."

"The old ones are the most horrid, aren't they?" Imogen asked, taking a sip of tea. "Can't ever finish the job no matter how many times they try."

Grace sipped at her own tea and nodded in agreement. She could feel the warmth of a slight flush spread across her chest and rise toward her neck. Imogen was correct. The doctor had never been able to consummate their marriage. He had blamed Grace for his failure—and for all she knew of such things, she *was* responsible.

"And when was the Wicked Widow born?" Imogen asked, a seductive smile curving her lips.

"The doctor died three weeks ago."

Imogen's smile disappeared. "You mean to tell me the man that secured this house for you is your first protector?"

Grace should have done more thinking on her supposed past. But really, how was she to know someone such as Imogen would suddenly appear in her garden—or within relatively close proximity, anyway.

"Is that surprising?" Grace countered, setting her cup down on its saucer.

Imogen returned her own cup and saucer to the silver tray then scooted her chair closer to Grace's. "Yes, very much so! I have only caught glimpses of him from the street, but he looks to be of some importance. Quite a coup for such an inexperienced woman. Brava, Wicked Widow!"

There had been very little to be proud of in Grace's life for quite some time. She looked at Imogen and let the woman's infectious smile kindle one of her own. "Brava, indeed, Imogen!"

⁂

Langdon had always been fond of the water.

Seawater, that was. But the Thames? He stared down into the murky dark river and a faint stench rising from the water reached his nostrils. The perfect place to meet the King.

"Have you been thinking?"

Niles appeared from the shadows and casually strolled up to Langdon, a sly smile upon his lips. "My question to you is humorous, because I already know the answer. You are a smart man and an excellent agent. Always prepared, ready with the latest information. So of course you have been thinking. The real question is, are you brave enough to accept my challenge?"

"Funny, I do not recall any being issued by you," Langdon answered, irritated by Niles's correct assessment of the situation, save the last part.

Niles released a gasp of surprise. "Oh, do not play

coy. It is beneath you. I very clearly issued a challenge. After the crossroads bit and before I suggested taking up the bottle."

Several sinister shadows formed along the timbers of the tall ships as members of the Kingsmen approached.

Langdon signaled to the Corinthians, who crouched behind shipping crates and boxes of goods stacked along the quay. "I am afraid our conversation will have to wait."

Niles slipped a knife from his boot and palmed it. "Lucky bastard," he murmured.

As the three men drew closer Langdon was able to make out Marcus Mitchell. He was accompanied by what looked to be standard-issue thugs. "Unless you are the King, I fear I am to be disappointed this evening," he called out.

"I do hate to disappoint," Marcus answered, stepping into the ring of light cast by a workman's lantern that hung from a pole some yards away. "But you could not have expected the most important businessman in all of London to go traipsing about in the dead of night? And on the wharves, no less?"

Langdon shook his head at the man's explanation. "Tell me, Mitchell. If I had done as your message said and met you at the Four Horsemen?"

"The King would not have been there, either. But we all would have been far warmer," Marcus answered, cupping his hands and blowing on them for warmth.

Langdon already knew what Mitchell had just confirmed. The King had no intention of meeting with him—ever. It was time to persuade the man otherwise.

"I love the water," Langdon said to Mitchell, sucking up a long breath of the putrid air. "Do not know that I would build on it, though. Would you?"

The man continued to rub his hands together while he considered the question. "Seems a rather good investment, considering the trade that's conducted day in, day out."

"Perhaps, but it is too *vulnerable* for my taste," Langdon replied, eyeing the two thugs as they listened.

The thug on the right reached within his coat and produced a pistol. The one on the left raised the club he'd been holding and pointed it menacingly at Langdon.

"You and I are too intelligent for such dancing about," Mitchell said, warning off his men with a steely glare. "Say what you mean, plainly. Before these two grow as impatient as you claim to be."

Niles flashed the gleaming blade of the knife he was holding. "Do not rush the boss," he spat out, his Liverpool accent spot-on.

"Now, now, boys," Langdon said, grinning at Mitchell. "No need to fight. After all, we'll soon be one big happy family."

"What do you mean, 'one big happy family'?" Mitchell asked, confusion clouding his brow.

Langdon reviewed the information in his mind, needing to get every last detail right. The King would not fall for a plan he could see through. "You see, Mitchell, I've outgrown Liverpool. It was an ideal town for me to learn my trade and build my business, but it is time for me to move on. That's why me and the boys will be coming to London—permanently."

"That still does not explain your inference that the Kingsmen will in some way be joining with your gang," Mitchell pressed.

"As you know, the Kingsmen currently rule London," Langdon continued, rubbing his hands together to thwart off the cold. "Which presents a problem. Therefore, your King will have to agree to join forces with me."

"And what's in it for him?" the thug with the bat asked.

"The Wicked Widow."

Mitchell narrowed his eyes. "I am afraid I do not understand."

"Do not try to pretend the King isn't anxious to get his hands on the doctor's wife," Langdon replied smoothly. "The King does as I say and the Widow is his to do with as he pleases. Otherwise, I dismantle the Kingsmen from the top down. I believe we'll start with the East India Company. An important partnership to the Kingsmen, wouldn't you agree? I would hate for there to be a falling-out between your organization and the Company. But these things do happen."

The bat-wielding thug charged Langdon and got off one solid swing of his weapon before Mitchell and the other man pulled him off.

"You see, even *he* understands what's at stake," Langdon said, swiping at the blood near his temple.

"I am expected to believe Mrs. Crowther possesses information so sensitive, the King would align himself with you in order to keep her quiet?" Mitchell asked.

Langdon accepted Niles's proffered handkerchief. "Well, if you will not believe me, perhaps you should ask your leader."

"He's telling the truth, Mitchell," the thug with the gun said, his nerves twitching in his voice. "Came down from the man himself. Find the doctor's widow at all cost."

Mitchell held up his hand. "Enough, Jones." He returned his attention to Langdon. "Obviously the King must be made aware of your . . . offer."

"Of course," Langdon agreed, dabbing at the wound on his forehead. "I am feeling generous of late. You have five days before I cut the King out of London completely. And every twenty-four hours that pass without an answer means something bad will happen to your business interests, Mr. Mitchell."

The man laughed out loud at Langdon's words. "You cannot be serious!"

"Deadly so."

10

"Lady Grace?"

Grace excitedly swung about at the distinctive, deep male tone. "Mr. Clark?"

"There, we know each other's names," he replied. "Now for my next question: what are you doing out of bed at this hour?"

Grace raised her candle and stepped forward, examining Mr. Clark's features including a fresh cut and growing bruise on his temple. "I could not sleep. And when I cannot sleep, I walk," she said, distracted by the injury.

"I see. Where is Midge?" he asked, looking down the darkened corridor.

"Here, sir," Midge answered as he appeared from the drawing room. "She said she couldn't pace properly with me chasing after her. So I have been skulking instead."

Grace smiled at the guard. "You are a good man, Midge, for putting up with me. And you, Mr. Clark," she said, frowning with concern at the wound on his temple, "how were you injured?"

He touched his fingers to his temple and winced. "Midge, you may go."

"Yes, sir." The guard nodded a good night, turned on his heel, and disappeared down the hall.

"Are you in pain?" Grace asked, holding her candle high to inspect the wound. "A bat?"

He gritted his teeth, his jaw visibly hardening. "How on earth did you know?"

"The doctor saw patients at the house," Grace explained as she stood on tiptoe and gently pushed his hair aside for a better view. "Often I acted as his assistant, of sorts. It is unbelievable what you men are willing to do to one another."

The feel of his hair against her fingers as she held it out of the way was unexpected. It was soft, like silk. Grace had admired his dark locks before, but never imagined they would be so seductively soft. Like a satin ribbon teasing her skin.

"Will I live?" he asked.

His lips, mere inches from hers, moved in a whisper of sound before returning to a measured frown.

"Barely," she told him. "Come, I will see to the wound."

"No, that's quite all right," he argued, stepping back. "I've plenty of experience with such things."

Grace truly wanted to tend to his wound. But more than that, she wanted to see Mr. Clark. She had missed him.

"But do you know how to relieve the headache?"

"I never said I was suffering from a headache," he countered, looking skeptical, then added, "but if I were, would you know how to relieve it?"

Grace desired the man's company, but she would not beg. "You will never know if we continue to stand here arguing."

"Lead the way," he replied reluctantly, rubbing his temples.

Grace turned toward the staircase, looking back over her shoulder to make sure he was following. Mr. Clark was quite close behind her, the masculine smell of leather and faint, spicy male cologne teasing her nose. She ascended to the upper floor then walked to her room.

She opened her door and walked in. "Go sit by the fire. I'll be with you in a moment."

He obliged as Grace moved about the room, lighting more candles and collecting the things she would need.

She joined him and set her supplies on the cherry-wood table.

"Do you always travel with medicinal supplies, Lady Grace?" he asked, inspecting the contents of her small kit.

Grace pulled the table closer so that the candlelight illuminated his wound. "It must seem strange to you, I suppose. But yes, I do. You never know when you'll need them."

"I wouldn't say strange," Mr. Clark answered, settling into the wingback chair and letting his head rest against the cushion. "I would say sad, though. No woman should ever have cause to consider such things."

"You are rather considerate of women, for a criminal," Grace said. She collected the basin of water and linen towel she'd requested before retiring for the evening and focused on wetting the length of fabric. "I'll have that explanation now. I am assuming it has something to do with the Kingsmen?"

He looked at her, hesitating for a moment, his eyes dark and unreadable behind the thick screen of his lashes. "Keeping you informed is part of our bargain, isn't it?"

"Yes, Mr. Clark, it is," Grace confirmed, wringing out the fabric and pressing it to his forehead. "I cannot help you if I do not know what is going on."

He sat perfectly still as Grace carefully washed the dried blood from around the wound, though even her gentlest touch was clearly painful. "Yes, of course. Let me see . . ."

Grace rinsed out the linen, the basin water turning pinkish with blood, and wrung the cloth free of excess water.

She leaned over and dabbed at the wound. "I'll need you to move your head for me," she told him, then gently grasped his chin and tilted it to the left. "There, now I can see what we are dealing with."

His nearness pleased her and she wanted more. But Grace sensed he didn't feel the same and was holding back.

She released his chin and leaned closer in order to inspect the wound.

He inhaled sharply, his body tensing beneath her gaze.

"Does it hurt?" she asked, reaching out to trace the skin surrounding the wound.

He exhaled but the tightness beneath her hands remained. "Does what hurt?"

"The wound, naturally," Grace replied, savoring the feel of his skin as she examined the injury.

"Yes, but it is the headache that's bothering me most," he answered, his voice rough.

Grace straightened and stepped back. "Tell me what is troubling you, then. Tension only adds to the ache."

"I know we are partners of sorts in this," he said, his shoulders visibly easing as he relaxed into the chair once again. "But it feels wrong to expose you to danger—as though I am using you without any regard for your safety."

The man's thoughtfulness warmed Grace's soul. Mr. Clark was not like any of the Kingsmen she'd known. "I suppose you are using me—but I am doing the same to you. Do not forget, once we are finished with the Kingsmen, you'll be funding my new life."

"I do not like it," he confessed in a low tone, closing his eyes.

Grace couldn't help herself. She smoothed the back of her hand along his high cheekbone. "Didn't anyone ever tell you that criminals are not supposed to have a conscience?"

She'd meant to make the man laugh with her witty observation, but it fell flat, probably because she herself was near tears, touched by his tender concern.

He leaned into her caress. "You've no idea what a bloody curse my conscience is to me. No idea at all."

Grace had known the power to be found in affecting someone with a glance or a smile. She'd practiced such naïve seduction as a debutante, giddy and filled with butterflies when the victim fell under her spell.

This was altogether different. Butterflies did not flit back and forth in her belly. No, from the feel of it, a tiger prowled within her, inspiring fear—and need.

He opened his eyes.

Grace suddenly realized that she'd leaned in further and was staring at him, much too close.

"Grace."

His honesty touched her and urged her on. She swallowed hard, attempting to stifle her reply. It was no use.

"Do not ever regret those parts of you that are good, Mr. Clark," Grace whispered, lost in his eyes. "They're what separate you from men like my husband."

At that very moment, Grace felt she'd never expressed anything more important in her life. She needed him to understand. She needed, desperately, to touch him more intimately.

Grace continued to hold his gaze as she closed what little space existed between them and pressed her lips tentatively to his. For one brief moment, he went perfectly still. Then he responded to her touch with careful coaxing, returning her kiss while asking for more.

❧

Her mouth was innocent, and Langdon reined in the urge to plunder, content for the moment with the press of her sweet lips on his. He cast off all other thoughts, including his conscience, which told him he shouldn't do this.

Her tongue shyly touched his and Langdon initiated an age-old dance meant to coax one's lover that much closer to surrender.

He wanted to reach out, place his hands on the curve of her waist, and pull her in until she rested on his lap. He wanted to breathe in her delicate floral scent as he tasted her skin and tested its silken softness.

He was aching, tired, frustrated, and unsure—everything he'd never been nor thought he would ever be.

Carmichael and Niles had only reinforced his own conviction that something was very wrong with him.

Lady Grace seemed intent on convincing him otherwise.

She pressed her hands to his cheeks and jaw, cradling his face in her palms.

The swift surge of emotion shocked him into awareness.

What the hell was he thinking? He couldn't, shouldn't be doing this. He was risking the little he had left in life, for what? A moment's pleasure?

He broke the kiss and quickly rose from the chair, forcing a safe distance between them. "I apologize, Lady Grace. I should not have taken advantage of you in such a manner," he said stiffly.

She turned to see to her supplies. "A moment of weakness—on both our parts, apparently."

Langdon was an ass. He almost felt sorry for Grace. It could not be easy, dealing with him in such a state.

He watched as she finished repacking her supplies and took a seat.

She attempted to appear unaffected by the kiss, but her breathing was too shallow, too fast.

Langdon could still feel her lips on his. Taste her on his tongue.

"Now, are you going to tell me what happened to your face?" Lady Grace asked, folding her hands in her lap.

Langdon knew he should be relieved she was not outraged by his behavior. Taking such liberties was not what a true gentleman would do.

Then why did he only want more?

"Yes," he finally replied, deciding he needed to do the opposite of what his gut craved. At least for the time being—and always in the company of Lady Grace.

"The Kingsmen made contact," he began, reclaiming his chair. "They suggested a meeting at the Four Horsemen. I insisted on the wharf, which your man Marcus reluctantly agreed to."

"And the King?" Lady Grace asked, her eyes narrowing with interest.

Langdon shook his head. "Only Marcus and two of his men."

"Ah, Brutus was there," she confirmed with a nod. "That's where the bat comes into play. He's as stupid as they come, but exceptionally talented with that bat."

Langdon gingerly fingered his wound. "You do not have to convince me. Thankfully Marcus called him off."

Grace's brow furrowed. "They must want you alive."

"Well, I did not go empty-handed," Langdon explained. "My best man accompanied me, with ten more lying in wait, in case there was trouble."

"All of this is because of me. What is it that they think I know?" she wondered aloud. "I've gone through every last scrap of information I gathered over the years. Nothing stands out. I'll keep trying, though. And we'll push harder."

Langdon fought the urge to growl with disapproval. As Carmichael had told him, the ends would justify the means.

They had to.

"Well, actually, I have begun to work on that," he said, dreading the words to follow. "I've offered you to the King in exchange for a partnership and gave them twenty-four hours to respond. If they fail to meet the deadline, I'll steal the East India Company's latest shipment—in the name of the Kingsmen. Every day that passes, I told them, they lose something that is integral to their business. And on the fifth day I've threatened to remove the King entirely from the equation."

Grace eyed him skeptically. "And how, exactly, did you convince Marcus of this? The Kingsmen have been threatened by rival gangs in the past—gangs that no longer exist."

"Other gangs did not have my connections," Langdon explained, his faculties beginning to fire as they should. "I planted a man inside the Company months ago. Not only has he gleaned valuable information, he's floated false facts concerning the Kingsmen. The Company has suspected for some time that the gang is cheating them. And if the King does not comply, I'll give them the final push they need to go after the Kingsmen."

"You'd force them out in the open," Grace said, raising one eyebrow in approval. "You'll need to be careful, though. Along with the Kingsmen will come their anonymous partners—some of whom hold high positions within the ton. They'd do anything to keep their good names from being tarnished."

"Let us hope it does not come to that," Langdon answered.

"Yes, of course," Grace agreed.

The two fell silent, the only sound in the room coming from the crackle of the fire.

Langdon's head began to throb in earnest. "It is late," he noted, abruptly standing.

Grace nodded, but remained seated. "Good night, Mr. Clark."

Langdon paused awkwardly, knowing he should go but feeling as if there was something more to say.

Giant ass, indeed.

"Good night," he replied, and turned to go.

❧

Lady Serendipity Theodora Hatch had not always been insane. There was a time—long, long ago—when she'd been quite normal, actually.

She looked about the Bentleys' ballroom and sighed as she watched the debutantes dance with their eligible young men. Serendipity could recall every last detail surrounding the evening she'd gone mad.

A liveried waiter paused with a tray of filled champagne flutes. Serendipity eyed him with contempt and waved him off.

Her dress that long ago night had possessed a sash of the most spectacular shade of blue. Matching diamond hairpins, given to her by a favorite aunt, had twinkled in her lush mahogany hair. And her mama had allowed her to wear a hint of rouge upon her cheeks.

Serendipity had walked into the Filburns' ball sure

that he would see her, and her alone. He would propose that evening. She felt it in her bones. Mama had suggested Serendipity should not be overly hopeful of the possibility. "After all," she'd warned, "he has not spoken with your father. Perhaps you should consider Lord Pinehurst or Lord Bates. Both men have asked for Papa's blessing, unlike *him*."

Serendipity would hear none of it. She'd danced and laughed the enchanted night away, only growing concerned as guests began to leave. She'd been a bold girl in those days. Sanity makes everything that much easier, she supposed. Serendipity had sought him out on the terrace. He was smoking with a few of his friends, discussing something wholly masculine and of no interest to her. She'd asked the other men to leave.

And they had. Then she'd asked him why he'd not proposed to her that evening.

And he told her he hadn't because he was not going to ask for her hand in marriage—ever.

She was a charming, lovely girl, he'd assured her. But he had no plans to marry.

Serendipity had not begged him to reconsider, though she'd wanted to. A girl had her pride, after all.

Half-lost in the memories, Serendipity continued to watch the dance floor, purposefully ignoring Lady Herbert as the silly woman attempted to gain her attention.

People always speak of suffering broken hearts when disappointed in love, she mused with scorn. Serendipity's heart remained intact, solid as ice and heavy as ore. But her mind had shattered like thin, cheap glass that night and she hadn't managed to repair it since.

"Lady Serendipity," Lady Herbert said with overwhelming enthusiasm. "You are looking well this evening."

She sighed. Enduring such company was the price Serendipity was required to pay for catching a glimpse of him. It seemed rather high at times. There were days when she hated him for forcing her into such a degrading position, suffering fools so that she might be near him.

In fact, there were times when she wanted to kill him. But Serendipity wasn't a stupid woman. To kill the only man she'd ever loved would defeat the purpose of remaining devoted to him for so many years. And so, she'd killed others in his place. The deaths relieved the tension and she'd found them a convenient way to ease the stress of unfulfilled dreams.

"You are too kind, Wilhelmina," Serendipity finally responded, aware she'd taken a touch too long, but caring little.

Several men sauntered into the room, not bothering to wait for the majordomo to announce them. And there he was, right in the middle of the pack of young lords, indulging their antics while remaining wholly above them. They looked even younger next to his seasoned, experienced character.

Women adored him and men revered him.

But Serendipity was the only one who truly loved him, she thought smugly.

"I did not see you at Lady Pickwick's garden party," Lady Herbert said congenially.

Serendipity knew what the woman was up to. Ever

since Serendipity's father had died and left his entailed estate to a distant cousin, the ton had made a habit of attempting to discover how, precisely, she paid her way.

She'd never married, of course. And the distant cousin was a tightfisted penny-pincher. Gossips spread rumors that a mysterious male benefactor had come to her rescue.

Little did the idiots know Serendipity had not required rescuing. She'd built her business brick by brick, employing many but trusting few.

And along the way, she'd donated to charitable causes and dropped enough coin the length of London to ensure even those within the highest echelons of the ton could not ostracize her—though Serendipity was quite sure they would like nothing else.

Lady Herbert wanted to know if Serendipity had been invited to Lady Pickwick's party because the fat, over-rouged woman had nothing better to do with her time.

It disgusted Serendipity.

But torturing her with a prolonged pause was the tiniest bit enjoyable.

"That's because I was not there, Wilhelmina," Serendipity replied, eyeing the woman with a condescending glare. "I had a previous engagement in Kent."

It was a lie, of course. Serendipity had been forced to miss the garden party due to an issue with her business. But she'd overheard Lady Filburn bragging to Lady Morrow about having received an invitation to Lord Carstair's house party, which occurred on the same day as Lady Pickwick's garden party.

"In Kent, you say," Wilhelmina asked, her skin slowly warming to a spring green, if Serendipity was correct.

"Envious?" she countered, failing to supply an answer.

Wilhelmina furrowed her heavy brow as if she did not understand. "Why would I be envious of your trip to Kent? I understand the weather is most unpredictable in that part of the country—especially during the spring."

"Oh, quite the contrary, I assure you," Serendipity replied with relish. "I can't remember the weather ever having cooperated in such a glorious fashion. You really should have been there."

A footman approached the two, a silver tray with a single, sealed note resting on its gleaming surface. "For you, my lady," he said to Serendipity, holding the tray out to her.

"Well, I will leave you to your correspondence," Lady Herbert said, clearly knowing when she'd been beaten and thankful for the opportunity to make her escape.

"Thank you," Serendipity answered, taking the letter in her hands and ripping it open.

Wilhelmina nodded then scuttled away.

The footman remained.

"Go," Serendipity ordered, anxious to read the missive in private.

The man remained. "I am to accompany you to your carriage should you agree to the meeting."

Serendipity captured the impertinent man with a critical eye. Was he one of hers? "Well, give me a touch of space, you idiot," she hissed.

The footman took three steps back and waited.

Serendipity read the short letter, which requested she leave directly to attend an urgent meeting. Annoyed, she looked up from the letter and once again at her true love. Would this have been the night he realized life was nothing more than a string of mundane interactions without her?

She read the letter once more then crumpled it in her hand. Now she would never know.

"Come," she ordered the footman, shoving the letter into her reticule as she stalked toward the stairs, the weight of her position—made heavier by male incompetence—ever so slightly bowing her normally erect, even regal, carriage.

11

"I adore the cut of your gown," Imogen complimented Grace as their barouche rolled along Regent Street. "But the bonnet seems a bit much. Actually, more than a bit—even for me. And your entourage, though discreet, smacks of arrogance."

Grace smiled. Not that anyone but her was aware of her amusement since her entire head and most of her neck were encased in a swath of black netting. Grosgrain ribbons were tied in a jaunty bow beneath her chin, anchoring the bonnet in place against a slight breeze. The playful gusts ruffled skirts and bonnet ribbons on strolling shoppers up and down the exclusive row of shops. "Mr. Clark can be quite protective."

Grace knew the bonnet looked ridiculous as did Mr. Clark's men trailing behind her. Nevertheless, she would have done anything within reason—or not, actually—to get away from Aylworth House. She'd followed her instincts and pursued Mr. Clark, only to be rebuffed. She was humiliated, but more than that, she was disappointed. She'd thought for certain there was a connection between them.

"Well, you do have a flair for the dramatic, I'll give you that," Imogen replied, arching one perfectly plucked brow as she discreetly looked behind, to where a number of gang members followed. "I don't know that there will be room for all the men in Madame Fontaine's, though."

Grace pulled her cashmere shawl more tightly about her shoulders and pictured Mr. Clark's men squeezing into the modiste's shop, thankful for the distraction. "I believe you are right, Imogen."

"Remember, it is Mademoiselle Louise, if you please," Imogen playfully whispered as the barouche drew smoothly to a stop. "Mademoiselle Louise LaRue."

Grace covered her mouth with mock embarrassment. "Of course. How could I have forgotten?"

"It is the bonnet," Imogen replied, stifling a laugh. She allowed their driver to take her hand, then stepped down from the carriage and smoothed her cherry-red pelisse over her gown. "The weight is muddling your mind."

Grace rose from the cushioned carriage seat and accepted the driver's hand, carefully stepping down onto the street. "Do you know, you may be right? Perhaps your Madame Fontaine might be able to help."

"Oh, Madame is truly the most talented modiste in all of London!" Imogen exclaimed, looping her arm through the crook of Grace's elbow. "You have heard of her before, haven't you?"

Grace let Imogen steer her toward Madame's front door. "I am afraid I have not," she replied as Imogen grasped the polished brass doorknob and pushed. "My husband would have liked for me to have taken more care with my appearance, but it seemed a trifling detail at the time."

"Well, your situation has changed. And so must your wardrobe," Imogen answered, a small, wicked smile curving her mouth as she opened the door.

Grace looked down at the handsome morning dress she wore. Made of soft muslin in a stylish blue pattern, she'd thought her appearance rather fashionable—especially when one remembered that it was Mr. Clark who chose the gown for her.

Mr. Clark.

She shivered as memory and vivid sensations flooded her.

Or rather, *Mr. Clark's lips.*

Grace fought the urge to run the pad of her forefinger across her mouth.

"*Bonjour,* Madame Fontaine," Imogen trilled, sweeping into the waiting area of the dress shop with a flourish.

A woman and her two daughters sat upon a striped divan, their backs as rigid as the expression on each face.

Grace's lungs filled with irritation, the doting mama and her matching offspring's reaction to Imogen's presence wholly insulting.

And then she realized it wasn't only Imogen's presence in the modiste's shop that offended the trio. It was Grace as well.

An impish woman appeared from behind a pair of fanciful, lace-over-brocade curtains that separated the front of the store from the back. Her coal-black hair was clipped and curled close to her head, the style perfectly showcasing her enormous hazel eyes and high cheekbones. "My dear Mademoiselle LaRue," she said in welcome, her husky voice musical with a delicious French accent.

The society mama huffed with indignation at the modiste's friendly hello.

"Lady Finnywinch, you have something to say?" Madame Fontaine asked the woman pointedly, her tone clipped.

Grace held her breath. She was not familiar with the Finnywinch name. But anytime "Lady" preceded a surname, one was advised to tread carefully.

Clearly, Madame Fontaine held an entirely different view on the matter.

"Tea, please," Lady Finnywinch ground out.

Grace exhaled.

Imogen preened.

And Madame Fontaine sniffed imperiously. "Cosette," she called, snapping her fingers as she did so.

A young woman appeared from behind the curtains, a tray laden with service for three in her capable hands. *"Oui, Madame,"* she answered quietly, gliding past Grace noiselessly.

She set the tray on the low mahogany table in front of the Finnywinch ladies and proceeded to pour.

Lady Finnywinch looked as though she might scowl.

Grace rather hoped she would, if only to witness Madame in action once again.

"This way," Madame ordered, turning toward the back of the shop and gesturing for Grace and Imogen to follow.

The curtains parted to reveal a neat hallway. A door

on Grace's right sat partially ajar and she peeked inside. A cozy, neat kitchen lay within.

Madame Fontaine reached the door at the end of the hallway and opened it. Bright light spilled out, rushing down the hallway, nipping at the toes of Grace's kidskin boots and quickly spreading sunny rays from her hem to her bodice to finally reach her bonnet as she neared the room.

"You must spend a fortune on candles, Madame," Grace remarked as she walked across the threshold and into the modiste's workroom.

"Au contraire," Madame Fontaine replied with a smile, closing the door behind Grace and gesturing to the high-banked windows that made up the entire upper half of the workroom's back wall. "Candlelight masks a woman's imperfections—this is why it is preferred by lovers, *oui?*"

Grace nodded in agreement as she lifted her veil, tucking it back over the crown of her bonnet. The woman's line of thinking made sense.

"Non, natural light is the modiste's brother-in-arms. Not the clients', it is true," she added, shrugging. "But that is neither here nor there. Once the garment is fitted and sewn, then is the time for candlelight and masquerades."

"And Lady Finnywinch approves of your methods?" Grace asked, hiding her curiosity by scanning the large fabric-strewn room.

Madame Fontaine chuckled, the low, throaty tone at odds with her tiny, feminine visage. "Now I see why you and Imogen are friends. Honesty, as you English are so fond of saying, is the best policy, *oui?* Lady Finnywinch is an exact replica of the last lady to darken the door of my shop. And the one before that, and the one before that . . ."

Grace turned to discern why Madame had paused in her explanation. The woman had bent down to retrieve a slip of creamy Belgian lace.

"That is to say, when one influential lady decides something, the rest follow," she went on, straightening and coming toward Grace. "In Paris, my mother was a wealthy man's mistress and I his bastard child. In London, a lie or two and voilà, I have dressed princesses and ladies most highborn. English ladies are easily fooled—present company excluded." She held the lace up to Grace's neck and smiled wickedly. *"Parfait."*

Ah, Madame was not who she appeared to be. Grace felt a touch of the tension that had tightened her shoulders slide away.

"Now you see why I am so fond of Madame Fontaine," Imogen said, walking to join Grace and the modiste. "She's one of us. Or might as well be. That does not sound right, does it?"

Madame Fontaine handed the lace to Imogen then patted her hand. "Do not worry yourself, *mon amie*. Now, what have you come for? Dresses?" She turned back to Grace and began to examine her green gown. "It is Mrs. Beecham's work, yes?"

Grace stood still while the woman looked at the lace on her sleeves. "I honestly do not know. I neither ordered nor paid for the gown."

"Before her recent round of luck, Grace was married to a horrid man—did not want him near her, so there was no need for pretty things," Imogen explained, admiring the strip of lace. "Lost in a game of cards by her father, if you can believe it."

Madame Fontaine's eyes rounded with surprise. "Is this true?"

Imogen ceased fingering the lace and looked at the two. "Did I say too much? I am sorry, Grace. Once I open my mouth it is almost impossible for me to close it."

"Do not worry, Imogen," Grace assured her new friend. "And yes, it is the truth. The father, the husband—the whole sordid tale, I am afraid. Are you quite scandalized? I am sure Lady Finnywinch would have an apoplectic fit if she knew even half the details of my history."

"Please," Madame answered, rolling her eyes. "You are amongst friends here. And if you truly do want to give Lady Finnywinch a fit, come with me."

Madame took Grace by the hand and led her to a pair of upholstered chairs. She gestured for her to sit and asked Imogen to do the same.

A low table stood between the chairs, a crystal decanter of amber liquid and three cut-crystal glasses placed precisely in the middle of the lacquered mahogany top. Madame knelt and decanted the carafe, lifting it gracefully and pouring a small amount into each glass before passing one to each younger woman.

"First, we drink," Madame explained, taking up her glass.

Grace lifted hers, the heavy crystal feeling good in her hand.

Imogen raised hers as well and all three women took a sip at precisely the same moment.

The amber liquid warmed Grace's lips at first, its

heat increasing as it slid down her throat. She gasped from the unexpected sensation and sucked in cool air in an effort to ward off the building fire in her mouth.

Madame swallowed the entire contents of her glass, an enthusiastic *"oui!"* escaping her lips before she returned the glass to the table.

Imogen followed suit, tossing hers back with wild abandon. "Hamlet's balls, but you best me every time!" She set her glass down on the table and fanned herself. "One day, Madame. One day . . ."

Grace smiled at the woman's antics—or was it the instantaneous effects of the drink? "I believe you are correct, Lady Fannywench—Finnywinch—would be appalled."

"Oh, no, this is not the scandalous portion of your visit," Madame replied, standing up and quickly crossing the room to a large chest of drawers. She opened the top drawer and reached inside, removing a pile of soft silken things and lacy bits. "This is."

The modiste returned and slid the decanter and glasses to one side of the table, then deposited the fabric and lace on the other.

"I do not find fabric and lace to be particularly offensive," Grace offered, looking at Imogen. "But perhaps I am missing something."

Madame carefully plucked one slim line of silk from the pool and held it up, revealing a soft, sensuous lilac gown, of sorts.

"Oh, it is lovely," Grace exclaimed, marveling at the intricate lacework that banded the bodice. "But where is the rest of it?"

"That is the scandalous part, *mon amie,*" Madame Fontaine responded, holding up the second shoulder strap. The gown consisted of only enough fabric to cover Grace just past her derriere—if that.

"Is it transparent?" Grace asked, quite befuddled by this point.

"Mmm-hmm," Imogen answered, admiring the scrap of silk and lace.

Grace could not fathom what one was meant to do with something so . . . so . . . so small. "Is that meant for sleeping?"

"Only if your protector is aged, blind, and infirm," Madame answered practically.

"Oh," Grace exclaimed, feeling rather foolish. If the night before was any indication, the last thing on Mr. Clark's mind was seeing her in such a gown.

✎

"Stonecliffe?"

Langdon scanned the room and spotted Niles in the far right corner just as his friend received a facer from his sparring partner.

The Young Corinthians was a demanding organization, expecting their agents to be brutes, politicians, Casanovas, and skilled spies all at once. Langdon excelled at anything he put his mind to. But that did not mean he enjoyed it. Boxing, in his opinion, was amongst the least likable.

Deep in the underpinnings of the Young Corinthians Club, Langdon picked his way toward Niles, dodging agents in various forms of combat, until he reached the ropes that separated the boxing area from the rest of the room.

"Was that quite necessary?" Niles asked Tamborlin

as he gingerly inspected the welt growing on his right cheek.

Tamborlin offered his fellow agent a cheeky smile. "Never take your eyes off your enemy, isn't that what you are always telling the new recruits?"

Langdon laughed, garnering a glare from his friend.

Niles pointed to the door. "Go, before I literally make you eat your words," he commanded the young agent.

Tamborlin did as he was told, turning away before Niles followed through on his threat.

"He's right, you know," Langdon told his friend, eyeing the red mark on his cheek. "You are always telling the new recruits to ne—"

Niles spit into a brass basin at his feet. "Not you, too. It is your bloody fault the boy had the opportunity in the first place. You, in the combat room? Why, an agent is more likely to see the ghost of King Henry VIII scrounging about for scraps in here than find you kicking about."

"You summoned me, remember?" Langdon asked, smirking. "And I am quite glad you did. Can't remember the last time someone managed to best you. And a new recruit? Even better."

Niles narrowed his eyes at Langdon as he snapped up a length of linen from a nearby chair. "I summoned you to the *Club*, Stonecliffe. Which, in your case, historically meant your office. Or Carmichael's. Or even the floor above—and always with a newspaper in hand. But never the combat room. You are lucky boxing does not agree with you. Otherwise I might have felt obligated to teach you a thing or twelve."

Langdon cleared his throat. "And what if I said boxing does have its appeal?"

"I'd say about bloody time, old chap."

Niles swiped at his sweaty forehead with the linen then threw it on the back of the chair. "Come on, then. Let's see what you've got." He put up his fists in a classic boxer's stance.

Langdon stripped off his cravat, shrugged out of his coat and vest, rolled up his sleeves, and ducked between the ropes to join Niles. He raised his fists, mimicking his friend's position. He knew enough of the sport to protect himself from the uneducated jabs and punches thrown by most opponents. But Niles was not most opponents. The man was known throughout the Corinthians for his boxing prowess.

Langdon hoped his friend was in fine fighting form. He needed to hit something—anything. Or better yet, be hit. Whatever might erase the memory of kissing Lady Grace.

Niles suddenly dropped his hands and stepped back warily. "This is too good to be true. What are you playing at?"

"Nothing, I swear," Langdon answered honestly.

Niles stared him down, his eyes narrowing as he watched Langdon closely. He raised his fists again, apparently satisfied with what he saw. "All right, then. Glad you've come around to seeing the virtues of pounding another man to a pulp." He shifted back and forth, grinning with anticipation.

Langdon tried to follow Niles's movements but the near-dancing motion made him self-conscious. "Why did you ask me to come to the Club?"

"Oh, did not I tell you? A letter came—from the King."

Langdon stopped moving and lowered his hands, frowning blackly. "When were you going to tell me?"

Niles tapped Langdon's unprotected chin with a right hook. "Well, why else do you suppose I summoned you?"

Langdon rubbed his jaw. "Hilarious. What did the letter say?"

"Put your fists up or I'll hit you," Niles ordered.

Langdon obeyed and began the ridiculous dance once again. "There. Now, the letter."

"You, my dear sir, have been invited to a masked ball. Along with your lady."

Langdon stared at Niles's mouth, sure he'd heard wrong.

Niles took advantage of the momentary lapse in attention and hit Langdon.

"Blast," Langdon ground out, bringing his fists closer to his face. "You must be joking."

"Oh, I never joke about a masked ball, my friend," Niles replied with mock sincerity. "And this masked ball? This one is to be held at Vauxhall."

Impossible, Langdon thought. "How are we to guarantee the safety of Lady Grace in a setting as public and crowded as Vauxhall? And with everyone in disguise, no less?"

"I rather think that is the point," Niles answered sarcastically.

Langdon suddenly remembered why he was there. He needed an outlet—he needed to hit something. Even if the frustration and pent-up tension had begun with Grace, Niles's face would do just fine. "And even more reason for you to have told me at once."

"Really, Stonecliffe, have you learned nothing during the course of our friendship?" Niles gestured for Langdon to lower his fists a touch. "Of course I know the location is a logistical nightmare. But they would not budge on their terms. I knew you'd find the situation less than ideal but I couldn't figure a way around it."

Langdon followed Niles's suggestion and dropped his fists an inch or two, only to be slapped on the temple. "Do you mean to tell me you feared I would be disappointed in you?" He lunged at his friend and tried to pay him back with a blow to the stomach.

Niles effortlessly avoided Langdon's attempt by shifting to the right. "You must know that everyone fears disappointing you, Stonecliffe. You are a bloody paragon around here—just below Carmichael on the saints list, I believe."

"Paragon? Please," Langdon growled with disgust. No one was further from sainthood than he.

"Come now, modesty is absolutely overvalued, in my opinion," Niles assured him as he landed a light blow to Langdon's gut. "You are a superb agent— that goes without saying. The real issue is your decency, your . . . I don't know, humanity? It all sounds a bit glossy for my taste, but there it is. You, my friend, are a first-rate human being. A rare breed these days."

The churning tension in Langdon's gut spun into full-blown rejection and outrage. "Take it back," he said through his teeth.

"I won't," Niles said, tapping Langdon on the temple once again. "It is the truth and you know it."

"Take. It. Back," Langdon snarled. He'd had enough of such testaments on his behalf. Sophia and his brother would no doubt also be willing to relate their own angelic view of him to anyone who asked. Carmichael, too. And Grace? She believed him to be the most perfect of all.

Darkness flooded his senses, edged with red, roaring in his ears until he heard nothing else but the echo of words from his family and friends.

"You are the heir this family has waited generations for," his absentee father exclaimed.

"I am not worthy of you—nor is anyone else, I fear. You are the most honorable man on earth," Sophia promised.

"No brother could ever compare. More than that— no man could," Nicholas praised.

"I can think of only one man capable of succeeding me as the leader of the Young Corinthians. That man is you," Carmichael pronounced. Langdon lashed out, slamming his fist squarely into Niles's face.

The sight of his friend lying on the floor, blood running from his broken nose, finally silenced the voices in Langdon's head. "What have I done?" Aghast, he bent over Niles.

"You've broken my bloody nose," Niles answered, sitting up. "You are really not yourself today. What is wrong, Stonecliffe?"

"Nothing. Everything," Langdon growled in frustration. "Come, we have a ship to loot."

"They're beautiful, my lady. Now, tell me, what do you do with them?"

Mrs. Templeton stood on the opposite side of Grace's bed. A colorful array of chemises, drawers, nightrails, and robes had arrived that morning from Madame Fontaine's shop. They now lay spread out across the bed, the jewel tones and silken fabric all but begging to be caressed.

"Well, a man's mistress would wear them to please her protector," Grace answered, picking up a gossamer ice-blue nightrail.

Mrs. Templeton's brow furrowed in puzzlement. "But they'd be hidden beneath her skirts."

"Not when her dress is removed, Mrs. Templeton," Grace further elaborated, stifling a laugh when the older woman smiled with sudden insight and her brows arched in amusement.

"Ah, now I see." She smiled as she lifted a ravishing robe in deep umber trimmed in wide bands of cream lace and held it to her own body. "Is it my color, then?"

Grace could no longer hold back. She burst into laughter, delighted when Mrs. Templeton joined her. "Oh yes, Mrs. Templeton. It is quite becoming."

That only made Mrs. Templeton laugh harder. She slid the flimsy pieces aside and settled herself on the counterpane, next to the rainbow of silk and lace. "I tell you, Mr. Templeton wouldn't know what to do with something such as this—nor would I, to be honest. What will you do with them?"

That, Grace recognized, was a very good question. "Well, Imogen brought me to Madame Fontaine's shop specifically to purchase these items. It would have seemed very odd if I'd not ordered a few."

"A few, yes," Mrs. Templeton answered, busying herself by beginning to fold the lingerie. "But the delivery boy told Midge there would be three more boxes coming next week."

Three? Good Lord, Grace thought, she must have ordered more than she realized. "You know that I normally eschew such frivolous purchases—especially anything of such an intimate nature."

"Yes, of course, my lady. You did not want to encourage the doctor. But the doctor is dead now."

Grace held the ice-blue garment against her, the soft silk beneath her fingertips pure pleasure to her long-denied love of feminine garments. Could the answer be that she simply desired to once again own pretty things? Indulging in wearing silk and lace underclothing and nightrails wasn't a crime, after all.

"I am sorry, my lady," Mrs. Templeton rushed to add, placing the umber robe in the growing stack of folded garments. "It is none of my business what you buy nor what you wear."

Or was it more? Grace wondered, distracted. Was her undeniable attraction to Mr. Clark fueling a desire to feel more feminine?

"Have I upset you?"

Mrs. Templeton's question startled Grace. "Oh, my dear Mrs. Templeton, nothing you could ever do would upset me, I assure you."

"Then what troubles you, my lady?" the woman pressed, pausing to pick up a pair of ivory silk drawers edged in rose ribbon. "I know your face as well as my own. Your mind is working at something, and it weighs on you."

"Is it wrong to want, Mrs. Templeton?" Grace

asked, pushing the lingerie aside and sitting down next to her on the bed.

Mrs. Templeton studied Grace with a practical, sympathetic eye. "You know it is not, my lady. Wouldn't be human if you did not want things. And especially you, married to that monster for so many years. He did not allow you one comfort, out of spite, that one."

"I know you are right. Spending so long living without makes it difficult to move forward with, if that makes any sense."

Grace's life with the doctor had taught her how to survive with only the most base of necessities—physically and emotionally. And after a time she'd learned to almost relish her lifestyle because she knew it pained the doctor to see her derive even the minutest amount of pleasure from her life with him.

"Come, now." Mrs. Templeton patted Grace's hand. "Tell me what this is really all about."

"Am I that transparent?" Grace asked wryly, taking the dear woman's hand in hers.

"To me you are," she answered, squeezing Grace's hand. "Though perhaps not to others."

Grace had never lied to Mrs. Templeton. Honesty was intrinsic to their bond, and she could not, would not, offend her friend by lying now. The problem lay in the very fact that answering her question truthfully might do just that. "I asked you if it was wrong to want. And you answered in relation to things. But what of people? A person. Is it wrong to want someone?"

"Are we speaking strictly biblically, my lady?"

"No," Grace answered, adding, "though I will not lie. Passion does come into play."

Mrs. Templeton's gaze did not waver as she looked at Grace. "And would you be speaking of Mr. Clark?" she asked calmly.

"I would," Grace replied in a whisper, suddenly feeling quite ashamed. "Have I disappointed you?"

The woman's steel gray eyebrows lowered and she frowned in confusion. "How could you ever disappoint me?"

"He is a criminal, Mrs. Templeton—some would say no better than the doctor," Grace explained, finding it difficult to meet the woman's gaze.

"Ah, is that your worry?" she asked, her brow smoothing once more. "Mr. Clark is a criminal, that much is true. And yes, he holds that one fact in common with the doctor. But that is where those two men part ways. Mr. Clark may be a cunning criminal, but he's not a monster. I never dreamt I would see the day that I'd make a distinction between the two, but there it is."

"He breaks the law," Grace offered, feeling overly vulnerable now that she'd confided her feelings.

"Would it interest you to know that I've broken the law—as has Mr. Templeton?"

"What?" Grace looked at the woman skeptically. "When?"

"When we lost our positions with Lady Deerfield," she replied, looking into her lap as if remembering. "Neither of us could find a job—no one wanted a pair of broken-down servants. So there were times our meals were pinched from street vendors. Once, a warm coat went missing from a tailor's shop so Mr.

Templeton would not freeze to death. And there's more. I am not proud of what I've done, but I'll tell you this, I'll do it again if the need arises," she said staunchly.

"You did what you had to. There is no shame in that—"

"And how do you know Mr. Clark does not act for the very same reason?" Mrs. Templeton interrupted.

Grace could not accept the comparison. "You and Mr. Templeton were thrown out on the streets for the crime of aging. Do you believe Mr. Clark suffered cruelty at the hands of fate? Is that what drove him to become the leader of a criminal organization—one that could be even more dangerous than the Kingsmen, for all we know?"

"It sounds to me as if *you* are the one who is disappointed in your own feelings for Mr. Clark."

Mrs. Templeton had done this before in their conversations, Grace reflected. Her friend knew better than to tell Grace what to do, so she made her work for the truth, pushing till it revealed itself.

Grace pondered and then sighed. "I believed myself to be more intelligent," she said finally.

"Is it stupid to be drawn to another?" Mrs. Templeton asked. "I suppose it is. Mr. Templeton tries my patience on a daily basis—has since the day we first met. But I wouldn't have life without him."

"You are confusing me, Mrs. Templeton," Grace said. "Is it foolhardy for me to be attracted to Mr. Clark, or is it not?"

The dear woman patted Grace's hand again. "I can't answer that question, my lady. You've boiled it down until there's meat and there's bones. But that's not life. Right or wrong is not a simple thing."

Throughout her years with the doctor Grace had learned to control her emotions, to view life and its unpredictable and callous nature with calm and practicality. Mr. Clark robbed her of this particularly useful talent. She was finding it exceedingly difficult to treat him with any common sense at all.

She couldn't stop thinking about him. She lay awake at night, restless, aching and needing . . . something. She was very much afraid that what she needed was him and she had no idea what to do about it. Her time with him, of necessity, would be brief, for as soon as he'd either taken over or wiped out the Kingsmen, he would no longer need her, and their relationship would come to an end. She would retire to the country with the Templetons and he would remain in London. She thought it unlikely their paths would cross again.

"I will say that it does my heart good to know the doctor did not ruin you for love, though," Mrs. Templeton added. "Mr. Templeton and I were afraid you wouldn't be able to bear having a man so close again."

"Yes, well, I suspect Mr. Clark does not feel the same for me," Grace admitted reluctantly.

Mrs. Templeton sighed. "Than he is not the man for you. There is a whole world out there, my lady."

But Grace did not want the whole world. She wanted Mr. Clark.

12

"If you do not pull your bloody head out of your ass, I will do it for you," Niles threatened Langdon. "Give in, already. Before I suffer a second broken bone. Your cowardly ways are doing no one any good."

They stood upon the *India Queen*'s deck as she made her way slowly up the Thames toward the dock. Darkness cloaked their arrival and the waterway was eerily silent. The Corinthians had boarded the ship at Weymouth and replaced the East India Company men with their own hired crew. "My head is not in my ass," Langdon countered. "But my fist will be in your face if you do not leave off."

Niles smiled widely, his teeth a brief flash of white in the inky night. "Sensitive subject?"

"Cowardly ways?" Langdon asked incredulously.

Niles shrugged off Langdon's displeasure. "You heard me. And you know I am right. You cannot be the man you were before, but you're afraid to move forward. Lady Grace represents a different future than you'd imagined. And that scares you."

Langdon breathed in a draft of salty sea air. Niles was right. He clapped his friend on the back. "When did you become so wise?"

"Oh, I always have been," Niles answered, gesturing to the docks as they came into view. "But my wisdom intimidated you."

Langdon smiled. "Is that right?"

"Completely understandable, of course."

The East India Company owned a line of docks along the Thames, just down from Clarence Street and the Mayberry district beyond. Langdon chuckled at his friend's verbal jab as he considered the upcoming attack.

The Corinthians around the two men moved into place as the Company's dock drew near.

"I might just hand you over to the Kingsmen myself," Langdon threatened Niles while his friend pulled a knife from within his boot and tested the blade.

As the ship adjusted its speed in preparation to dock, Langdon suddenly felt very thankful for his friend. "Shall I ruin everything and say thank you for forcing me to see the fault in my thinking? And for nagging me until I did?" he asked Niles, unsheathing his knife and testing the weight of it.

Niles pretended to slit his own throat. "God, no. We are men, Stonecliffe. Save your pretty words for Lady Grace."

"Very well," Langdon replied, clapping his friend on the back once more.

The two watched as the crew rimming the perimeter of the ship began to throw the heavy lines out to men waiting on each side of the dock. What should have been impossible in fact began to take shape, the *India Queen*'s bulk reacting to the brute force of the men as they guided her safely in.

Niles returned his knife to the hidden pocket in his coat and offered his hand to Langdon. "Just in case you die a horrible death tonight, you should know working with you has not been the worst thing to happen in my life."

"I thought we were dispensing with the pretty words," Langdon said, taking Niles's hand in his and shaking it.

"I like to keep you guessing, Stonecliffe," his friend replied, then yanked his hand away and strode off toward the stern.

Langdon smiled at Niles's uncharacteristically sentimental farewell as he scanned the shadowy wharf for any sign of additional men. Other than those assisting with the docking of the *India Queen,* no one appeared to be about.

"Are you prepared, sir?" one of a handful of agents aboard asked.

"The men are ready?" Langdon countered, continuing to look out into the dark night.

"And waiting, sir."

"Then let us proceed."

Langdon walked across the deck and waved for the men to move out of his way. "Wait for my signal," he instructed them, then walked to where the men standing on the dock could see him.

"Long journey, eh?" one shouted by way of a greeting. He looked to be in his fifties, his face tanned and lined from too many hours in the salty sea air.

Langdon smiled in response, readying himself for action. "Too long."

"Aye, the Company does not mind sending you halfway 'round the world, that's for sure," the man said, offering Langdon a grin that revealed his six teeth. "My name is O'Donnell. Me and my men will get you started with the forward hull. Drop the gangplank."

Langdon casually stretched, offering a large, lionlike yawn. "Do you know, I am too tired to go through the trouble of lowering the plank. I believe there is a better way."

The man smiled a second time at Langdon and let out a bark of laughter. "Been drinking, have you? Do not blame you. In my sailing days the bottle's the only thing that got me through."

"Indeed I have," Langdon said, reaching for the cask at his feet and lifting it so that O'Donnell could see. "The Company's brandy is hard to resist." He tossed the cask over the side of the ship and watched as it hit the water, then bobbed gently away.

O'Donnell's friendly countenance turned hostile. His mouth dropped into a somber thin line and he widened his stance. "You'll be paying for that out of your wages, of course. Now lower the plank before I lose my patience."

"I'm afraid I can't do that, Mr. O'Donnell."

Langdon raised his arm, the signal to his men. All at once, casks of brandy, reams of silk, and enough spices to make an insignificant country wealthy were flying from the men's hands, over the side of the ship and into the deep waters of the Thames.

"Stop!" O'Donnell shouted as he reached into his coat pocket and produced a pistol. "That's Company property!"

Langdon smiled down at him, as the man's first shot narrowly missed. "You're mistaken. This here belongs to the Kingsmen. And we will do whatever we like with it."

A second shot landed in the wooden railing near where Langdon's hand rested.

A piercing whistle sounded and Langdon looked to where Niles stood at the stern. "Time to go," his friend called, then gestured at the longboat that waited on the water.

Langdon turned back and saluted O'Donnell. "A pleasure doing business with you," he shouted before signaling his men to abandon ship, making a run for the stern himself.

"I always did fancy myself a pirate," Niles told Langdon as they reached the railing and prepared to jump.

"Why does that not surprise me?"

∗∗∗

Langdon returned to Aylworth House from the wharf much calmer than when he'd left. Breaking Niles's nose had felt good. Looting the ship even better. Telling Lady Grace of his feelings for her would be the best. But he wanted to compose himself first, to clear his mind and prepare for what would come next.

He'd decided to walk the library, the scent of old books pleasingly familiar and calming. One complete tour of the large room failed to prepare him. And so he ventured forth on a second.

A third trip around the room had him closing his eyes to see if he could navigate the enormous room blind. The tall French case clock in the entryway unknowingly aided him when it chimed, announcing the two o'clock hour. The melodic tones allowed Langdon to orient himself in relation to the front of the house.

He was in the farthest, most northern corner of the room, nearing the end of his circuit, when a familiar feminine voice spoke behind him.

"I see you've come around to my favorite pastime."

Langdon stopped walking at the sound of Grace's voice and opened his eyes. "I'd no idea how useful pacing could be," he replied, infusing his voice with a careless note. The sight of her took his breath away.

"Oh yes, quite useful," Grace agreed, walking down the library carpet toward him, the golden light from the candlestick she carried softly illuminating her.

Her deep rose robe was tied at her waist with a satin ribbon, glimpses of the paler pink of her nightrail revealed as she walked. Her hair was loose, a thick mane of silk that fell past her shoulders, and she was barefoot, her small feet almost ghostly against the deep blue and gold of the carpet.

Botticelli? Yes, he thought, the Italian artist. Langdon had mastered the least amount of art knowledge he could, having never felt a particular affinity for the discipline. But something in Grace's ethereal appearance certainly spoke to him.

Her eyes narrowed. "Are you well, Mr. Clark?"

"That depends."

She held the candlestick aloft and studied him. "On what?"

Her clear concern shook him, even more than the pull of her curved, feminine body.

"On you."

She took a slow step back, then another. "If I've done something wrong, please tell me what it is."

"What could you possibly have done wrong?" Langdon asked.

"Please, Mr. Clark. Tell me what you mean," she urged, taking a step toward him this time.

Langdon closed his eyes for a moment, afraid to begin. "I've been such a fool."

Lady Grace set her candlestick on a nearby bookshelf. "In regards to what, Mr. Clark?"

"Not what, whom," he gently corrected.

"May I assume you are speaking of me?" she asked, coming dangerously close to him.

"You may," Langdon replied hesitantly. The room began to spin a bit. "I want you—need you. But I am afraid, Grace."

She looked at him with surprise, then reached out and laid her palm on his coat, right over his heart. "I have been afraid as well. Terrified of my husband, of the men he worked for and the things I saw. But here you are. And here I am. I want you, too, Langdon. I need you. And I will not let fear keep me from you."

Even through the layers of his coat, waistcoat, and linen shirt, her delicate hand branded his skin. He pulled in the intoxicating citrus and floral notes of her scent each time he drew a breath. Her face, so beautiful, so earnest, filled his vision. All he could feel, smell, hear, and see was Grace.

"I don't know what comes next," Langdon got out, his heart beating too loud in his ears. "I only can see right now. Right here, with you."

Grace trailed her fingers from his chest up his throat

to his face to cradle his cheeks in her soft, warm hands. "That is all I need," she whispered, then lifted on tiptoe and kissed him.

He wrapped his arms around her waist and pulled her against him. Lowering his head, he covered her mouth with his.

※ ※

Grace succumbed to the urgent, hot seduction of his mouth, without a thought. She felt surrounded by him; his arms crushed her against the hard, heated length of his body and she wrapped hers around his neck in an attempt to get closer.

He tore his lips away, lifting his head just far enough to look down at her.

"I want you in my bed." His voice was gravelly, smoky with passion.

Grace never thought to say no. Instead, she nodded mutely.

His eyes flared with heat and he caught her hand, grabbed the candlestick she'd set down, and tugged her after him, out of the library, to the stairway, and upstairs. The hallway was quiet, deserted, and they saw no one as they reached Langdon's room.

The door closed after them and Grace barely registered the quiet click as he turned the key in the lock. Langdon took her to the bed, set the candlestick on a table beneath the window, and without pausing swept her into his arms again.

This time, the kiss was slow, sensuous, and very thorough. When he lifted his head at last, Grace was heated, needy, and she murmured a protest when he unwound her arms from around his neck.

"Patience, love," he murmured, bending to press a kiss at the corner of her mouth before trailing his lips down her throat.

Grace purred with satisfaction, tilting her head to give him better access and clutching handfuls of his coat in a vain effort to pull him nearer.

He untied the sash that held her robe together and it fell open. Then he lifted his hands, slipped them along the neckline of both robe and nightrail and slid both off her shoulders in one movement.

Grace would have protested the sudden brush of cooler air against bare skin but then he kissed her again and she was lost. His hands cupped her bare bottom and lifted her, fitting her more perfectly against him, the cove of her hips against the hard thrust of his. Grace gasped, awash in sensation.

She was heated, flushed, and panting when he tore his mouth from hers.

"I have too many clothes on," he told her, his mouth quirking as she stared up at him, uncomprehending, unable to adjust to the sudden switch from heated passion to conversation.

Then she translated what he'd said and nodded.

"Yes, you do." She brushed his hands aside and tugged at his cravat, then abandoned her efforts, leaving him to unwind it while she moved on to his shirt.

She couldn't help pausing to stroke and explore each part of his body as he shed clothes. Her curiosity and fascination made his undressing take longer than it should have, but at last he shoved his breeches and smalls to the floor and stepped out of them.

Grace caught her breath, staring. He was amazingly built, with sleek powerful muscles layering his broad chest and down his abdomen, which tapered to narrower hips and strong thighs.

Her bare feet looked delicate and narrow, so close to his much larger ones.

Her gaze traveled back up his calves and thighs. Her eyes widened as she took in the aroused length of him, and caught her breath.

"Oh my," she breathed when he visibly thickened beneath her stare.

"Did you never see your husband unclothed?" His voice was deeper, rougher than before.

"Oh yes," she replied. She tore her gaze from the fascinating sight and looked up at him. "But never like"—she gestured at the jutting length of him—"like this."

A faint frown of confusion creased a V between his brows before it cleared. "You mean aroused? Your husband didn't get hard when you had sex?"

Grace felt the heat of embarrassment move up her throat and warm her face. "We didn't, actually, um . . ." She cleared her throat, her gaze chasing away from his. "He couldn't, so we never had sexual congress." She laced her fingers together, staring at them. "He said it was my fault. I suppose I should have told you earlier . . . that I'm not good at this."

Langdon's low growl yanked her gaze back up to his.

"It was *not* your fault, sweetheart. He was older, maybe that's why he was incapable, but whatever caused his problem, it damn sure wasn't you." He lowered his head and pressed a hot, openmouthed kiss against her mouth and set her simmering once again, relieved and aroused. "You have to be honest with me," he said when he lifted his head, his voice rough with desire. "Are you a virgin?"

"Of course." She frowned at him, confused. "I just told you that I didn't have marital relations with my husband. Why would you ask if I'm a virgin? What else could I possibly be?"

His eyes turned darker, more slumberous. "Oh, Grace, I've never met a woman quite like you. What else could you be, indeed?" He cupped her face in his hands and brushed cherishing kisses over her cheeks and closed eyelids until she shivered.

"And since you are," he continued, breathing the words against the shell of her ear. "I'm thinking you might like to explore a little, yes?"

She nodded, her cheeks hot, and he chuckled before releasing her and easing back. He dropped his arms to his sides and nodded. "I'm all yours, Grace."

She caught her breath, hesitating. But when he didn't move and waited patiently, she reached out and closed her hand around his penis.

He twitched, going completely still, fists curled at his sides, his breathing labored, as she explored, smoothing her fingers over the head and testing the fascinating contradiction of silky smooth skin over steely hardness. He throbbed beneath her palm, pulsing with a rhythm as fast and hard as her own heartbeat.

At last, he groaned and covered her hand with his. "Grace, sweetheart, any more of that and I'll be finished before we've started."

"But . . ." she protested, not ready to cease exploring.

Gently, he took her hand from him and bent to swing her up in his arms, turning to lay her down on the bed. The sheets were cool against her back but she did not have time to do more than briefly notice before he came down on top of her. His much broader body blanketed her as he wedged a place for himself between her thighs. She felt a brief moment of panic but then his mouth took hers once more and desire claimed her, erasing her fear. He cupped her breasts, his big hands warm as he caressed her. He touched her everywhere, smoothing his palms over her throat, shoulders, and down her arms, stroking over the smooth skin of her abdomen and lower.

She loved every slide of his hand, every brush of his mouth against her throat and breasts. She'd never really been touched with affection and love by a man, and he tore away her defenses and loneliness with each glide of his hands and press of his lips.

His slow, heated seduction had Grace twisting beneath him, pleading, when he finally shifted, settling deeper between her thighs. She felt the hard length of him nudge against her, then a slow, heavy penetration that pinned her and had her clutching his shoulders to pull him closer.

He slowed, then surged forward and held himself still when she couldn't hold back a moan. Braced on his elbows, he lifted his head and looked down at her, eyes molten.

"Are you all right?" His voice rasped, deep and gravelly.

"Yes," she murmured. Threading her fingers into

his thick hair, she urged him back down. "Do not stop."

He obeyed, his mouth taking hers as his hips shifted against her. Within moments, she was gasping, begging him for release from the tension that strung tighter with each slide of his body against hers.

Then the world exploded and she cried out, catching him tighter as he climaxed, then fell with her into a deep well of pleasure.

Exhausted, Grace fell asleep and was only vaguely aware that he left the bed, returning with a warm, damp cloth that he stroked gently between her legs. When he slid back into the bed beside her, she rolled against his side and murmured her pleasure as he wrapped her in his arms, and she slept.

He woke her again during the night and they made love with an intensity that left her feeling vulnerable, her emotions laid bare.

When she woke the next morning, she was in her own bed.

Langdon must have carried her back to her room, she thought. She smiled and wondered if he would come to her bed, or take her to his, that night.

The possibility made her heart beat faster.

She couldn't wait. And she was giddy with the good fortune that had let her first lover be Langdon and not her husband. She couldn't imagine spending those hours with anyone else.

She tossed back the covers, crossed to the armoire and pulled its door open, then bent to rummage through a stack of nightrails.

"Where did Mrs. Templeton put the umber nightgown?"

She wanted to wear it tonight. A mischievous smile curved Grace's lips.

She now understood exactly why women became mistresses, she thought. It was time to embrace all the benefits of being the Wicked Widow.

13

Grace adjusted the intricate mask of silver and gold she wore. "Well, I suppose an uncomfortable mask is better than the oppressive hat," she said to Langdon, burrowing closer to his side as the crowds of Vauxhall Gardens pressed against her.

He tightened his arm about her waist. "Very pragmatic of you," he confirmed, a charming smile appearing just below his fanciful mask.

Grace smirked in reply. "Are you teasing me for being practical?"

"Not at all," he replied in earnest. "It is one of your most admirable traits. And until you came along, one of mine."

"What do you mean, until I came along?" she asked, narrowing her eyes as she considered whether he'd meant to pay her a compliment.

Or not.

The crowd around them seemed to pulse with excitement. Cries of delight and anticipation broke out in the cheaper boxes. Wearing concealing masks apparently made the revelers feel anonymous—and more uninhibited.

Langdon bent closer and his lips brushed against the shell of her ear. "I mean, when you are in sight, I cannot think rationally, let alone practically. All I want is you and damn all the rest."

"Oh," Grace replied, delight flooding her. "Is it wrong that I find the idea of holding some sort of power over you enjoyable?"

He laughed out loud, a charming dimple creasing his cheek. "Not at all."

"Very enjoyable? Extremely so?" she pressed, desperate to see him smile.

"Power monger," he muttered good-naturedly, the delicious dimple appearing once more.

Flirting again, after she'd spent so long avoiding innuendo and affection, felt good to Grace. She was elated to learn she'd not forgotten how to do it.

A man stepped in front of them, a sly, wily grin on his long, narrow face. "Good evening to you, Mr. Clark."

Grace did not recognize him as a member of the Kingsmen, but that meant very little, especially in light of his jaunty scarlet mask. New recruits were forced into service every day. She was glad she still wore the serviceable dagger strapped to her thigh.

"Mr. Davis," Langdon replied in a relaxed manner. "We've been looking for you everywhere."

"You've not been able to see me, as you've been admiring the Widow, here," the man countered, his smile friendly as he bowed politely to Grace. "And who would blame you."

Langdon looked down at Grace, consideration on his face, laughter in his eyes. "Should I introduce you to Mr. Davis? His charm is well known. He might just steal you away, right out from under my nose."

"Impossible," Grace assured him, then held out her hand to the man.

"Very well," Langdon proceeded. "Lady Grace, may I introduce you to Mr. Richard Davis, my second in command."

Mr. Davis carefully clasped her fingers and bowed with polite deference, his eyes twinkling as he looked up at her from beneath his lashes.

Amused, Grace laughed softly.

"That is far too sweet a sound to have come from the Wicked Widow," he remarked, winking rakishly.

"And that is far too grand a mustache to spring on unsuspecting strangers, Mr. Davis," Grace replied, looking pointedly at his upper lip.

Surprised, Mr. Davis let out a hearty bark of laughter and smoothed his fingers over the brushy length. "All part of the masquerade, I'm afraid."

She cast a critical eye over the man's face, finally offering a nod of judicious approval.

"I see where the 'wicked' in your name was earned," he said, then turned to Langdon. "It is a pity she will not be meeting the King this evening. She might have been able to thaw his heart a bit."

Mr. Davis gestured toward the luxurious guest boxes located near the end of the promenade. "He awaits—with very little patience, I might add."

"We are on time," Langdon said, scanning the boxes. "Besides, we hold the upper hand. Surely the King understands this. Otherwise, he would not be here."

"I agree. But even if he knows how this will play out, that does not mean the King has to be at peace with the impending takeover of his organization."

Grace had heard countless men and women make references to the King. His reputation alone did not frighten her, but the thought of sitting near to the notorious gang leader who had given the order for her own death made her heart beat faster. She turned her body into Langdon's until she was as close as she could possibly get to his hard strength.

He tightened his grip about her waist, which eased her concern . . . a little. "And you can assure me the night will proceed as planned?"

"What good would I be if I could not?" Mr. Davis asked dryly, rolling his shoulders back and standing tall. "I've had eyes on the gardens since you received the summons. The Kingsmen are well represented tonight, but we still outman them three to one. Seems they've underestimated just how seriously you desire this partnership to work."

Mr. Davis's information eased Grace's nerves. "Then we'll be safe?" she asked, wanting Langdon to confirm. Only hearing the words from his lips could completely convince her. And she needed to be convinced. Otherwise, she'd not be able to play her part in the evening's charade. And she wouldn't—no, couldn't—disappoint Mr. and Mrs. Templeton. Nor herself. The Kingsmen would pay for Timothy's death, and Grace would have a say in just how high the price would be.

"Sounds rather weak, I suppose," she added, sorry that she'd said the words out loud in front of Mr. Davis.

Langdon tipped her chin up to look into her eyes. "You will always be safe now."

Grace's fear slipped away from her just as the collective noise from the surrounding crowd did, until there was only one thought that existed in her mind:

She did not feel afraid.

For the first time in her life, fear did not accompany her initial steps toward the future. She knew her time with Langdon would end when all this was over, but she would be settled, safely, in the country. Away from London. But also away from Langdon. So for now, she was determined to make the most of every moment with him.

"I believe you," she murmured. Langdon's dark eyes flared with heat. His hand tightened on her waist.

Mr. Davis cleared his throat and Grace realized that Langdon's associate still waited.

"I suppose we've kept the King waiting long enough," Langdon said, then asked Grace, "would you agree?"

His words. His presence. Him. Langdon could reveal her vulnerability with a touch and convince Grace of her strength with one word.

She took a half step away from him and squared her shoulders. "I would."

※ ⅋

"So it is true. The doctor's widow stands at the usurper's side."

The Queen held the spyglass up to her eye. "Why the gardens?"

"They seemed the perfect choice. Mr. Clark will not see us coming—and if he does, he won't know to defend himself. One bloody harlequin domino looks the same as another at these events."

"Do not use such foul language in my presence," she ordered, lowering the spyglass and glaring at him. "I am your Queen."

"Of course, Your Grace," Beaufort humbly replied, hoping he'd managed the right touch of feigned obeisance.

God but he wanted to kill her. He'd dreamt of it many times—too many times, strictly speaking, until now he feared he was obsessed with it. He watched as she adjusted the gold mask that hid her eyes and upper face, her beaklike nose sniffing delicately as if she'd smelled something offensive.

"And how will it be done?" she asked, resting back in the gilt-wood chair.

Beaufort had already explained the plan to her two times. Details were beginning to muddle her, only the eventual death of the doctor's widow fastened in her mind.

"We'll wait until the fireworks are almost over," he began, barely able to hide his annoyance. "Jones sawed through the back left panel of the box—though no one would be able to tell. He's rigged it so that when the time is right, he can pull the panel out and take Mrs. Crowther. The crowd will be looking at the sky, just before all goes black."

The Queen's thin lips pursed. "Won't the light from the fireworks reveal you?"

"That is why our timing is key, Your Grace. We know how long the fireworks will last and when to take Mrs. Crowther. You've nothing to be concerned about."

He regretted the implication the moment the words left his lips. He groaned silently. Sometimes it felt as if he would never learn when it came to the Queen.

She sucked in a long draw of air and held it for interminable moments. Her face reddened from the effort until Beaufort thought she just might pass out.

And then the *sound*. The low, hissing release of pressure as she breathed out her displeasure. She was livid.

"I have nothing to be concerned about, you say? With one quick strike the man has managed to nearly destroy our agreement with the East India Company. He has in his possession the doctor's wife. Have I forgotten anything?"

Failing to answer was not an option. Beaufort had played this game before. He knew she wanted him to meekly place his neck in the noose.

"No, Your Grace." It took all his control to manage the subservient tone he knew was required.

Her unblinking, glittering gaze pierced him.

"I'll not remind you of the power I wield—power I earned all on my own. No one gave it to me. No one laid the foundation, built the house, and then invited me in."

"Are you suggesting I contribute nothing to the Kingsmen?" he ground out, his control slipping as he wiped a bead of sweat from his temple.

She did not move, her face frozen in superiority. "I am suggesting you remember your place, Mr. Beaufort."

The Queen never used his given name. She was making a point. Would in blood, if necessary.

"I remember," he said, the anger that had threatened his common sense beginning to cool.

"This Mr. Clark, is dealing with him the reason for your impudent behavior?"

Well, Clark was as good an excuse as any. Besides, there was some truth in her question. If Clark succeeded in taking over the Kingsmen, life for Beaufort and all of his men would change.

He looked at the bloody bitch seated before him and believed he could almost guarantee it would change for the better.

"Yes, Your Grace," he finally replied, avoiding her eyes. "I did not want to worry you. But you are far too intelligent for such games. Mr. Clark is a very real threat to all that you've worked so hard to build."

"And the doctor's wife, do not forget to factor her in," the Queen added. "If she should realize who I am . . ."

Beaufort had half a mind to question Crowther's widow himself and wring the information from her before handing her over to his men. He'd no idea what-all Mrs. Crowther knew. But from the Queen's reaction, there was enough for blackmail. "I have to think Mr. Clark would have used any information the doctor's wife had by now."

What was it that the blasted woman knew? Had she somehow seen the Queen's face? Beaufort looked again at his employer. Nothing about the mask or her fine gown and turban spoke of anything incriminating. Of course, the light was poor in the box, as he'd purposely lit few candles, so he supposed something about her might stand out in the light of day.

If he could somehow be responsible for capturing the woman . . .

"Good point, Mr. Beaufort," the Queen intoned, then muttered something to herself.

It would mean taking out Clark and his men. He kept the Widow under constant guard.

"Unless she has not told him yet."

Hate to lose a man like Clark. If he could negotiate a partnership with him, it would be highly profitable. And if it meant he could get out from under the bitch's thumb?

"Well, we'll have her all to ourselves soon enough," the Queen finished, raising the spyglass to her eye once more and pointing it through the velvet curtains of the tent. "They're very nearly to the box."

"Yes, Your Grace," Beaufort replied, glad to be released.

"Do not fail me, Mr. Beaufort," she said coldly, not bothering to look at him. "Disappointing me would be a mistake."

He glared at the woman, wanting to reach over and throttle her. Only iron control kept him from acting on the urge and allowed him to silently stand and leave the box.

14

Langdon escorted Grace toward their box, his arm entwined with hers. The mask accentuated her intelligent eyes, turning them into mysterious pools of dark, shaded violet, while the golden velvet cloak she wore hid her curves from all.

Except for him. Every inch of Grace's soft, supple body was catalogued in his mind for easy reference. The hollow at the base of her throat, the sensual weight of her breasts. Even the mole in the middle of her back—all there within reach, waiting for him to savor.

Niles walked just ahead of the couple. He glanced over his shoulder. "Are we ready, then?"

The question forced Langdon to rein in his wayward thoughts and focus on the Corinthian plan. It was essential that he not allow Grace's presence to distract him. Otherwise, she would be in danger's way. He nodded at Niles. "Ready. Be a good man and do not let Lady Grace out of your sight."

Niles looked back at him, one eyebrow raised in surprise. "Do you question my abilities?"

"Not at all," Langdon murmured in his friend's ear, careful not to let Grace hear, "but I need to know that she's safe."

Niles's eyes sharpened. "You have my word—"

"Gentlemen."

Langdon straightened, slipping seamlessly into his role of criminal leader as Marcus Mitchell strode toward them. "Mr. Mitchell," he said coolly.

"Good evening, Marcus." Grace's hold on Langdon's hand loosened. "I'd hoped you would be in attendance this evening."

"You flatter me, Lady Grace," Mitchell replied, his tone too familiar for Langdon's taste.

Langdon released Grace's hand and placed his palm on the small of her back. "Mr. Davis will be dining with you," he told her, easily cutting off the conversation between her and Mitchell. "I'll return shortly."

Grace smiled and allowed him to kiss her hand. "Do not be long."

Langdon savored the feel of her delicate, gloved fingers beneath his lips, and then turned to Mitchell. "Shall we?"

"This way." Mitchell smiled at Grace before turning and walking up the path toward the King's box.

Langdon pretended to adjust his mask and scanned their surroundings as they wove their way through the crowd. Vauxhall Gardens had never held much interest for him. Now it possessed even less. The crowds of people would have presented a problem no matter the location. But in the dark, it was worse— although, he did take some comfort in the fact while the night put the Corinthians at a disadvantage, it did the same for the Kingsmen.

The orchestra, situated in a building of its own in the center of the Grove, struck up a cheery tune. Apparently inspired by the music—and, more important, by the champagne and ale—people began to clap in time and even a few cheered. The din of music, raised voices, and bawdy laughter filled the cool night air.

A woman staggered toward them down the path. Dressed as a fairy, her wings swayed behind her as she lifted up her skirts to keep from tripping. "Beg your pardon," she said as she passed, her breath reeking of wine.

The savory smells of Vauxhall ham wafted from the kitchens, the aroma of roast chicken and freshly baked bread blended with the woman's stench until Langdon's nose twitched from the overwhelming combination.

"A friend of yours?" Langdon said dryly to Mitchell, tilting his chin toward the inebriated woman.

"The Kingsmen enjoy females and we are nothing if not predictable," he replied over his shoulder. "And you? Surely a man of your standing does not make do with only Mrs. Crowther for entertainment?"

Anger flared and Langdon bit off a curse, reining in his urge to make Mitchell apologize for his words. What he wouldn't do to give Grace his name and the protection it afforded. But he had a game to play tonight and he couldn't let personal feelings interfere with solving the case.

"Mrs. Crowther is a name for a dour, beaten-down soul, wouldn't you agree? While Grace . . ." He let his mind's eye travel from her lovely eyes to her full, luscious mouth.

"We are in agreement—for once, Mr. Clark," Mitchell replied, his face somber as he looked at Langdon. "Our Grace has never been a beaten-down soul—nor will she ever be."

"No, I am certain that she will not," Langdon answered, infusing his voice with a lightness he did not feel in the least.

"You are a lucky man," Mitchell said, his voice hard. He looked ahead as they neared the King's box. "And here we are, Clark."

Langdon shifted his attention from Mitchell to the box. Four men and one woman sat within. The grim atmosphere looked to be the opposite of the crowd's loud celebrating that reigned outside the King's box. No one seemed to be engaged in conversation. In fact, they looked not to be acknowledging one another at all, their faces so stony they could have been awaiting the executioner.

"I see my reputation precedes me," Langdon commented.

Mitchell halted and turned to face him. "In a manner of speaking, yes. Your business proposition piqued the King's interest, of that you can be sure. Which is why you are about to meet the Queen."

"The Queen? Not the King? You lied to my men." Langdon's mind quickly recalibrated the evening's plan in light of the news. "You lied to me," he said, his voice lethally cold.

"I did not know myself that he wouldn't be here until this evening," Mitchell countered. "But you should not be disheartened. No one meets the King until they've entertained the Queen—well, in theory anyway. I can't recall the last time anyone made it as far as even this. Well done, Mr. Clark."

Langdon scowled at Mitchell. He had a swift, strong urge to wipe the smirk off the other man's face with his fist. "Do not lie to me again. Or you will regret it. Do you understand?"

"I will do my best. But keeping promises is not my strong suit," Mitchell replied, the smirk fading.

Langdon's blood rose at the man's continuing impertinence. "Is that right? Well, it is one of mine," he said softly. "You've been warned."

Mitchell ignored him. Without another word, he gestured for Langdon to follow and within a mere twenty or so steps, they reached the King's box.

Mitchell knocked at the entrance and waited. The door opened and one of the four men Langdon had seen earlier appeared. "Mr. Mitchell," the giant said by way of a greeting, his thick dockside drawl lingering in Langdon's ears.

He was one of the largest men Langdon had ever seen. In fact, if he were someone prone to believing in fairy tales and such, Langdon suspected the giant would have played a starring role in one of the Grimms' works.

The man looked at Langdon and grunted, clearly less than impressed.

"Thank you, Isle," Mitchell replied, gesturing for the man to move. "Now let us pass."

Isle continued to stare at Langdon. "Aye," he eventually agreed, and moved aside.

"Isle?" Langdon asked as he followed Mitchell into the box. "An interesting name."

Mitchell paused to watch the giant close and lock the door. "More descriptive than interesting. It is short for 'island.' Because he's the size of one."

"Mr. Mitchell is endlessly creative when it comes to christening our men. Wouldn't you agree?"

Langdon waited for his eyes to adjust to the candle-light as he considered the Queen's words. "Christen-ing?"

The woman sat in profile, watching the festivities through a spyglass. Her features were hidden behind an intricate mask. "Yes, of course. Our men are born anew when they join the Kingsmen. Is this not com-mon practice where you come from?"

"I am afraid not," he answered, sure he was meant to be insulted by the lack of eye contact. "We are far too busy seeing to our success."

That got her attention. The Queen instantly dropped the eyeglass in her lap and swiveled her head about to face him. "And are we to be properly intro-duced?" she demanded imperiously.

"My Queen, may I introduce Mr. Clark of Liver-pool," Mitchell began.

The Queen nodded, the tassel on her aubergine tur-ban swaying.

"Mr. Clark, the Queen."

Langdon bowed as if he stood before a real queen. "Your Grace."

"Ah, you do have manners," she exclaimed, disbe-lief coloring her tone. "And here I'd been taught to believe pirates are nothing more than savages."

Langdon rose. "Pirates, Your Grace? Ah, you must be referring to the *India Queen*. Well, don't say I didn't give you fair warning."

"Hemlock, move," the Queen ordered the man on her left, ignoring Langdon's teasing.

The man obeyed, unfolding his long, wiry frame and standing.

Langdon assumed from the man's name he specialized in poisoning people. Hemlock's stained fingers and shifty gaze only deepened his belief.

"Come," the Queen commanded, gesturing for Langdon to claim the seat vacated by Hemlock.

Langdon moved across the box, stealing a glance at the two unnamed men. Both stared straight ahead, their eyes lifeless in their identical faces.

"Tweedledee and Tweedledum, for obvious reasons," she explained, holding up the eyeglass once more.

So Mitchell is the highest-ranking Kingsman in attendance, besides the Queen?

Langdon mentally filed away the telling fact and sat down next to the woman. "As I was saying, someone has been telling stories."

"Do you not plan to plunder the Kingsmen? To take what is not yours?"

Now that he was close, Langdon could better see the Queen. She was older than he'd first guessed, perhaps in her fifties. The skin on her neck drooped slightly and her fair hands were wrinkled. Her high-necked muslin gown and cashmere wrap were of fine quality and her kidskin boots peeking out from beneath her hem looked to be brand-new. She sat with her spine rigid, her shoulders rolled back and straight.

All of these things could be learned or bought with money. After all, dance masters, modistes—anyone required to make a lady into a lady, really—had to make money to survive.

But something about the Queen told Langdon she wasn't a street urchin who'd rose from nothing and paid her way to gentility. Instinct told him she'd been born a lady; he'd stake his life on it.

"Mine is a business proposition, Your Grace," Langdon answered her, accepting a glass of wine from Hemlock. "Not a hostile siege."

The Queen lifted a glass that rested on a small table next to her. "Stealing what rightfully belongs to someone else is not hostile?"

He had to admire the woman's skill with treachery. She needed to know how many details about the Company delivery Langdon had managed to procure.

"Oh yes, that," Langdon replied with casual charm. "Necessary and wasteful, but hardly what I would call hostile."

The Queen took a slow sip of her wine, her sharp, dark eyes watching Langdon over the rim of her glass.

She returned it to the table with a snap and pursed her lips in derision. "I see. And the Widow Crowther?" she asked, raising her chin haughtily. "What does she make of her part in all of this?"

Langdon swirled the wine in his cup slowly. He'd yet to drink. Nor did he plan to. Poison was all too easily disguised in wine. "It is a touch premature to be speaking of such things, wouldn't you agree? I was disappointed that you missed my deadline."

The Queen visibly paled at his condescending tone.

"Tell me, Your Grace, how much longer will we play this game?" Langdon asked purposely, stripping his voice down to nothing more than danger and intent. "I would hate to miss the famous Vauxhall ham."

The Queen took up her spyglass again and turned to the crowd beyond. "We've yet to even speak of terms, Mr. Clark."

"I'll not discuss terms with you."

"Because I am a woman?" the Queen asked, her hands visibly tightening as she held the spyglass aloft once more.

Langdon handed the untouched glass of wine back to Hemlock and stood. "No, not because you are a woman. Because you are not the King."

He strode toward the door, his gaze cold, lethal, as he purposely looked at each of the four men as he passed. "This situation appears to be quite difficult for you to address, my Queen. Therefore, I will allow you two days to respond before I find it necessary to teach you a second lesson. Good evening."

15

Grace had never been able to understand why everyone fussed over the Vauxhall ham. She speared a piece from her plate and placed it in her mouth. Thin, salty, and ridiculously expensive.

A footman appeared in their box and began to douse the candles.

"Did anyone ask you to do that?" Mr. Davis snarled, standing up from his seat next to Grace.

"It is for the fireworks, my lord," the young man explained, staring at his boots.

"Leave them. Go. Now," Mr. Davis ordered the footman just as the colorful display began.

"Mr. Davis," Grace said, gesturing for him to reclaim his seat. "Come, or you will miss the show."

"I am not here for the fireworks, my lady," Mr. Davis replied, reluctantly returning to his seat.

"You yourself said we outman the Kingsmen three to one. I do not know about you, but I rather like those numbers," Grace reassured him.

The first of the fireworks exploded across the darkened sky, streaks of light racing against one another. Though she'd never had the opportunity to view a fireworks spectacle, Grace had always assumed it would be entertaining. And if the opening sequence was a promise of things to come, her assumption had been correct.

"Oh," Grace murmured, more impressed than she'd hoped to be. "It is beautiful, isn't it?"

Mr. Davis humphed with disapproval. "Considering it is akin to setting coin on fire for entertainment? Yes, I suppose it is."

The shape of a flying horse appeared overhead in shades of gold and blue. A unified "ooh" of awe rose from the dinner boxes and Grace smiled. "Come now, surely a flying horse in the sky is impressive— even to you, Mr. Davis."

The horse slowly melted just as a woodland rabbit hopped across the stars. Suddenly the outline of a large hawk appeared. In pursuit, its wings were fully extended and his beak parted as he swooped down toward the rabbit. His claws dropped and he scooped the helpless animal up in his powerful talons.

Grace squeaked in surprise, as did many of the other women around her. Thankfully, the creators of the light show brought the image to a thrilling end before the impending carnage.

"I must admit, I found that impressive," Mr. Davis commented, his eyes now fixed on the display high above.

"That is very male of you," Grace said, glad for Mr. Davis's presence. The rest of the box was absolutely filled to bursting by Langdon's men, including Midge. She liked Midge, but he, much like the rest of their party, was not the loquacious type. Grace was too practical to react to such treatment in a sensitive manner. She understood that the men had a job to do. And talking to her was not one of their duties.

Mr. Davis, on the other hand, while nowhere near chatty, was at least willing and able to carry on a conversation.

He puffed out his chest and clapped his fist against his coat in a comical gesture. "Well, I am a man, my lady. And this display," he gestured at the night sky, "involves loud explosions and marauding hawks. Both are decidedly male interests."

Grace laughed and looked up at the dark sky just as a gathering of fairies in pinks and lavenders floated away. "Surely you are comfortable enough in your manhood to admit when something more tender, such as fairies, tickles your fancy?"

Before he could reply to her teasing comment, a loud crash directly behind them startled Grace. Davis pushed Grace to the floor. "Stay right here. Do not move until I tell you it is safe to do so."

Long strides carried him across the box and the wall of Langdon's men parted, quickly closing behind him, and he disappeared from Grace's view.

Every inch of Grace's body and brain screamed for her to run away. She pressed her back against the wall of the box. Dealing with the doctor had been fertile ground for training her how to deal with dangerous circumstances, though her preferred method had always been to hide.

Grace fumbled with her skirts and slipped her knife from its sheath. She braced for the yells and screams that would surely accompany the attack. Men never fought without the horror of the battle being expressed in as many different ways as was possible. The smell of sweat and urine. The sight of torn flesh and broken bone. The sounds were the worst of all.

You could close your eyes and bury your nose in your wrap. And try to block out the horrific sounds by covering your ears with your hands. It never worked, really. Men's violent efforts and ensuing pain were far too strong to be muffled.

Grace braced herself for the terrifying sounds—but none came. Instead, she heard the low scuffle of boots on the plank floor. Straining, she then heard the wet suck of a knife being withdrawn from flesh. And finally a man's last whispered gasp for life, air dragging against his windpipe, desperate for working organs that would guarantee its usefulness.

The group of men parted and Davis emerged, stalking toward her, followed by two of Langdon's men. One of them took her hand and pulled her to her feet while another took a stance behind her. The three formed a protective circle around Grace, blocking her from the rest of the men.

"What is it? What's happening?" She went up on tiptoe but couldn't see past her guardians' broad bulk.

"Stay down, my lady," Davis urged, his large frame easily blocking Grace.

Determined to know what threatened her, she ducked and peered around his upper arm. The sky lit up with another burst of fireworks, illuminating the scene just beyond. Midge stood with his back to Grace, a man lying silent and unnaturally still at his feet. Just behind the two, more of Langdon's men appeared to be securing the back panel of the dinner box.

The outer door of the box slammed open, drawing the attention of all within.

"Where is Lady Grace?" Langdon's deep voice was hard, demanding an answer.

"Here," Grace called out. The agents around her stepped back and she saw past them to the doorway. "I am here."

Langdon strode toward her, his men clearing a path, moving out of his way. "Are you all right?" he asked, controlled fury lacing his tone.

"She's safe," Davis answered.

Langdon reached her and cradled her face in his hands. His fierce gaze scanned her pale features in an all-encompassing sweep. "Lady Grace?"

"I am unharmed," she answered, a tremor building within her as she looked into his eyes. "I promise."

The tremble transformed into violent shaking and Grace collapsed against him.

With a muttered curse, he instantly gathered her in his arms.

"I cannot stop shivering," Grace muttered between her chattering teeth. He was blessedly warm and she wrapped her arms around his neck, pressing closer.

His arms tightened.

"You are in shock, my lady," Langdon explained, carefully maneuvering his large frame through the door. "Davis, come with me. Bring four men with you. Leave the rest to clean up."

Grace clasped her hands more tightly around Langdon's neck. "I am able to walk," she insisted, pressing her face against his strong shoulder. She knew her words were contradicted by her actions. Still, instinct compelled her, the need to feel Langdon's warmth seemed essential.

"You are not," he replied, his voice grim. They

took the shortest path toward the boat landing, the five men with them forming a wall of protection around them. "And even if you were, I would not allow it. I need you in my arms."

"Sir," Davis said, breathless as he caught up with them.

"Is the intruder dead?"

Davis took off his coat and tucked it around Grace. "Yes, sir."

Langdon swore under his breath. "Do we know who sent him?"

"He bears a tattoo of a chess piece."

Grace turned her face into Langdon's chest and closed her eyes.

"The mark of the Kingsmen," Langdon said, his voice hard.

"We'll make them pay, sir," Davis assured him.

Langdon's heartbeat hammered beneath Grace's cheek. "Oh, of that you can be sure."

❦

Langdon swept Grace into Aylworth House, an arm around her waist. He was reluctant to let her go. He'd held her on his lap, close in his arms, on the coach drive home. He still needed her under his hand, the feel of her slim body next to his was necessary to his sanity and uncertain temper.

"Have water brought up immediately for her ladyship's bath," he told Yates, pausing inside the entry.

"Right away, sir." Yates cast a concerned glance over Grace's pale face and hurried away.

Langdon strode across the marble-floored entry-way and up the stairs, taking Grace with him.

"I am perfectly well, Langdon," she protested as he closed her bedroom door behind them and untied her domino.

"You are still trembling," he said grimly, pushing the encompassing cloak from her shoulders and tossing it across a nearby chair. "And you are too pale."

"I am a bit chilly, that's all," she insisted.

"That's not all of it," he told her as he quickly and efficiently stripped her out of her clothing and bundled her into a robe. "You shouldn't have been there tonight."

"I wanted to be there," she reminded him. "I would have been most put out with you had I not been."

Langdon ran his fingers through his hair and shook his head. "You could have been hurt. And it would have been my fault." The thought terrified him. He shrugged out of his coat and tossed it over a nearby chair, then unwound his cravat as he walked to the small table beneath the window. A decanter half-filled with brandy sat on a silver tray with several glasses.

He poured brandy into two of the heavy cut-glass goblets and handed her one.

She eyed it dubiously.

"Just sip it," he told her. "It will warm you and steady your nerves."

"Very well. If you insist." She took a tiny sip and shuddered, waited a moment, then sipped again. The second taste went down easier. "Langdon—" she began but a knock on the door silenced her.

"Your ladyship?" Yates said through the closed door. "Your bath is ready."

"Thank you, Yates," Grace called out.

"It is about time," Langdon muttered. He took her hand and opened the door to the bathing room just beyond.

The large tub was filled with gently steaming water. Langdon slipped her robe off her shoulders, letting it fall to pool at her feet, and caught her waist, lifting her up.

Grace gasped, her hands closing over his forearms, her eyes wide.

"Shhh, I've got you." Langdon gently set her down in the rose-scented water.

"Ahhh, this is lovely," she murmured, closing her eyes as she eased back to rest her head on the rim of the tub. A smile of pleasure curved her lips.

Langdon couldn't resist her. He bent and pressed his mouth to hers. She responded instantly, lips soft and inviting, coaxing his, her damp hands cupping his nape to urge him nearer.

Langdon lifted his head and looked down at her. Her violet eyes were smoky, darkened, and sultry. The silky curves of her breasts and shoulders were flushed pink from the heat of the water and their kiss.

"You are feeling warmer." It wasn't a question. Still, Grace nodded in response.

"As am I."

His dry comment made her laugh.

"You would be much cooler without your clothes," she said, eyes sparkling with mischief.

He eyed her for a moment, delighted by her daring. "You are right," he said at last. "I believe I would be."

He removed his onyx studs and set them on the

table that held a stack of linen drying cloths, some washcloths, a bowl with soap, and a jar of rose-scented bath oil. Then he shrugged out of his shirt and sat on one of the chairs, where he managed to tug off his snug boots. Then he stood and without ceremony shoved his breeches down his legs.

Throughout his disrobing, Grace watched him silently, her eyes darkening even further, lashes half-lowered.

"Move up, love," he told her.

Grace scooted forward and he stepped into the bath behind her, water sloshing dangerously close to the rim as he sank down.

"Oh, this is so nice," she murmured as he stretched long legs out alongside her hips and slipped an arm around her waist, drawing her back to lean against his chest. She rested her head on his shoulder, her damp hair tickling his throat when she turned to look up at him. "Are you warm, sir?" she teased.

He brushed a kiss against her temple and chuckled. "I am, madam. As you no doubt can tell." He spread his fingers over her belly and nudged her back against his solid erection.

Her gaze turned sultry. "So I can," she murmured with a soft laugh.

Langdon scooped the bar of French soap from the bowl and rubbed it between his hands until bubbles dripped from his fingers. Then he set the soap back in the bowl and smoothed his hands over the wet curves of her shoulders, before moving on to the delicate line of her collarbone. Then he cupped her breasts, her wet skin slippery beneath his palms.

She sighed, moving against him restlessly.

He stroked his thumbs over her rosy nipples, pulled them into tight peaks.

"Langdon," she murmured, her small hands closing over the back of his much larger ones to press him closer.

"Yes, love." He kissed the curve of her ear, the rose scent of her skin surrounding him.

Any pretense of bathing her forgotten, Langdon smoothed his palms over the curve of her midriff and stroked the soft dark triangle between her thighs. Grace moaned and pushed against his hand, twisting to reach his mouth with hers, her fingers gripping his forearms.

Water sloshed, spilling over the rim of the tub and onto the floor.

Reluctantly, Langdon took his mouth and hands from her. "I want you in my bed." He stood, water streaming down the length of his body, bent to pick her up, and stepped out of the tub. He set her on her feet and she leaned against him as he grabbed a linen towel and wrapped it around her, rubbing it over her wet skin. Then he did the same perfunctory drying job on himself before leaving the damp towels on the water-soaked floor and lifting Grace once again.

"You are always carrying me." Her lazy, passion-husky voice held amusement.

"I like carrying you," he told her as he stalked into the bedchamber. "I like touching you."

He strode swiftly across the room to toss back the coverlet on the high bed and lay her down on the sheets, immediately covering her body with his.

"I like having you under me in bed." He brushed openmouthed kisses over her face.

He wedged a thigh between her slighter, softer ones and stroked his hand down her throat, over the sweet high curve of her breasts, the indent of her waist, and the hollow of her belly button, until he unerringly found the softest part of all. She was hot and wet. More than ready for him.

"And I like being inside you." He knew his voice was raspy, guttural, that he couldn't smoothly speak sweet words and give poetic compliments. It was all he could do to carefully nudge against her, and he breathed a sigh of relief when she immediately surged upward. Her hands tightened around his shoulders, her mouth urgent as she pulled him closer, and he gave in, thrusting forward until they were locked together.

She cried out, tightening around him, and he stilled, breathing hard. Then she wrapped her legs around his waist and pulled him closer, her mouth urgent on his, and he began a pounding rhythm that in moments sent them both spinning over the edge.

Langdon lay on his back when they could breathe again, Grace tucked against his side with her head resting on his chest, just below his chin. Her damp hair smelled like roses where it brushed across his lips and her arm hugged his waist. One slim, bare thigh was draped over his, her soft skin silky smooth against him.

He'd never felt this level of driving passion and need to possess with any other woman before Grace.

How was he going to let her go when the King was caught and their masquerade ended?

16

"Was she injured?"

Langdon chewed a bite of succulent roast game hen before answering Carmichael. "Thankfully, no."

"Good." Carmichael nodded in satisfaction, dabbing at his mouth with a linen napkin.

Langdon took advantage of the pause in their conversation to scan the Young Corinthians dining room. It was brimming with agents and club members alike, some fresh from the card tables while others looked to be fortifying themselves for a long night ahead. Footmen bustled back and forth between tables, busily serving various courses from the massive sideboard along the far wall.

He knew all of the agents in the room were most likely discussing details and status reports concerning Corinthian cases. Each man there worked endless hours to ensure the safety of the country, becoming intimately involved with, yet detached from, the lives of those on both sides of the battle.

Langdon could recall that world. Professional comportment and a keen sense of justice had allowed him to operate as a Young Corinthian without forming any sort of attachments. He lived in a different world now.

"And the Queen?"

Carmichael's question drew Langdon's gaze back toward their table. "Now, she is interesting," he began, setting his fork and knife down. "I would swear upon my father's grave that she is one of us. A member of the peerage, that is."

"And why is that?" Carmichael asked, taking a sip of wine.

Langdon lifted the linen napkin from his lap and dropped it on the table. "Some things can be bought. But others?"

"Meaning?"

"Not one person in the world lives who has the ability to teach such . . ." Langdon paused, eager for Carmichael to understand him. "Such bravado as that which is innately present in members of the ton."

"Present company excluded, of course," Carmichael commented dryly.

Langdon smiled. It felt good to be on familiar ground yet again with his superior. "Of course."

The man nodded with approval. "Anything else about her that would be good to know?"

"Unfortunately she was draped in costume from head to toe," Langdon replied, settling back in the heavy oak chair. "Does not give you much to go on, I know."

"Strictly speaking, no it does not."

A footman approached and waited until Carmichael gestured for him to clear their plates. Both men paused as the man saw to the finished meal and left.

"From time to time, noble families find themselves in need of funds," Carmichael continued. "For most, such a state is cured through marriage or other, more common means. And then there are those who go about replenishing their coffers in much more creative ways."

Langdon himself knew of many families who had resorted to unsavory matches or ill-advised business investments in an effort to sustain their privileged way of life. But partnering with a criminal organization?

"Sounds a bit far-fetched," Langdon suggested, waving off the returning footman.

Carmichael countered Langdon's instruction and beckoned the man forward. "We will take our brandy here, thank you."

The footman bowed and noiselessly disappeared.

"You would think so, wouldn't you?" Carmichael answered Langdon. "But there are some for whom nothing is more important than money. Not morals nor common decency, even. I will look into it."

"Grace knows something of that," Langdon added. Her father gambling her away certainly qualified the bastard for such recognition.

The footman returned with a second man. "My lords," he said, making way for his companion to place a cut-crystal glass in front of each man, then shooing him off before pouring. He returned the stopper to the top of the decanter and bowed before turning away.

" 'Grace' is it now?" Carmichael asked. His face remained unreadable, no hint of innuendo in his eyes.

But Langdon knew his superior never asked a question simply to make conversation. Carmichael was as careful and precise with his words as he was with everything else in his well-ordered universe.

Langdon could lie. And he wasn't entirely sure that Carmichael wouldn't prefer a fabricated explanation to the knowledge that one of his agents was in love with a woman intimately tied to a Corinthian case.

Yes, he could lie. And he probably should.

Still, he would not.

"I love her, Carmichael."

His superior's face remained fixed. In fact, Langdon would have wondered if the man had heard his confession at all if not for the slightest intake of breath that registered in Carmichael's chest and puckered his waistcoat for a split second.

"I know," he finally answered, reaching out and taking his glass in hand. "The change in you is palpable. Let us drink to your good fortune."

He raised his glass in salute.

Langdon only stared at his superior, dumbfounded by the man's words.

"This is where you raise your glass, too, Stonecliffe," Carmichael instructed.

Langdon obeyed, the clink of cut glass ringing softly.

He took a drink of the brandy. "How did you know?"

"Rising to my rank within the Corinthians was not an easy task," Carmichael answered, slowly rolling the glass between his hands. "The job requires many things, including knowing your agents inside and out. You are not the first man under my command to fall in love."

Langdon watched the brandy in Carmichael's glass slowly revolve. "And you? Have you ever known love?"

He could not say why he'd asked the question. But now that he had, Langdon desperately wanted to know.

The glass stopped.

Langdon looked up at Carmichael, whose face appeared to be a shade paler than it had been a moment before.

"I have," he answered simply. "Unrequited love, that is. She was promised to another and did not return my affection."

Langdon sipped his brandy, thankful for the liquid heat of the liquor and its momentary distraction. "I am sorry, Carmichael—I should not have pried."

"I would not have answered you if I did not want you to know," he explained, his color returning to normal. "My experience makes me uniquely qualified to oversee the Young Corinthians. I have no attachments to speak of, and all the inducement needed to keep things as they are. As it turns out, a broken heart can be quite useful."

He took up his glass again and knocked back the remaining contents with one swift swallow. "Does she love you?"

"I cannot say for sure," Langdon replied, still considering Carmichael's admission.

"But you suspect she does?"

Only a handful of agents during Langdon's time had left the organization to pursue a life outside service. And he knew Carmichael had attempted to convince every last one to reconsider.

"Is this where you tell me leaving the Corinthians in favor of a life with Grace would be a colossal mistake?" Langdon asked, avoiding Carmichael's question.

The older man chuckled low in his throat, as if he realized he'd been caught. "So you have heard of my methods?"

"Do not take this the wrong way," Langdon said somewhat sheepishly, "but your methods are legendary."

"Perhaps. Nevertheless, do me a favor and answer my question anyway," Carmichael replied, his countenance settling into an expression of quiet confidence.

He clearly had a strategy in mind.

"Yes," Langdon answered simply. "Yes, I believe she loves me."

Carmichael's chin lifted at Langdon's words. "Ah. In that case, do not let her go. Ever."

Langdon stared at Carmichael, struck speechless for the second time in as many minutes. He looked at the man's empty glass. Then back at the man. "You are not foxed, are you?"

"No, Stonecliffe, I am not drunk."

"Then why would you suggest such a thing?" Langdon pressed, feeling as if he stood on shifting ground. "You know what it would mean. It is nearly impossible to maintain a happy marriage when working as an agent."

Carmichael leaned in and rested his elbows on the table, suddenly appearing fatigued. "Of the men I've asked to forsake a life outside of the organization, do you know how many have stayed?"

"No. It isn't something we are encouraged to discuss," Langdon replied, still attempting to decipher Carmichael's strategy.

"Precisely," his superior replied gravely. He slowly twisted the signet ring he wore on his left hand, the movement absentminded. "Nearly eighty percent continued on with the Corinthians. And of those, almost all have risen to become integral members of the organization. They have little in life but the Corinthians. As for the twenty percent who left the brotherhood? They went on to marry, have children, fight with their wives, spend money, lose money . . ."

Langdon watched his superior wrestle with what to say. "They loved and were loved. Unlike those men who chose to stay."

"Precisely," Carmichael repeated. "I could lose my position for what I am about to say. Perhaps even my head. But I will not willingly keep one more man from happiness. Stonecliffe, see the Afton case through. Then grab on to your Grace and never let her go."

17

Grace smelled Imogen before hearing her. The woman's lilac scent drifted on the chilled breeze and tickled her nose.

"It is not polite to sneak up on someone, Imogen," Grace said, looking up from the book she was reading. She closed the leather-bound volume on her lap and turned in her seat to look at her friend.

Imogen pursed her lips and bustled across the garden, her puce muslin gown billowing about her ankles. "Whoever said I was reaching for polite?"

Grace laughed at the woman's reply, mainly because she knew it was true. "Well, you have me there."

"And here is one more question for you, my lady," Imogen offered as she sat down and carefully arranged her morning dress. "Why are you sitting outside on a day such as this? The breeze is positively arctic *and* the sun has made an appearance. It is as if Mother Nature cannot make up her mind. I believe I will both freeze to death and acquire more spots on my skin than my father's old nag Matilda."

"Spots? Oh, freckles. Come now, Imogen," Grace playfully chided. "We are not the sort to allow a bit of brisk air to dampen our spirits. And as for *spots*? I rather like them."

"Bite your tongue!" Imogen implored, adjusting her bonnet so that it sat lower on her brow. "Men prefer a woman with a milky complexion. You should know that."

Grace had obtained quite a few freckles since coming to stay at Aylworth House. And she could not remember Langdon complaining about them. Not when his tongue had traced a trail from her ear to her toes. Maybe when he'd opened her legs and kissed the very core of her? No, not then, either.

"Perhaps I do not care what men think," Grace answered, her nipples tightening at the memory of making love with Langdon.

Imogen's mouth formed a charming O of understanding. "None of my protectors have been men who prefer women with much of a will. Lucky you."

You have no idea, Grace thought to herself.

She leaned over and retrieved the parasol she'd tucked underneath the bench. "Mrs. Templeton insisted I bring it outside. She never mentioned anything about using it, though."

"Naughty girl," Imogen teased, taking the lace parasol in her hands and opening it. She twirled it this way and that before finding the perfect angle. "There, that is much better. Now, what news, Wicked Widow?" Imogen asked, her perfectly plucked eyebrows wriggling with innuendo. "Have Madame Fontaine's creations come in handy of late?"

Grace realized she'd not put the garments to the test yet. Langdon did not seem to care what she wore as long as it was easily removed. "Oh yes. Please do tell Madame I am most thankful for the help."

"You can tell her yourself when we visit her next," Imogen replied, pulling her cashmere shawl tightly about her shoulders. "Which will not be far off, I think. I've need of a new riding habit and a morning dress or two."

A pang of sadness poked at Grace's heart as she realized there might not be a next time she'd venture out with Imogen. Once Langdon took over the Kingsmen, there would be no reason for Grace to remain at Aylworth House.

There would be no reason to remain at Aylworth House.

Of course Grace had thought about her future. She still very much wanted a quiet life in the country with Mr. and Mrs. Templeton. Only she now required Langdon as well.

What was the likelihood the leader of England's most powerful crime organization would be willing to retire at the zenith of his power?

"Why do you suddenly look so sad?" Imogen asked, unwrapping her shawl and spreading it over both her lap and Grace's.

Grace attempted a smile, but her lips would not co-operate. "I wonder, Imogen . . . to your knowledge, has any woman ever spent the entirety of her career with one protector?"

"Oh heavens," Imogen breathed. Her eyes widened and she dropped the parasol dramatically. "You've not fallen in love with the man, have you?

Grace shook her head adamantly.

"Say the words," Imogen demanded, ignoring the

open parasol as the breeze caught it and sent it slowly sailing across the lawn toward a hydrangea bush.

Grace shook her head a second time, reluctant to out-and-out lie to her friend.

"You've broken the most important rule, my lady," Imogen nearly wailed. "A woman never—ever—falls in love with her protector. Ever."

"Is it really so wrong?" Grace asked, aware her tone bordered on desperate. "After all, wouldn't love only improve upon the relationship between the woman and her protector?"

Imogen took Grace's hands in hers and squeezed. "To the best of my knowledge, not one woman has ever spent the entirety of her career with one protector. And do you know why? Because ours is not a world in which 'relationships' exist—not in any real sense anyway. These men already have enough relationships to fill the Tower, my lady. What they want in a mistress is not love. Affection, yes. And sex. And their egos stroked along with other bits and bobs. But not love."

"And if a man says he is in love?" Grace pressed.

"He is lying," Imogen answered, her expression pained.

Langdon had yet to say the words to Grace. There had been a few instances when she'd wanted to tell him she'd fallen deeply in love with him. But she'd held back—out of fear or pride, who knew.

Perhaps it did not matter why now.

"Surely you do not know the heart of every last man on earth," Grace suggested, positive that mathematics was on her argument's side.

Imogen bit her bottom lip as she considered Grace's

question. "Well, no, I do not. But tell me this: if your man is in love with you, and you are in love with him, then what will happen?"

"Well, we will marry . . ." Grace had not realized until that very moment that she'd been looking at her life with Langdon as though she was still a lady and he was not a criminal, but a lord. "That is not right, is it?"

"Do not think on what is right or wrong," Imogen instructed as the parasol blew by. "You will marry, and then?"

Grace closed her eyes and focused on the sun's warmth upon her face. "We will marry and move to the country—far away from London and its sordid memories."

"And who will see to Mr. Clark's business interests?"

The most powerful criminal organization in the whole of England could not be run by an absentee overlord. Everything Langdon had built and spilled his blood, sweat, and tears for would be lost.

Imogen squeezed Grace's hands reassuringly. "Yours is not an impossible match. He is not a lord—which would make marrying you absolutely out of the question. But it is complicated. I tell you these things because I want you to be prepared, my lady. You need to pursue what is in your best interest. And I do not know that Mr. Clark is."

Grace was not sure letting Langdon go was in her best interest. But she was convinced it was in his.

"Thank you, Imogen," Grace said, slipping her hands from her friend's and embracing the woman.

"You treat me as a true and good friend would by telling me these things."

"I do not want to see you hurt, my lady," Imogen replied. "You've lived through too many bad things in life to miss out on the good. Just keep your mind on that little cottage in the countryside. Your dream will see you through."

※ ↗

Langdon stood right outside the entrance to Niles's drawing room and listened to the man while he played the violin. Langdon had returned home from his meeting with Carmichael and been informed that Grace had gone to bed early, blaming a headache. The Corinthian who'd delivered news of the Kingsmen's failure to provide any communication had arrived just after dawn, and Langdon had departed for Niles's apartment shortly after that. He'd been desperate to interrupt Grace's sleep and steal a kiss before leaving, but had not wanted to disturb her.

"I had no idea you played the violin," Langdon said to Niles as he walked into the man's drawing room. "And so well. Really, keeping such talent a secret truly is a crime."

The bow screeched across the violin's strings as Niles stopped playing. "Why did Strout not announce you?"

"Because I paid him. And promised to bring him into my service should you fire him."

"Oh, you would like that, wouldn't you, Stonecliffe?" Niles said accusingly, walking over to retrieve his violin case. "Leaving me to my own devices. Really, man. First you physically attack me, and now this?"

Langdon chuckled as he watched his friend settle the instrument into its case before snapping the lid latches closed. "How is your nose, by the way?"

"Still broken, thank you very much," Niles replied dryly. "And in the interest of saving myself any further injury, let us discuss why you are here." He placed the case on the floor then claimed a chair for himself. "I would hate to once again be the victim of your mercurial temperament."

"It was an accident," Langdon explained as he walked across the room and sat next to Niles. "And besides, I am the one who sought you out this time. Not the other way around."

His friend rolled his eyes. "Details. Nothing more than details. Now, tell me, what news have you?"

"Another twenty-four hours have passed and the Kingsmen have failed to make contact. It is time to burn down the Four Horsemen."

"The popular gaming hell?" Niles asked, crossing one leg over the other. "Seems likely we would run the risk of injuring civilians."

"True, there are very few hours when the building is empty, which is why we will need to be quick," Langdon explained. "We've a man on the inside who will search all three floors for anyone present, then unlock the main door and let us in."

Niles carefully considered the information. "I see. And you are certain the Four Horsemen is a worthy target?"

"Yes," Langdon replied confidently. "Our man took a look at the books. Between the rigged games, marked-up pricing for the inferior alcohol, and the prostitutes, the Kingsmen are earning nearly five hundred percent more than what they put into the hell each year."

Niles emitted a low whistle of appreciation. "Who says crime does not pay?"

Langdon chuckled as he flexed his fingers.

Niles propped his elbow on the arm of his chair and rested his chin in his hand. "Though I fear it makes us appear an old married couple, I know what you are doing there, with your hands. What is bothering you?"

Langdon looked down at his hands, now balled into fists. "I am concerned for Grace's safety. With each attack, we anger the Kingsmen more. What if the King—"

Niles held up one hand, urging Langdon to stop. "We are prepared for any eventuality—you know that better than I. She is unharmed, Stonecliffe, and will remain so. We knew going in that Vauxhall would be a difficult location to manage. Aylworth House is not Vauxhall. Hell, you've enough agents guarding the premises and surrounding grounds, we might as well move the whole of Corinthian operations there."

"The Afton case is one of the Corinthians' most important," Langdon countered, Niles's comment putting his back up. "Do not forget there were many other agents who were either killed or lost family members in the aftermath."

"Easy, my friend," Niles said, holding his hands up in mock surrender. "I am well aware what solving the Afton case means to the Young Corinthians. What I find more important is what Lady Grace has come to mean to you."

Langdon's hackles lowered. "What are you suggesting?"

"Do you remember when we first met?" Niles asked, lowering his hands. "We were paired up for the better part of our training period—which I'll never forgive Carmichael for, by the way."

"Yes," Langdon replied. "You were rather full of yourself then—still are, actually. When I introduced myself, you said, 'Your name is of no consequence. But your motive is. Tell me why you are here.'"

Niles smiled wryly. "Yes, well, as you mentioned, I was rather full of myself. But do you recall what your answer was?"

"'I am here to solve the Afton case,'" Langdon answered, picturing himself and Niles as the young men they were then.

"Because?"

They'd trained that day until they dropped, then dragged themselves to the room they shared at the Corinthian facility outside London. When Langdon had introduced himself to Niles he'd intended to shake the man's hand then collapse onto his bunk and sleep until forced to do otherwise.

The man's question had caught him unprepared. And he'd answered without even thinking upon it.

"Because it is my job," Langdon replied. "You reprimanded me for such reasoning. A man's calling was not his job. It had to be his love—his very life. Otherwise, he dishonored the effort and himself."

"God, I was rather an ass, wasn't I?" Niles asked.

"And you never forgave me for it—would not even allow me to speak of it."

"You questioned my motivation without knowing a single thing about me," Langdon countered.

Niles shrugged his shoulders. "I'll give you that. Which was why I then set out to learn the truth for myself. You four—Sophia, Carrington, Bourne, and you—all of you had more than enough reason to pursue the Afton case. Though, and I say this with the deepest respect, yours was not quite as much of an emotional one as the other three's."

"What are you saying, Niles?" Langdon asked, his eyes narrowing.

"Lady Afton was a mother to the three. Only a surrogate one to Dash and Bourne, but still, the only mother they could claim in any real sense. As for you? Whether you wanted a closer relationship with the woman I cannot say. But if I had to guess, I would say no. You were stronger than your friends, more independent. You had to be—you are the eldest son, heir to an earldom. Which means, from the time you could walk you understood what it meant to be the firstborn son. To manage the lands, marry the right girl, and protect the family name. You understood your job and accepted it—even relished it. But it was never something that consumed you. It was not your calling."

"It is true enough that I did not require Lady Afton's attention in the same way as the others," Langdon responded, his patience fraying, "but that does not mean I wanted to solve the case any less than they did."

Niles nodded as he uncrossed his legs. "That is precisely my point, Stonecliffe. You *wanted* to solve Lady Afton's death. The others? They *needed* to. Needed it more than air, from what I understand."

"Get to the point," Langdon ground out.

"You have finally found your calling. The something you need more than air is Lady Grace."

The sentence was short and simple. Less than twenty words, no more. And it held the truth of Langdon's universe.

He did not know what to say. So he sat there, staring at his friend, and breathed. Just breathed.

"Do not think this means you may abandon me," Niles added in a menacing tone. "Capturing Lady Afton's killer may not be your purpose in life, but it is still integral to who you are."

"And absolutely necessary to Grace's happiness," Langdon added, his instinctive response only proving Niles's theory. "The same man responsible for the death of Lady Afton is to be blamed for Timothy's death, too."

"Yes, yes, that as well," Niles agreed with little enthusiasm. "Now, let us hammer out this plan so you and Lady Grace may get on with your happy ending, shall we?"

18

"There you are."

Grace startled at the sound of Langdon's voice and the accompanying click of his bedchamber door closing. "I missed you today," she told him.

"And I, you," he answered, the flickering light from his candlestick coming closer to where she lay, his bed linens pulled up and tucked beneath her chin. "The plans of men never do come together as quickly as one would prefer."

He set the candlestick down on the fireplace mantel and ran both hands through his hair in a weary gesture.

"Will you join me now?" Grace asked, needing the weight of him against her.

Langdon turned and looked at her, a rakish smile playing on his lips. "You did miss me, didn't you?"

"Yes, but . . ." She was going to cry. Though she'd practiced the conversation most of the day and well into the quickly disappearing night, she knew the telltale signs. The pressure behind her eyes began to build. A lump the size of Sisyphus's burden lodged in her throat. Grace bit her tongue and met his gaze, willing herself to remain calm.

"Grace?" he asked, his smile fading and a confused

frown lowering his eyebrows. He strode toward her, knelt down next to the bed, and gently stroked her cheek, his fingers gentle as he studied her face. "What is wrong? Please, tell me, and I will make it right."

Grace reached up and took his hand in hers. She kissed his fingers as though she would never feel them pressed against her again. "Undress and get into bed. Then I will tell you what is on my mind—and in my heart."

Langdon rose and shed his clothing, unwinding the cravat from his neck and tossing it on the floor. He quickly shrugged out of his coat and linen shirt, then set to work on his boots and breeches.

Grace caught sight of his perfect form for only a brief moment. All sinewy muscles and sculpted bone, Langdon's body made her ache with need. She closed her eyes and waited for him to join her.

Cold air brushed her back as he lifted the blankets and slipped into bed beside her. He wrapped his arm about her waist, his palm on her belly, fingers spread over her nightrail, and pulled her toward him until she nestled against his bare, warm, hard body.

"Now tell me. What has upset you?" he asked, his chin resting in the curve where neck met shoulder.

Grace melted against him, allowing his heat to warm them both. "Do you love me?"

"Why are you asking—"

"I am aware this is hardly the right way to go about asking such a question," Grace interrupted him, afraid she would lose her courage and instead allow his closeness to lull her into a sense of security. "But I need to know."

Langdon exhaled, a deep sigh filling the quiet room.

"I do love you. More than I've ever loved anyone else—so much so that it scares me. So much so, in fact, that I want to leave everything behind except you. You, Grace. I love you."

"And what does that mean?" Grace pressed, pushing her hope far back into the recesses of her heart.

Langdon nudged her onto her back and he leaned over her. "Precisely that. I will gladly give up my old life if it means a new one with you in it."

"That is what I both hoped for and feared," Grace whispered, unable to stave off the tears any longer. "I cannot stay in London and you cannot come to the country unless you relinquish your position. And I will not be the reason your dreams are unfulfilled. You would grow to resent me, Langdon. I would rather we part in love than stay together in eventual anger and hatred."

In one swift movement, Langdon straddled her, his knees on the mattress next to her hips. "Are you saying that you love me?" He planted his large, capable hands beside her temples and bent to press a soft kiss against her mouth.

"I do," Grace breathed, then turned her head and kissed the inside of his wrist. "Which is why I cannot allow you to come with me."

He kissed the corner of her mouth, then trailed kisses from her chin to her temples. "What would change your mind?"

Langdon's question struck Grace as somewhat odd. "Nothing short of no longer loving you."

"Are you sure?"

"Langdon, please do not make this any more difficult than it already is," Grace pleaded, kissing his wrist tenderly once more before turning to look at him.

He lifted away from her, the darkness hiding his expression. "What I am about to tell you . . ." He paused and Grace heard him inhale deeply, then exhale with equal force. "What I am about to tell you is something I have kept hidden from all for most of my life. But if it will convince you to stay, I will happily share it with you."

"What is it, Langdon?" Grace asked, equal parts hesitant and impatient.

"I am not who I appear to be."

Grace's mind began to sift through different scenarios, none of which provided the answer to their problem. She squinted against the shadows in an attempt to better see his face. "And who are you? Exactly?"

"Langdon Bourne, Earl of Stonecliffe," he replied simply, as if rattling off the name of his tailor.

"That is impossible," Grace exclaimed as she swiped at the tears staining her cheeks. "I know that name. It belongs to one of the most honorable families in England. Why would an earl be posing as the leader of a criminal organization? It makes no sense whatsoever."

"Which is exactly why I am the perfect man for the job," Langdon replied as he moved to sit next to her. "As are all of the other men in service to the crown. No one would think to link the nobility to a government network of spies. We are all too busy gambling our inheritance away and ruining the young women of the ton. Or seducing desirable young widows."

Grace pushed the blankets to her knees and sat up, turning to face Langdon. She took a moment to consider the stunning information he'd just revealed. "But don't you see? Your title makes our situation even more impossible. An earl and the ruined daughter of a dissolute drunk cannot be together."

"A dissolute drunken *duke*," Langdon corrected her, reaching out to take her hands in his. "Though a poor excuse for a man, your father was a member of the peerage. And you were not ruined, my love. Your marriage to Crowther was legal."

A spark of hope ignited within Grace's heart. "Legal or not, the doctor was well beneath me. I have been absent from the ton for many years, but I feel certain people's attitudes concerning such things have not changed completely."

"I do not give a fig what my peers think," Langdon answered with conviction. "I am a bloody earl—and furthermore, a bloody earl with a spotless reputation. I have spent my entire life devoted to the happiness of others and service to my country. And now I am going to spend the rest of my years loving you. If you will have me, that is."

The tiny spark of hope began to pulse with pure, white light. "What of leaving London?"

"I own homes in Kent and Devonshire. And if neither of those pleases you, I will purchase another home wherever you like. Multiple homes, if necessary."

Langdon squeezed Grace's hands, his long, strong fingers urging her to agree.

"It cannot be that simple," she argued halfheartedly, hope's light beginning to burn hot within her. "Can it?"

Langdon pulled her into his lap and released her hands. "Will you marry me, Grace?"

"But your family—"

Langdon silenced her with a kiss. "Will you marry me?"

As a girl, Grace had dreamt of the moment when the man she well and truly loved asked her to marry him. The reality was quite different from her dreams, with far more life having been lived and learned before he found her. But he had found her. Just as she was meant to be found. And that was all that mattered.

"I will."

❦

Grace caught a glimpse of the fierce joy that blazed in Langdon's eyes before he covered her mouth with his. He lifted Grace, turning her in his lap. Her knees bracketed his hips, her body aligned with his, and she wrapped her arms around his neck, swept away by the passion that soared between them.

His hands swept up her back, trailing over her shoulder blades and up her spine to her nape, before cupping her breasts.

She leaned back to give him better access and his lips left hers to trail down her throat. His mouth was hot as he pressed openmouthed, tasting kisses against her skin, and she burned everywhere he touched. His arm at her back held her securely as his mouth closed over the tip of her breast and she groaned, arching, pressing her nipple against his tongue.

Even the air she took in felt hot, too heated to

breathe, and she gasped, burying her fingers in his hair to anchor her while the world spun dizzily.

Langdon muttered a curse and he buried one hand between her thighs, unerringly finding the wet heat that begged for his touch.

Grace squirmed, pressing frantically against his teasing fingers. Then they left her and she protested, trying to pull him back.

"Shh, love," he murmured. He lifted her just far enough to position his erection against her aching center and then lowered her, surging upward and filling her.

She moaned louder and rocked forward, forcing him deeper into her. His groan joined hers as the movement seated him hard within her. With his hands at her waist, he lifted her just enough to partially retreat, then lowered her in a long smooth slide that had her clenching him, her nails scoring the skin of his shoulders.

"Langdon," she begged, tortured, needing more. She put her arms around his neck and clasped him, pressing her breasts against his chest. His hair teased her sensitive nipples as she moved up and down his shaft.

"Grace," he growled, grabbing her backside with both of his hands. He flipped her onto her back, his heavy weight pinning her to the mattress, and began a pounding rhythm that made her cry out with pleasure.

"Let go, my love," Langdon urged.

"With you," Grace panted. "Only with you."

Langdon sunk himself into Grace's core, his eyes wild with passion. "Now."

And Grace let go. Her body shattered into a thousand points of white light as she climaxed.

Langdon pressed his forehead to hers and groaned loudly, his own release exploding within her.

"I love you," he whispered over and over, reverently.

Grace pulsed with pleasure and wrapped Langdon in an embrace. "And I love you."

Much later, after Langdon had taken Grace once more, and Grace had done the same to him, she lay in his arms, her head resting on his bare chest. She listened to his steady breathing, the strong beating of his heart against her cheek like music to her ears.

Home. Langdon was her home.

19

"Do you know, I think I would make quite an accomplished criminal."

Langdon looked at Niles, the man's face almost entirely shadowed by the dark night. "Considering a change in careers?"

The kitchen door of the Four Horsemen rattled, drawing the men's attention.

"All I am saying is that it is never a bad idea to have options," Niles explained.

The door slowly swung open and the Young Corinthian agent assigned to the gaming hell emerged. "Sir, the name is Rawlings," he said to Langdon in greeting. "You will have no more than an hour before the first of the employees begin to arrive."

Langdon looked at Niles, then swept his gaze over Cleese, the second agent he'd brought along. "Do you hear that, men?"

Both nodded in understanding.

"Good," Langdon said. "Let's not waste a minute of it."

Rawlings stepped aside and Langdon gestured for Niles and Cleese to move.

"Watch the door," he ordered Rawlings, waiting

for the other two to enter before crossing the threshold himself.

"I will," Rawlings replied, then quietly shut the
door behind them.

Langdon took a moment to let his eyes adjust to the
almost entirely dark room. Slowly, the layout of the
space came into focus. They were in the Four Horsemen's kitchens, a set of stoves on the far wall and
work areas to the right. A large wooden worktable
stood directly in front of them.

"Cleese, light a candle and unload the supplies."

The young agent walked to a lit sconce on the wall
opposite them and produced a tallow candle. Lighting it, he returned, then bent to retrieve the large
rucksack he'd brought with him.

"The gunpowder has been encased in wooden
tubes, all sharing a common fuse," he began, gently
setting the sack down on the worktable. "We will
start upstairs, in the northern corner of the building,
then work our way counterclockwise. I will place
the tubes approximately in the middle of each corner room. Then we will return to the main floor. We
will prepare that floor in the same way, then return
to the kitchens. Once you two have exited the building and moved a safe distance away, I will see to the
wick."

"Simple enough," Niles commented dryly.

Cleese gave him a pointed look, then picked up the
sack and moved toward the stairs.

Taking two at a time, the line of agents made quick
work of the two flights and headed for the northern
corner of the Four Horsemen. Cleese set the sack
down on the floor and unbuttoned the flap, revealing

an intricate web of gunpowder tubes and lines that attached each one to the next. "You'll find it tedious work, but it is absolutely essential that we stay together."

Cleese picked up the first batch of tubes then stepped aside. Langdon saw to the sack and Niles followed behind.

"Let me place this one before anyone else touches the next unit," Cleese instructed. He moved slowly toward the middle of the room with Langdon and Niles following closely behind.

"Like you're cradling a baby, gentlemen," he told the two as he knelt down and gently placed the tubes on the floor.

"Rather less dangerous than a baby," Niles replied.

"Only you could make a joke while we risk blowing ourselves up," Langdon commented, watching closely as Cleese saw to the unit.

Cleese stood up and chuckled at the comment. "It's actually quite safe—as long as you do not move too quickly. Or drop anything. Or speak too loudly."

"I feel so much better now, Cleese, thank you," Niles replied dryly. "Come, let us see to these babies before I lose a limb."

The three carefully covered the top floor with the black powder tubes, keeping close track of the shared fuse as they went. They moved on to the main floor and set about repeating the meticulous ritual. Returning to the kitchens, Langdon clapped Cleese on the back. "Be quick about it."

"I always am," the young agent assured him.

Niles opened the door and shooed Rawlings away, then followed.

"We will be across the street waiting," Langdon told Cleese before exiting the Four Horsemen. He ran west along the building, looking both ways before crossing the street and taking up his spot behind the tobacco shop that faced the gaming hell.

Cleese appeared two minutes later, running faster than Langdon had ever seen a man move. He made it to the corner of the tobacco shop when suddenly the Four Horsemen exploded, knocking the young agent into the air.

Langdon ran to Cleese's side, glad when the agent turned over and frowned.

"I was off by two seconds," Cleese groused. "So much for perfect execution."

Langdon looked across the street to where the Four Horsemen once stood. Rubble, splintered wood, shattered brick, and broken glass were all that remained of the Kingsmen's popular business.

"Oh, I don't know about that," he told Cleese, then offered the agent his hand. "Looks pretty near perfect to me."

❦

Serendipity stared out the elegant French doors to where her perfectly cultivated garden grew. In her hand, a letter from the King. The man was sorry to have to tell her that the Hills Crossing gang had burned the Four Horsemen to the ground. The building was completely lost. All of the furnishings had been reduced to ashes. A supply of French wine smuggled in from Calais was gone, too, along with the rest of the spirits. Not to mention the beef and poultry, potatoes and carrots. Even the salt, Serendipity reflected.

Luckily, the King had relayed, not one person had been injured.

Serendipity crumpled the letter in her hand. People were dispensable. Easily bought, easily sold. While furnishings, fine food, bricks, and mortar? Those took time. And effort.

But especially money.

Mr. Clark had cost her all three.

Mr. Clark had cost her quite a bit more, actually. Serendipity could count on one hand the number of restful nights she'd experienced since his arrival in London.

He plagued her mind with his machinations and scheming. Why would one man—one unimportant, common man from Liverpool—think he had any right to her kingdom?

It was beyond comprehension, Serendipity realized. As was the idea that Mr. Clark clearly believed she would release everything she'd built because he said so.

The audacity! The nerve. His hubris would be his downfall, Serendipity felt sure. Stealing the East India Company's shipment was something she could almost admire. Indeed, given the same situation, Serendipity would have more than likely made the very same move. It had cost her dearly, the Company men demanding their required payments for the Kingsmen's protection be cut in half. And she had not been pleased.

But the Four Horsemen? Serendipity had seen to

the gambling hell herself, taking special delight in overseeing the project. Not one pathetic excuse for a man who darkened its door would have done so if they'd known of her connection to the hell, simply because the establishment was owned by a woman. And still, they spent their money as if they could not get enough of the very things Serendipity had chosen so carefully in order to entice them. To ensnare them.

It began to rain outside, darkening Serendipity's mood further. She moved away from the window and walked down the main hall of her townhome, taking note of the priceless art that lined the walls—pieces by the Masters and a handful of more modern work carefully arranged to highlight exquisite artistry. She savored the softness supplied beneath her feet by the finest of Aubusson runners in peach and blue tones that covered the floors. Stopping in front of the entry-way to the drawing room, Serendipity cast an approving eye over the luxurious settee and matching chairs, the silk wallpaper and flawless oaken tables. Breathtaking crystal candlesticks adorned the large marble fireplace, along with a pair of busts depicting Aristotle and Plato.

"My lady, you are bleeding."

Serendipity looked back to where the voice came from. Her maid stood nearby, concern creasing her features.

"I am?" the Queen asked, following the maid's gaze. Blood dripped from Serendipity's closed fist. She unclenched her fingers and discovered several scoring marks in the flesh of her palm from her own nails.

"I am," Serendipity said again, this time with anger. "Go at once and fetch a length of linen for me," she commanded.

The maid bobbed a bow then scurried toward the servants' stairs.

Serendipity looked at the letter from the King, now crumpled and stained. The words "Mr. Clark" stood out from the rest of the smudged missive. She curled her bloody fingers into a tight fist around the paper once again and swore under her breath.

Mr. Clark intended to take everything away from her. Without the Kingsmen, Serendipity would lose her home and everything inside of it, including the artwork and furnishings, the busts and crystal candlesticks. Next would be her standing within the ton—something she felt sure her peers would gleefully applaud. And finally, she feared, the last scintilla of sanity she possessed. All of her work, her careful planning. The sacrifice and years spent hiding behind that imbecile Adolphus Beaufort. Going without the respect and recognition she fully deserved. And everything without the man she loved.

Her vision narrowed and all Serendipity saw was Mr. Clark. He was responsible for everything that was not right in her life. Why had she not recognized it before? Mr. Clark had to be dealt with severely and with finality. He could not be allowed to go on living and reaping Serendipity's rewards.

He would remain alive, but she would ensure his life was hell on earth. Seemed a much more fitting punishment for his crime.

The Kingsmen did business with a prison-ship captain by the name of Mr. Croy. The man operated under unattainable quotas put forth by his company. And when he needed men to fill the cells on his ship, he consulted the Kingsmen. It would not be difficult to arrange passage for Mr. Clark on Mr. Croy's ship. Every last man aboard claimed innocence, therefore his own cries of injustice would be ignored by crew and captain alike.

Serendipity had been on Mr. Croy's hulking ship once. It was indeed hell on earth. And when she told Mr. Clark of the Widow Crowther's painful death, his slow, tortuous journey to Australia would be the end of him.

☙

Grace plucked a strawberry from one of many trays laid out before her and maneuvered it beneath the netting of her heavy, concealing hat. She bit into the juicy fruit, savoring the sweet, slightly tart taste.

"Well, at least one of us was good and thoroughly bedded last night."

Imogen's outrageous statement found Grace almost choking on her bite. She swallowed the tangy flesh and furtively glanced about her. Thankfully, only a few others had come to Hyde Park to enjoy the appearance of the sun. While Grace and Imogen relaxed by the banks of the Serpentine and feasted on the gourmet picnic, a handful of ladies strolled the many man-made paths that cut through the large green space, presumably discussing the latest *en dits* rather than Grace's possible night of passion.

"Come now, you are not going to deny it, are you?"

Imogen prodded, waggling her eyebrows in comedic fashion.

Grace popped the last bite of strawberry into her mouth and chewed slowly—either to buy herself some time or to torture Imogen, she could not say.

"And what led you to such an assumption?" she finally asked, widening her eyes and pretending innocence.

Imogen sighed and pursed her Cupid's bow lips. "Please, my lady. Recognizing such things is nothing more than a trick of the trade. Now, stop stalling and tell me all about it. Did you attempt the magic carpet ride? Where your leg wraps about his—"

"Imogen," Grace hissed, tickled by her friend's bravado though she tried not to be. "I did not mean to insult you, Imogen," she assured her friend. "It is only that I would prefer to keep some of our discussions more private than a public park allows. Do you understand?"

Imogen rolled her eyes in true Imogen fashion. "Oh, all right. Does this mean we will not be discussing any gossip, either?"

"I am reserved, Imogen, not cruel," Grace answered, with a decidedly wicked wink.

"Oh well, that *is* good news." Imogen beckoned her closer and waited while Grace scooted over. "You've forgotten your parasol."

Grace looked at the sunshade lying alone just on the edge of the blue wool blanket. "No, actually, I did not."

Imogen frowned and leaned in until their shoulders touched and her parasol shielded both from the sun. "There. Now, would you like to go first or shall I?"

In truth, Grace had very little to share in the way of gossip. Mrs. Templeton always told her any news she had gathered throughout the day, but it was hardly titillating. The latest to-do involved a deliveryman who had possessed the temerity to suggest the house could make do with substandard potatoes.

Grace looked at Imogen. The woman's expression was jubilant, clearly delighted at the very idea of a fine bit of juicy gossip.

The tale of the potatoes would not satisfy. "Why don't you start?" Grace suggested, sure she would remember something interesting by the time Imogen had finished.

"Well," her friend began, drawing out her L's for added effect. "Last night, poor Kirby fell asleep while waiting for me to change into Madame Fontaine's latest creation. He has been rather preoccupied lately, so I was not overly surprised."

"And who is your Kirby, again?" Grace asked, holding her hand out beyond the parasol's protective boundary of shade.

Imogen smiled widely. "Lord Cuthbert. An absolute dolt in the bedroom, but very sweet, and rich as they come. Now, where were we?"

Grace's fingers flexed in the sun's heat and she sighed. "Um, Kirby was asleep."

"Yes, of course," Imogen replied. "How silly of me. Well, I am rather used to being awake and active well into the wee hours. And try as I might, I could not fall asleep. And so, as I am wont to do in such circumstances, I wandered down to the kitchens in search of a little something to eat. And who should be there?"

Grace had grown bolder. The lower half of her arm now brazenly defied Imogen's circle of shade.

"Are you not going to guess?"

Grace roused herself from the sun's relaxing effects. "The cook?"

"No, thank heavens," Imogen replied with a shudder. "That woman hates me. But I did take your advice and managed to befriend a kitchen girl, Maisy. Charming young thing and pretty as a picture—which is where our story begins."

Grace could not help but think that Imogen had missed out on a splendid stage career. Every conversation was a performance, and this one was no exception.

"Do continue," Grace prodded her friend, reaching for a biscuit.

Imogen cleared her throat, signaling her performance was about to resume. "Well, it seems our Maisy has an admirer. Actually, I believe she has many. But there is one in particular who has caused quite a stir within the circle of servants."

"Not up to snuff?" Grace ventured a guess. She nibbled on her biscuit and awaited Imogen's disclosure.

"Worse," Imogen answered, gesturing for Grace to pass her a biscuit. "Apparently he is a member of the Kingsmen, the most dangerous gang in all of London."

At the mention of the Kingsmen, Grace's skin went cold. "The Kingsmen, you say?"

"Yes, that's right. I narrowly escaped a brush with them when I first arrived here," Imogen answered, then took a bite of her biscuit.

Grace finished her own, chewing slowly as she willed herself not to react emotionally. "Is that right?"

"Yes, but that is not the story I am telling today," Imogen answered while brushing stray crumbs from her skirts. "Now, Maisy's admirer is apparently young and handsome—and charming, too, but aren't they all? So when she saw the boy at the market, she allowed him to walk her home."

Grace had to admit the situation sounded entirely innocent despite the young man being linked to the Kingsmen. She relaxed slightly and rolled her shoulders to ease her tension.

"Aren't you going to ask what happened then?" Imogen demanded, ever the showman.

"I thought you had come to the end of the story," Grace explained, reaching for a second biscuit.

Imogen caught Grace's elbow and pulled her back. "What kind of story would that be?"

"My thoughts exactly," Grace countered, focused on the biscuit tray.

Imogen rolled her eyes. "The young man turned out to be quite loquacious and kept Maisy talking long after she should have gone to bed. But, as I mentioned before, he was handsome and charming, so she stayed and listened to his dangerous tales of life within the Kingsmen. Until he told her something Maisy knew could get her in trouble."

Grace forgot about the second biscuit and focused more intently on her friend's words. "What was that?"

Imogen glanced about them, then leaned closer, her voice dropping to just above a whisper. "Apparently a powerful gang from outside London has threatened to overthrow the Kingsmen and take everything," Imogen explained with great enthusiasm. "This young man told Maisy he heard the King was out of his mind with anger. So angry, in fact, that he's going to double-cross the gang's leader and trap him in one of those prison ships bound for Australia."

"What do you mean?" Grace pressed, her heart beginning to race.

Imogen smiled with satisfaction, clearly pleased with Grace's piqued interest. "The Kingsmen have their fingers in every sort of unsavory business there is, including prison ships. Captains are issued a quota, and if they do not meet this quota, they do not get paid. The Kingsmen supply the numbers needed in exchange for money."

"But surely this man will protest," Grace countered vehemently. "You cannot punish a person for something they did not do."

Imogen patted Grace's shoulder. "It is terrible, I know. But it happens every day. This man will only be one in a sea of men claiming their innocence. I imagine the crews of these prison ships no longer bother to listen."

Grace could hear the loud pounding of her heartbeat in her ears, the drumming drowning out everything except for one thought: she had to tell Langdon.

"Do you know, I believe the sun is a bit too much for me today," she told Imogen, leaning on her friend's arm for support.

Imogen gasped and placed her palm on Grace's forehead. "I told you, did I not? And now you are burning up. Baylor!" she called to the footman who stood at a respectful distance from the two.

The poor man sprinted toward them and fell down on one knee in front of Imogen. "Yes, miss, how may I help?"

"Have the driver bring the carriage at once, please."

"At once" didn't seem fast enough to Grace. She wondered if the Hills Crossing men watching from nearby would allow her the use of one of their horses.

"There, there, my lady," Imogen crooned, wrapping her arm about Grace's shoulders. "We shall have you home as soon as is humanly possible."

Grace searched the trees and grassy areas behind them, but could not manage to spy even one of Langdon's men.

"Here he comes," Imogen announced as she hauled herself to her feet. She offered her hand to Grace and waited. "We will have you home soon."

Unfortunately for Grace, soon was not soon enough.

Langdon looked out the bank of mullioned windows that occupied the south side of his study and closed his eyes. He pictured the *Resurrection,* the prison ship that the Kingsmen insisted would be the site Grace was given over to them in exchange for the King's co-operation. "Again," he commanded.

"We have reviewed the plan more times than I can count," Niles groaned, the sound of his crystal glass clinking against the mahogany desk, punctuating his annoyance.

"And we will continue to do so until I am able to

cast a critical eye forward and back without finding a weak link," Langdon replied in a short, clipped tone.

The truth was he was feeling impatient. Corinthian business used to fire his blood with excitement and anticipation. Now Langdon only wanted to be on the other side of the attack, the King in shackles and Grace in his arms.

"I apologize for the interruption, gentlemen."

Langdon turned at the sound of Grace's voice. She stood in the doorway behind him, visibly upset.

"Not at all, Lady Grace," Niles addressed her, sitting up a touch straighter in his chair. "An interruption would be most welcome at this point."

Langdon beckoned her into the room. "Pay no attention to Mr. Davis. He is attempting to shirk his duties—with very little success."

Grace stepped over the threshold and closed the oak door behind her. She eyed Niles hesitantly before speaking. "I wonder, Langdon, if we might have a word in private?"

"I will plug my ears," Niles interjected, placing one finger in each ear. "You see, I cannot hear a thing."

"It is to do with the prison ship," Grace whispered to Langdon.

He looked at Niles and mouthed "Enough."

"Well, that was surely the shortest conversation of importance in the history of important conversations," Niles proclaimed, standing belatedly in deference to Grace.

Langdon walked to the chair next to Niles and waited for Grace. "You look as if you could use a brief rest. Sit."

"I do not want to rest," she answered, though she did as he asked. "I need to speak with you. Alone."

Langdon walked around his desk and took his own seat, watching as Niles reclaimed his chair, then stared at Grace.

"You are up to something, my lady," Niles said, narrowing his eyes in suspicion.

Grace's lips thinned at his accusation but her face remained unreadable.

"It is all right, Grace," Langdon told her, then looked at his friend. "Though he often appears the fool, Niles is one of the most accomplished agents I've had the good fortune to work with."

Niles's jaw dropped. "First, thank you for the compliment. They are, unfortunately, too few and far between coming from you. Second, you've just told Lady Grace my real name and that I am an agent. Have you lost your mind?"

"I was wondering the very same thing," Grace added.

The two stared at Langdon, a similar mixture of anger and disbelief coloring their gazes.

"For the record," Langdon began, "yes, I am as sane today as I was yesterday. And I have it on good authority that that is very sane, indeed. As to why I am revealing Niles's identity?"

Langdon considered his next words carefully. From a practical standpoint, it made no sense to keep Niles's real identity from Grace. It would prove to be an inefficient use of his time at a point in the case when every last minute of each day needed to be dedicated to capturing the King.

And from a wholly selfish side, Langdon no longer

wanted to hide anything in any way. Now that he knew what his life was meant to be, it felt dishonorable.

"Because it would not be right to do otherwise. Each of you plays an integral role in capturing the King. Therefore, what good would it do to continue this charade?"

Niles opened his mouth, closed it, and opened it again. "Oddly enough, I do not have an argument."

"Nor do I," Grace agreed. "However, I *do* have something of importance to speak with you about."

Langdon nodded. "Yes, what is it?"

"Imogen has learned the Kingsmen are planning on taking you prisoner aboard a prison ship docked in Weymouth."

"I am sorry," Niles said, raising his hand. "But who is this Imogen and why would we trust her information?"

Langdon began to look through the sheaf of papers concerning the most recent events in the Afton case that lay open on his desk. "She is Cuthbert's mistress."

"The Lord Cuthbert who would quite literally lose his own head if it were not attached to his neck?" Niles asked incredulously.

"I do not see how the intelligence or lack thereof possessed by Imogen's protector has anything to do with the information she supplied," Grace countered. "Imogen learned of the Kingsmen's plan by way of her kitchen maid—"

"Oh, well then," Niles interrupted rudely. "By all means, if a mistress's kitchen maid claims it is the truth, let us all stand corrected."

Langdon speared his friend with a murderous look. "If you would shut up for one minute I feel certain Grace will provide a reasonable explanation."

"Thank you," she said, adding, "Langdon, that is. Now, Imogen's kitchen maid has many admirers, one of whom is a member of the Kingsmen. The young man told Maisy that the King is nearly mad with rage over your attempt to take over his gang. So much so that he plans on imprisoning you aboard the ship and sending you to Australia as a convicted criminal."

"While your theory is plausible," Niles said, watching Grace as she began to pace back and forth, "let us not forget the months of Corinthian work that have gone into securing the most accurate of information. Are we really going to trust a kitchen maid over our agents?"

Langdon could not ignore Niles's argument. Imogen's kitchen maid was a young girl whose skills included washing cookery and fetching the white sauce for the fish. She was not a highly trained agent with the experience to know when someone was telling her the truth.

"We've received word from the Kingsmen, Grace, with the name of the ship, its location, as well as the day and time to meet," he began respectfully. "They've agreed to our terms. You will stay here and an agent, dressed as you, will go in your place. I'll be accompanied by a number of Corinthian agents."

Grace stopped in front of his desk and placed both palms flat on the oaken slab. "Please," she asked, her voice low, pleading, "do not ignore this threat."

Langdon closed the folder of papers and sat back in his chair. "Though I know you have your doubts, we must make an attempt to determine the validity of the maid's claim," he told Niles, then looked at Grace. He hated to see the clear disappointment and concern that flashed in her eyes, but could think of no other way to proceed. "There is not enough time to do a proper job. But it is all we have."

20

Grace groaned as the carriage wheels struck a rut in the road.

"Will she be all right?" Midge asked, eyeing her as though she might die on the spot.

Mrs. Templeton rubbed her hand in a circular pattern on Grace's back. "Once we get her to Master Chow, yes," she answered. "Which we should have done an hour ago," she added repressively.

Grace bent at her waist and kept her gaze on the coach floor, afraid Midge might discover this was all a charade. An urgent missive from Marcus had been waiting for her when she'd arrived home. Smuggled in by way of one of the housemaids, the letter stated that Marcus had something extremely important to share with her. With less than twelve hours to confirm the Kingsmen's plan, Grace knew she had no other choice but to pay the man a visit.

Mrs. Templeton had been enlisted to concoct a story that would convince Midge to allow Grace to leave Aylworth House. She never dreamt the woman would use Grace's monthly courses to embarrass the man into submission.

"Why does she have to go out to see the doctor?"

Midge asked, concern in his voice. "Surely I could have fetched him to the . . ."

Grace felt badly for deceiving Midge. She could only imagine what the young man assumed Master Chow would prescribe her. Potions? Lotions? Eye of the tiger and tongue of a serpent?

"Master Chow cannot provide treatment unless he examines the lady for himself. And once he has, it is necessary for him to have access to all of his herbs and such," Mrs. Templeton answered with a huff. "We are not all alike, Mr. Midge. Some of us suffer from back pain while others bloat up like spoiled fish—"

"All right!" He cut off Mrs. Templeton, an audible sigh escaping his lips. "I should not have asked after such things."

Grace let out another groan just as the carriage came to a stop.

"Wait here," Midge instructed, opening the carriage door and jumping out.

Grace looked at Mrs. Templeton pointedly. "Did you have to embarrass the man?"

"It worked," Mrs. Templeton countered proudly. "And besides, we women have very little in the way of weapons. Might as well use what is at our disposal."

"Come," Midge said, offering his hand to Grace and assisting her from the coach.

Grace hunched over and stretched to press her hand to her lower back, managing a pitiful moan. "Do hurry, please."

Midge did not bother helping Mrs. Templeton. Instead, he simply grabbed her about her thick waist with both hands and lifted her to the ground, gently setting her next to Grace. He took each woman by the arm and hustled them toward Master Chow's shop.

A young Chinese girl opened the glass-paned door and stepped aside to allow them in.

Midge nodded in abrupt thanks to the girl and gently pushed Grace over the threshold first, Mrs. Templeton following closely behind.

"Mei, my child, you've grown," Mrs. Templeton said to the girl, wrapping her arms about Master Chow's daughter and hugging her tightly before letting loose.

Mei looked suspiciously at Midge before giving Grace an enchanting grin. "Lady Grace, we have missed you."

"And I you, Mei," Grace answered the dear girl, reaching for Mei's hand and clasping her tiny fingers in hers. "I would like nothing better than to talk with you, Mei, but I am in need of your father's help. Is he here?"

"He is, my lady," Mei answered, casting one more suspicious glance in Midge's direction. "Come, I will take you to him."

Mei pulled Grace toward a narrow set of stairs to the right of the door.

Midge started after them.

"And where do you think you are going?" Mrs. Templeton asked the man in a loud voice. "Master Chow will need to *examine* my lady, Mr. Midge. I believe Mr. Clark would be quite displeased to learn you accompanied Lady Grace on such an intimate errand."

Grace looked over her shoulder and caught sight of Midge. The poor man looked about to explode from worry and indecision.

"Tell Master Chow to be quick about it," he said through tight lips.

Grace nodded, looking away from him just in time to manage the first stair tread. Mei's steps hurried faster as they ascended. She was practically running by the time they reached the landing and turned down the hall toward Master Chow's study.

Mei stopped in front of his door and knocked gently.

"Come," Master Chow answered.

Mei opened the door and stepped inside, dragging Grace behind her.

"Close the door," Master Chow told his daughter as he rose from behind his large lacquered desk and walked to Grace. "Lady Grace," he said, bending at the waist and bowing low before her. "Mei and I feared we would not see you again."

Grace smiled at the man with genuine pleasure. "As did I. But that is of no matter now, is it? I am here, in one piece."

"Yes, you are," Master Chow said, his stoic facade betrayed by the shimmer of tears in his eyes. "And I cannot tell you how happy my heart is to see you. But I would urge you to go. Mr. Mitchell still resides upstairs. It is too dangerous for you here." From the day Marcus had moved into the Chows' apartment for let above the shop, Master Chow had decided he did not like him. Marcus was a member of the Kingsmen, and in Master Chow's eyes that meant he was not to be trusted. Even though Grace had assured her friend that Marcus was different from his fellow gang members, Master Chow would not change his mind.

"He lives here because he believes you have magical powers," Grace told her friend, knowing the Chinese doctor's ego was not above a bit of stroking.

Master Chow pursed his lips at Grace's attempts. "He lives here because his fellow Kingsmen are fools who believe the tales they've been told."

"Then you do not possess the gift?" Grace asked, rather sure herself that the man had hidden otherworldly talents.

Master Chow was a man who knew when he'd been beat. "He is at home. Go quietly. Do not stay long. And promise you will call on us again."

"I promise, Master Chow," Grace replied, fully intending to keep her word.

She turned to Mei and kissed her on the forehead. "Stay close to your father until we've gone."

Mei nodded and noiselessly opened the door.

Grace stepped out to the hall and went toward the landing, carefully picking her way across the aged wooden floors.

Mrs. Templeton's voice drifted up from the shop below. "Try some tea, Mr. Midge. It will do you a world of good."

Grace placed one foot on the first stair tread and nimbly stepped up, taking two stairs at a time thereafter. She made quick work of the flight and hurried toward Marcus's door.

Knocking quietly, Grace listened for sounds from within the apartment. The scuff of a chair leg against a bare floor was followed by footsteps, and finally the door creaked open.

Marcus's eyes widened and he stared, an alarmed expression on his face when he realized it was Grace standing in front of him.

Grace clapped her hand across his mouth before he was able to utter a word and pushed him back into the room. She closed the door with her other hand and looked at him sternly. "We must be very quiet. I am going to remove my hand from your mouth now." She relaxed the muscles in her fingers and slowly pulled her hand away.

Marcus's mouth remained closed as he walked around Grace and locked the door. He turned back and frowned at her.

Though they'd been allowed to spend very little time alone together, Grace had thought of Marcus often and wondered at the little details that come together to form a person. His quarters were neat and elegantly furnished, a preference for the finer things in life evident in such possessions as the deep brown silk coverlet upon the bed in the room beyond the half-closed door and the ornately carved period desk situated in front of the window. Even the carpet upon which she stood spoke of Marcus's good taste. The wooden floor beneath it was no doubt as scarred and neglected as those throughout the building, but the expensive Persian rug hid such truths.

Marcus beckoned Grace over to a chair and waited while she sat down.

"What in the hell are you doing here?" he asked, his tone low but lethal.

Grace shook her head in confusion. "Marcus, your letter asked that I come straightaway. You promised information that would help our cause."

The half-closed bedroom door suddenly opened and two men walked in.

"Mitchell here knows nothing of the letter, Widow Crowther," the first man said, his sharp, broken voice shocking Grace's senses. "Because he didn't write it."

"Crow," Marcus said as he abruptly stood, "what is going on?"

Grace pushed her chair back, the legs screeching across the planked floor. "Marcus?"

"The King was right about you, Mitchell," Crow growled. "You, too, Widow Crowther. Seems you two are thick as thieves."

Marcus casually walked around Grace and roughly shoved her chair in. "What do you mean, 'the King was right'?"

"The King suspects you'll turn traitor and let the Widow go," Crow's accomplice said, a gap-toothed grin breaking across his face. "And you know what the King does with traitors."

Marcus claimed the chair next to Grace. "While this might be difficult for a man of your limited mental capability," he began, staring down at the gap-toothed man with superiority, "I do hope you'll try your best to keep up. The Widow and I are close. And do you know why?"

The accomplice shrugged his sloped shoulders.

"Because that is precisely how I want it to be. If I deliver the Widow to the King, he will be most grateful—so grateful, one might even say, he would consider allowing me to leave the Kingsmen. But first, it was necessary to gain the Widow's trust. Without it, I could not have pried her away from Mr. Clark."

Marcus offered the two men a condescending

smirk, while beneath the table he reached out and clasped Grace's hand in his. "And then you two showed up, tromping about my rooms while Clark's men wait below."

Crow quickly glanced at the door, unease in his eyes. "I knew you didn't have it in you to go against the King."

"Thank you?" Marcus replied, squeezing Grace's hand reassuringly. "Now, what is your plan? Clearly the King does not intend to meet Mr. Clark's demands."

"The King's tired of playing games," Crow began, pulling a menacing knife from an interior coat pocket. "Pushed him too far, Mr. Clark did. Destroying the Four Horsemen was a mistake, and the King's intent on making the man pay."

Grace listened to the man, his distinctive voice cutting through her mind, forcing her back to the hidden room in the house on Bedford Square. Her flesh crawled as she watched his mouth form the explanation and realized she stood before the man who'd taken Timothy's life for no reason. Killed an innocent boy simply because he wanted to. And he'd enjoyed it. She looked about the room frantically, searching for a weapon.

"I assume there is more to your explanation," Marcus announced, anger seeping through his tone.

Crow eyed his partner and chuckled, the sound low and gargled. "He thinks he can tell us what to do, doesn't he?"

The gap-toothed Kingsmen sneered at Marcus. "Always has. Can I tell him?"

"And deprive me of the pleasure?" Crow asked, moving closer to Marcus and Grace. "Not a chance."

He scratched his chin with the hilt of his knife. "The King wrote a letter to the Widow. Said there was information to be had and she better come quick. He signed your name, Mitchell, because he suspected the Widow just might do what you asked. And he was right, wasn't he? She came running as fast as she could. Smart man, the King."

Grace looked hard at Crow, sizing up his knife.

"You were there, weren't you?" the man asked her, his eyes narrowing. "In the house when I killed the doctor and the boy."

Grace nodded, unable to find her voice. She cleared her throat, loosening the hatred and disgust boiling within her. "I was. I heard everything. Timothy did not deserve to die. There was no reason for you to murder him."

"You needn't bother trying to make me see the error of my ways, Widow," Crow replied dryly, his indifference palpable. "I've killed those who didn't deserve to die before, and I'll do so again. Makes no difference to me. You can keep your shame and force it on the next person who does you wrong."

Grace lunged forward and slapped the man in the face as hard as she could. "You will pay, one way or another, Crow. I will see to it."

Marcus yanked her back then held up his arm to ward off Crow. "She won't be of any use to us dead."

"Will be hard to do while locked up in the hull of the *Resurrection*. But I'll enjoy watching you try," the man spat out, gingerly fingering his red cheek.

"We best be going," the second man urged as he

moved toward the window. "Before anyone comes looking for her."

"So that is the King's plan? Take the Widow by force? Then what?"

"Mr. Clark wasn't going to let the woman go—you know it as well as me," Crow answered, gesturing for Marcus and Grace to join the second man across the room. "This way, he has no choice in the matter. He'll be right upset, I imagine, too. And before you know it, we'll have him on board as well. Like I said, the King is a smart man. Wouldn't you agree, Mitchell?"

Grace looked up at Marcus with determination. If he disagreed, Crow would take him for a traitor and end his life right then and there. But if he agreed and played along? There was a chance both of them could stay alive—and even catch the King. She squeezed his hand hard.

"That is why he is the King," Marcus confirmed stonily.

"Good," Crow replied.

The second man opened the casement window and peered out, waving his hand as if sending a signal.

Crow pointed to the window. "Now, jump."

Marcus hauled Grace up and shoved her toward Crow. When they drew nearer, both stuck their heads out and looked down. A cart, piled high with hay, stood in place beneath the window. And two Kingsmen waited.

"You cannot be serious?" Marcus asked incredulously.

Crow nodded. "Afraid? It's only two floors. We can't risk running into any Hills Crossing men on the stairs. And we won't put up with no screaming either,

Widow," he said, looking pointedly at Grace. "Go quickly and quiet-like, or I'll kill you here."

"You wouldn't," Grace countered, though she knew the answer.

Crow smiled at her bravery. "Oh, I would, and you know it."

Marcus leaned in and whispered in her ear, "You will be safe, I promise you." He helped her up onto the ledge, holding her waist tightly. "Don't go and break your neck."

Grace looked down at the cart once more and signaled for Marcus to release her. And then she jumped, landing squarely in the middle of the hay.

21

The great hulking prison ship loomed in the distance, the violent cries and shouted expletives that carried on the wind from it chilling Grace's blood.

Marcus's hand held tight to Grace's shoulder as Crow and the others led the way along the wharf.

"You are a fool to trust me with your life," Marcus whispered in her ear. "You are smarter than this. You never should have come to see me."

"I was desperate," Grace replied, anger rising in her throat. "And you are a true friend, Marcus. Besides, you lied on my behalf."

"Though it is hard to imagine, you are in even more dire straits than I believed you to be, if I am your most trustworthy of friends," he replied. "And what makes you think I lied? We are on our way to meet the King, are we not?"

Grace searched his face for the goodness and respectability she knew existed within him. "You will not betray me. You will help me. And when the Kingsmen are destroyed, you will be free to build a life for yourself in America. To practice law. To marry and have children."

"Is that why you are risking your life? For my benefit?"

She continued to watch him. Had she not been looking so intently, she might have missed the brief flicker of pain in his eyes. "No. I ask this of you first and foremost because it is in my best interest—and that of the man I love. Though I am no less happy that you, too, will be given the chance at a new life outside the gang."

Crow looked back and scowled. "Hurry it up, you two."

Marcus gently shoved Grace forward to please the man. "You always were the most honest individual of my acquaintance, Grace. A trait I would normally appreciate—though I find it rather difficult to do so at the moment."

"Mr. Clark is not who you believe him to be," Grace offered, treading softly. "He is a good man, Marcus. I hope, as my friend, that will give you some comfort."

"It does," he replied, then fell silent.

The wind picked up, carrying more cries from the *Resurrection*. Grace waited for Marcus to respond.

"Well," he said at last, a measure of defeat in his voice. "If you dared to trust me, it must mean you truly believe I will do the right thing."

Grace smiled with relief. "I've always known you were the sort of man who would act honorably when given the chance."

"I would not claim a victory just yet," he warned her. "First, tell me what you need."

"Understand that I have no other choice, Marcus," she began, the stale river air whipping about her. "I would never ask you to put yourself in harm's way."

"But you are about to, aren't you?" he asked somberly.

Grace squeezed her fingers together until they ached. "I need you to play along with Crow as long as is needed. And when he decides what to do with me, you must find Langdon. You must find him and fight by his side."

His gaze searched Grace's eyes as if attempting to read her soul. "Why are you here, Grace? You had planned to leave London—to disappear and never return. Do you remember when you told me of a favorite spot in Devon where your family once holidayed and where you hoped to return? I would not have betrayed your secret, Grace. Not for anything in the world."

"Marcus," she replied, his words bringing her close to tears. "I still believe in that life—with all of my heart, I do. But I was given the opportunity to destroy the Kingsmen. And now I am offering you the same chance. Help me, Marcus. Help me make them pay for taking a young woman's life, full of dreams for the future, and turning it into a nightmare even God himself would cower at. For stripping a man's soul of hope until he believes all that remains is spoiled and unworthy. He kills. He maims. He destroys. Isn't it time we stopped thinking on what the King can do and began to ponder what he cannot? The King cannot stop those he's wronged from coming for him. Let's see if he cannot stop us from succeeding, too."

"Did she get the best of you, Mitchell?" Crow shouted, a sharp, broken laugh punctuating his joke. The rest of the Kingsmen joined in, a chorus of rude, rough chortles ricocheting off the growing wind.

"Please, Grace, do not ask this of me," Marcus said, shoving her ahead of him. "I want nothing more than for you to have the justice you deserve. But if it means endangering your life? Let us leave, right now. We will find a cottage in the wilds of Devon and never think on London again."

Grace tucked her chin and looked down, fearful Crow might see the concern creasing her forehead. "You know we cannot, Marcus—I cannot. I must see this through. With or without you."

Marcus quickened his step and came to walk beside her. He nodded, a small, sad smile forming on his lips. "I would have regretted not having asked, Grace. And I fear I am overburdened with regrets. Could not fit one more in my pocket if I tried."

Marcus looked again at the prison ship, then back at Grace. "And if the King is not on board? What then? I cannot guarantee your safety. Even if he is, there is no telling whether he will question you and keep you alive or question you and have you killed."

"Not odds I would have wished for," Grace answered honestly. "But I can live with them for the chance to take down the Kingsmen. Can you?"

Marcus scanned their surroundings, his brow furrowing as his eyes settled on the prison ship. "I do hope that man of yours is as trustworthy as you believe him to be."

"He will come, Marcus. That I would be willing to bet my life on."

"You already have," he replied grimly, then grabbed her hand in his and set off for the *Resurrection*.

22

Langdon was frantic. Enraged. Terrified. And he had been from the moment Midge had tracked him down at the Young Corinthians Club. Grace had been lured to Mr. Mitchell's apartment with the promise of information, that much Mrs. Templeton could attest to. And by the time Midge had forced his way upstairs and broken down Mitchell's door, Grace was gone, a letter from the King requesting the honor of Langdon's presence aboard the *Resurrection* left in her place. Carmichael had promised to send all the men he could to the *Resurrection* and Langdon had left.

"Faster," he urged his horse, the chestnut snorting with effort as he flew through the empty streets of London.

Langdon had once gone aboard the *Resurrection*'s sister ship, the *Providence,* to interrogate a prisoner being held there. What he remembered most about the visit was the smell. Desperation, mixed with sickness and a heaping dose of hopelessness, had joined the Thames's fetid stench to create one of the most memorable and miserable smells he'd ever had the bad fortune to encounter.

Even now, as Langdon raced toward the prison ship, with Niles following closely behind, he could swear the rancid odors tickled at his nostrils. Or perhaps it was the stink of his own fear.

Niles brought his horse even with Langdon's and shouted, "It will do no good if the horse dies beneath you!"

Langdon looked down at his mount's neck and shoulders, where sweat darkened the chestnut hide but, thank God, he could see no foam as of yet. "I will capture the King tonight. Not kill a horse. I promise you that."

The two riders and their mounts pounded recklessly through dark streets, the bay's and chestnut's hooves slipping on the wet paving stones as they raced down Hastings Street.

Bent low over the chestnut's neck, a hunk of his mount's mane clenched in one fist, leather reins in the other, Langdon looked straight ahead, hardly aware of the dangerous pace. Truth was, he'd been hardly aware of most everything since Midge had told him of Grace's abduction. More and more questions piled up in his mind. Did Marcus force her to go with him? Would he offer her up to the King? Or could the man be trusted and it was Grace who was risking her own life to capture the King?

He urged the gelding on at an even faster clip. God Almighty, but Langdon would kill the King himself if anything happened to Grace.

His nerves jolted with every last pebble and pothole the horse's hooves encountered. He should have listened to Grace when she'd come to him with Imogen's information. He should have ordered Niles to look into the rumor more seriously. He should have investigated the threat himself.

He should have done so many things differently. Langdon yelled, catching Niles's attention, and pointed toward Highchester Street. The two horses took the turn without slowing, wheeling in unison as if they were in harness.

Regrets would do him no good now, Langdon knew. All he could focus on was what came next.

Saving Grace—no matter the cost.

The wharf came into view, and with it the briny reek from the Thames. Langdon pulled up the gelding, slowing him to a trot, and scanned the river beyond, searching for the *Resurrection*.

"There," Niles said, pointing down the wharf toward the hulking ship that rested west of where they stood.

"What the hell is it doing there? Why isn't it anchored further out in the river?" Langdon couldn't believe his eyes.

"It is supposed to be," Niles said, his voice hard. "I'm sure the location fits snugly into the Kingsmen's plan. We should wait for the rest of our men."

Langdon looked at his friend as though the man had sprouted a third eye. "There is no way in hell I am waiting. If you would prefer to, by all means do so. But I'll be boarding the *Resurrection* now."

"I was required by Corinthian code to suggest such a thing," Niles explained, nudging his horse into a walk. "Of course I bloody well knew you'd refuse. Would have been disappointed if you had not," he added over his shoulder.

Langdon's heart warmed at his friend's loyalty.

"God knows I would not want to disappoint you." He caught up with Niles and the two settled their mounts into a brisk walk.

"And as much as I love a martyr, you must know our current predicament is not your fault."

The situation was what it was. "On a purely practical level, I am in charge of this investigation. Therefore, any missteps are to be attributed to me and me alone."

"Did you kill Lady Afton?" Niles asked simply. "Are you responsible for Grace being gambled away to the highest bidder?"

"Of course not, you imbe—"

"Therefore, on a purely practical level, our current situation—which stems from a hundred different decisions that had nothing to do with you—is not your fault," Niles said, then patted his horse's neck. "Damn, but it feels good to be right."

"I cannot lose her now, Niles. Not when I've just found her."

"You will not lose her, Langdon," Niles said with certainty. "Not now. Not ever. So, let us cease with the self-pity and devise a plan. And by 'us,' I mean you. Put that enormous brain to good use."

"A plan, then?" Langdon breathed deeply, pushed every ounce of fear from his mind, and considered Niles's words. "Whether Marcus took Grace by force or she went willingly, they are on that ship. The battle will be fought aboard the *Resurrection*." He focused intently on the ship's dark bulk, wondering where was the most likely place on board for the Kingsmen to hold her.

"And if Marcus was not knowingly part of her abduction?" Niles asked.

Langdon knew Grace was capable of much more than anyone knew—even herself. Still, when pitted against a criminal mastermind who had managed to go undetected for decades? God, he wanted to believe it was possible that she was alive on board the *Resurrection*. He needed to believe. Otherwise . . .

"I do not know, Niles," Langdon admitted, though it killed him to do so. "Get me on board that ship. Then we shall see."

"No plan, then. I like it. I like it very much."

❦

"Is that Crowther's whore?"

Grace flinched as the man halted their progress down the ship's stairs, but said nothing. She bit her tongue until she could taste blood.

"It is, Comstock." Marcus gestured for him to move aside. "And I will be sure to tell the King she was delayed by your curiosity."

Comstock snarled but did as he was told, stepping out of their path.

"Last cabin on the left," Crow muttered as Marcus led Grace past him and farther down into the prison ship.

Grace stared straight ahead, keeping her eyes focused on the narrow stairwell as they descended. The noise grew exponentially with each tread, as did the stench. She breathed through her mouth as they reached the ship's lower deck.

"I must admit, this is not as terrible as I would have

expected," Grace whispered as Marcus pushed her against the wall in order to avoid a pair of Kingsmen running the other way.

He plucked her forward by the shoulders and set off again. "The prisoners are kept on the deck below us. That is the area we need to avoid."

"I will try to remember that," Grace said, ducking behind Marcus's shoulder when a Kingsmen she knew appeared in the corridor.

"Well blow me down," the squat, surly man exclaimed as he came closer.

Grace knew the man only as Four Fingers. Her husband had never bothered with his associates' real names—something to do with Kingsmen protocol.

"The doctor's wife?" Four Fingers asked, holding his hand up, palm out, in a silent command to halt.

"And here I'd believed up to this point you were stupid," Marcus replied coldly, his knife clearly visible in his rock-steady grip. "Now move. We need to see the King."

Four Fingers growled low in his throat. Grace watched the struggle between hatred and common sense playing out in the man's eyes.

Eventually, common sense won and he stepped aside, making room for them to pass. "I'll come lookin' for you, Marcus. After we find what the King's wanting."

"You do that," Marcus replied, not bothering to even look back.

Four Fingers reached over and grasped a lock of Grace's hair that had come undone. "You, too, Mrs. Crowther."

His sharp tug on her hair was painful, but then he

released her, disappearing down the narrow steps to the level below.

"How much farther?" Grace asked, a shiver creeping up her spine.

"Not far at all."

Marcus suddenly stopped and Grace bumped into his back. She peered around his shoulder and discovered they had reached the end of the hall. Crow stood just ahead of them, along with another Kingsmen, who looked to be guarding a door.

"'Bout time she was caught," the guard said to Marcus, then gave Grace a black look.

Marcus reached behind him, caught Grace's hands and pulled her forward to stand next to him. "Insightful as always. Now open the door," he instructed impatiently. "Or should I?"

The guard pounded his fist against the heavy wood portal three times. "Marcus to see you. And he's brought Crowther's wife with him."

A chair scraping against wood flooring could be heard from within the cabin. Footsteps sounded next. With each heavy tread, Grace willed herself to remain calm. Yes, she was about to see the man responsible for causing incomprehensible pain and misery to so many people. But crumpling before the man would do no one any good. It was time for Grace to play her part.

She locked her knees and straightened her spine.

A key rattled in the door's lock. The hinges squeaked with effort as the heavy oak swung inward. And there stood a man.

"You are late."

Marcus sighed with disgust, then shoved Grace into

the chamber and followed after her. "I believe this shall more than make up for my tardiness."

Grace tripped on her skirts and fell forward. She landed on her knees, the rough wooden flooring biting at her skin.

"No need to injure her just yet," the King said, grabbing Grace's elbow and yanking her up. "Have a seat, Mrs. Crowther."

He pushed her down into a chair against the wall of the chamber, then walked to a desk opposite and tossed the keys at Marcus. "Close the door and lock it."

Grace's gaze followed her friend as he shut the door. She took a deep breath, steeling herself for the roles they both must play, as he placed the key in the hole and turned it. She sent up a prayer when he turned back toward her and eyed her with contempt.

"I always believed Mrs. Crowther to be a bright woman." Marcus shook his head in derision. "Apparently, I was wrong. She believed your forged letter. Can you imagine a more stupid move?"

Grace began to cry. It wasn't hard to do. She was far more frightened than she'd believed possible. Though she knew Marcus was pretending, his feigned betrayal still sliced at her emotions. She felt weak at a time when she needed all of her strength. "You said you were my friend."

"Marcus says a lot of things, Mrs. Crowther," the King responded, crossing his ankles. "That does not make them true. I've even found myself questioning the man's intentions from time to time. Fortunately, today he has proven himself to be a loyal Kingsmen."

Marcus chuckled without humor. "You see, Mrs.

Crowther, he knows me well. Unlike you." He walked across the cabin to a large porthole. "Do you mind? Never have been able to abide the stench of prisons."

"Nor I," the King answered, nodding his permission.

Marcus unlatched the round window and pushed it open, a waft of briny sea air filling the room. "Now, what shall we do with Mrs. Crowther? And, more important, where is my reward for so loyally following your plan?"

"I admire your ability to focus on what is important, Marcus," the King replied. "What would you say to freedom?"

Marcus eyed the man with deep skepticism. "Whose freedom, exactly?"

Grace watched the King re-cross his ankles. Something in his demeanor struck her as being off. He was the leader of a very powerful organization. The King had killed at will, taken whatever he desired, and ruled with an iron fist.

So why did he appear nervous?

"Yours, of course," the King said, waving an impatient, dismissive hand at Grace. "You did not think I meant Mrs. Crowther here, did you? No, she will not see the outside of this chamber. But you? You I can do something for—something you've wanted for a very long time, if I am not mistaken."

Marcus turned his back to the cabin wall and leaned against it casually, as though the King was not offering him a second chance at life. "As simple as that? You would grant my freedom in exchange for the woman?"

"I already have the woman, Marcus," the King

warned, uncrossing his ankles. "No, for your freedom I require one more favor. Mr. Clark will be coming for the Widow, here. And when he does, you will
kill him. Then, and only then, will you be free."

"Done."

23

The round, hard end of a pistol muzzle jammed against Langdon's back, just below his left shoulder blade.

"Listen to what I have to say. Then you may consider killing me. Agreed?"

Langdon knew that voice. It belonged to Marcus Mitchell. "Where is Grace?" he demanded.

The point pressed harder against his back. "Agreed?"

"Agreed, Marcus," he begrudgingly told the man.

"I found your friend scouting on the north side of the ship. Unfortunately, he attacked me. I did not kill him," Marcus said. "But he will be out for quite some time. Now turn around slowly. I want to see your face—talking to the back of your head feels rather unproductive."

Langdon obeyed. Marcus was dressed all in black and nearly blended in with the night shadows, the brim of his hat pulled low over his brow, shielding his face. He held a cocked pistol in one hand and a bloodied knife in the other.

"Whose blood?" Langdon needed to hear him say it wasn't Grace's.

"Not your friend's," Marcus assured him.

"Or Grace's?" Langdon asked, the question nearly sticking in his throat.

Marcus scowled at him. "Do you honestly believe I would kill the one woman I've ever loved?"

"I do not know what to believe about you," Langdon replied, watching the man's expression carefully. "If she is not dead, and she is not here with you, then where is she? Did you deliver her to the King?"

Marcus wiped his blade clean on his leather breeches. "She is with the King. A forged letter was delivered to Grace, asking that she come to my apartment. I knew nothing of this, nor that Crow and his men would be waiting for her. I had no choice but to go along with their plan. It was the only way for me to stay close to her."

"How do I know you're not lying?"

"I may hate you because she loves you, but that does not mean I would hurt Grace. She believed you would come. And here you are."

So Marcus had not forced Grace onto the *Resurrection*. Langdon was relieved that she'd not been betrayed by a man she considered a friend.

Still, she was now the King's prisoner. She was in danger. And Marcus had played a part in her capture.

"Why didn't you fight for her?" Langdon asked, unable to keep the anger from his voice.

"Crow, the man sent to fetch Grace, is not someone to be trusted. He's killed many whom the King had insisted be taken alive. I wanted her alive and she wanted justice. And Grace wanted justice—for herself, of course. And for you."

"You endangered her life for justice?" Langdon countered, believing Marcus lied. "Is that what you are telling me?"

"She promised me you would come," Marcus said simply. "I've seen many women who've needed so desperately to believe in something that they've trusted men they bloody well knew did not deserve the honor. But Grace? She does not need you—nor me, nor anyone or anything. Grace is everything strong and good in this world. Still, she chose you. She believes in you. I saw it in her eyes. I heard it on her lips. That is what convinced me. And if you fail her, I will breathe my last breath with my knife in your back. Do you understand?"

Langdon looked hard at Marcus, willing himself to be angry with the man. But something in him would not allow it. Marcus loved Grace, that much was clear. He understood who she was and what made her so special. He might be a member of the Kingsmen, but he was also Grace's friend. And the only other man on the planet who came close to understanding how Langdon felt about her.

"I will not fail her." Langdon held out his hand and waited. "I cannot. Not with your help and that of the men who ride with me. You have my word."

Marcus reluctantly took Langdon's hand in his and firmly shook it. "I am glad to be fighting on the same side, Clark. But it does not mean we are friends."

Langdon returned the firm handclasp then turned toward the *Resurrection*. "God, no. Never."

"What is it that you are afraid of?" Grace asked the King. She fidgeted with the rope that bound her wrists, the coarse braided hemp cutting into her skin as she attempted to loosen the knot.

Marcus was gone. And still, there the King sat, one leg crossed over the other as he tapped the heel of the boot on the floor.

"I will ask the questions, Mrs. Crowther," the man replied, his tone taking on a slightly desperate quality that had not been there before.

"Question, you mean," Grace corrected him. This was not what Grace had expected. She was glad, of course, to still be alive. And the longer she kept the King engaged, the more time it gave Langdon and his men to arrive. But something was off. The infamous leader of a criminal organization did not waste time. And yet, it felt as though that was exactly what he was doing, as he asked her just one question, over and over.

"Why would I want you dead?" he asked for what seemed the thousandth time.

Unfortunately, the repetition was not helping jog Grace's memory. "I have never been good at guessing games, I am afraid. Not even as a child. So you will need to be patient with me."

The man uncrossed his legs and stood, impatience flushing his face with ruddy color. "Do not play coy with me, Mrs. Crowther—you will not like the results. Tell me now and there is a very real chance you might survive the night. Keep the truth to yourself and we will both assuredly die a very painful death."

Rather cryptic, Grace thought to herself. As if he

had forgotten why he wanted her dead in the first
place.

Or as if he'd never known.

"If I tell you, my life will be spared?"

"Then you do know? Ha!" the King barked and
slapped his thigh with one meaty hand. "I'll bend that
bitch to my will yet."

Bitch?

Grace felt the pressure against her right wrist ease
and continued to work at the knot with her fingers.
"Then you promise to free me, unharmed?"

"Yes, yes, of course," the King replied impatiently,
turning to his desk and gathering up what looked to
be nothing more than odds and ends. "Now, tell me
what you know."

Something powerful slammed against the cabin
door. The King dropped what he was doing and spun
to look at Grace with wild eyes. "Now, woman. At
once. Or I cannot promise you anything!"

The door took a second blow and crashed inward,
wood from its center panel splintering around the
shape of a man as he stepped through it.

The deafening noise from the chaos below poured
into the cabin as the man stopped just over the threshold and turned back to offer someone his hand.

"Jesus Christ," the King swore as he backed up
against the outside cabin wall. His gaze darted about
the room, most assuredly looking for a way out.

"I am afraid your God will do you no good now,
Adolphus."

Grace's gaze flew to the doorway. The man who'd
acted as a battering ram only a moment before stood
inside the cabin, a woman at his side.

"I sent Marcus to fetch you," the King blurted out. Even Grace, who knew very little about the man, could tell he was lying.

"Are you certain of that?" the woman asked, her crisp, proper, distinctly upper-class voice surprising Grace. "According to the guard outside, Mr. Mitchell was ordered to lock the door and go in search of Mr. Clark. No one mentioned anything about informing me. Which is odd, considering you took Crowther's whore a day earlier than we'd agreed to."

"Isle," the King addressed the battering ram, "listen to me. Crowther's wife knows something that could put an end to the Queen. Help me and you will become second in command. You have my word."

Isle eyed the King with patent suspicion. "You think I am as stupid as they say, don't ye?" the man asked, then walked forward, all menace. "But I am not. You'd lead the Kingsmen straight to hell. You've not got the bullocks to pull it off. And I've no interest in seeing hell any sooner than I need to."

Isle's tree limb–sized arm moved with surprising speed. He grasped the King's neck with one hand and lifted him off the ground.

"Eloquently put," the woman said, gracefully crossing the cabin to join Isle.

She drew a knife from within the folds of her skirt and pointed the tip at the King. "I never cared for you, Adolphus. You are intelligent, yes. But too ambitious. Dealing with you has become quite tedious. I must thank you, I suppose, for giving me a reason to kill you."

She drove the knife point into the King's heart, sinking the steel to its hilt before pulling it free. Blood gushed from the wound and the King cried out, clutching his chest. The woman attacked once more, this time twisting the knife until his entire body convulsed, then stilled.

Isle released the King's neck and the dead man landed with a thud on the wooden floor.

"Clean this," the woman instructed the battering ram as she handed over the knife, then reached inside her reticule and produced a hanky.

Isle kicked the King's lifeless body, then spat on him.

Grace slipped her fingertips between the two pieces of the knot and twisted back and forth, the rope loosening more quickly.

"Do you know, your mother and I were quite good friends," the woman addressed Grace as she wiped drops of blood spray from her hands. "The best of friends, some might have even said."

Grace froze. Then she forced herself to look away from the King's corpse. With a calmness that surprised her, she managed to meet the woman's gaze without flinching and studied her patrician features. "Is that so? I apologize, but you are not familiar to me. Have we met before?"

"Long ago, when you were only an infant," the older woman answered, tossing the soiled handkerchief to the floor.

Grace watched the delicate fabric float downward, the salt-scented breeze from the open porthole catching the square mid-flight. Fluttering, it changed direction and finally settled on the King's limp, lifeless arm.

"Odd," Grace said, examining the woman's fine

dress and reticule. "I cannot recall my mother ever speaking of a woman with such an unusual hobby."

Grace's gaze reached the woman's face, where a cold, hard, slightly eerie smile played upon the woman's lips.

"Killing?"

"Not specifically, no," Grace answered, the hairs on her neck lifting with unease. "I refer to your connection with the Kingsmen—though murder is a most unexpected pastime, to be sure."

Grace could just fit her entire finger through the loop now, which gave her some small measure of comfort.

"Connection, is it?" the woman asked, her voice sharper.

Grace shivered at the change in her demeanor. Something shifted within the woman. Even Isle, who was now fishing in the King's pockets for God only knew what, stopped what he was doing and looked up at her with concern.

"Leave us," she commanded the giant.

Isle looked only too happy to oblige. He hefted his weight upward and stood, turning for the door.

"Wait outside," she added impatiently. "Let no one in."

He stepped across the cabin threshold and closed the splintered door behind him, leaving Grace alone with the woman.

"Do you know why your mother never told you about me?" she asked Grace, walking around the desk and claiming the King's seat. "Because she believed I'd gone mad. And she was not the only one.

And do you know, they were all correct. I had lost my mind—in a manner of speaking, that is."

Grace swallowed her fear and forced an uninterested expression. "I did not know one could go mad by degrees, Mrs. . . ." She paused, taking note of the insecurity that flashed in the woman's eyes.

"The Queen, Mrs. Crowther," she replied icily. "You may call me the Queen."

"No, no! You need me, I can tell you where she is—and the Queen's neck . . ."

The conversation between the doctor and his killers flashed in Grace's mind. She'd been terrified by the encounter she'd heard and would not have known she was hearing valuable information. Had she missed something? Had the doctor been about to tell Crow and his man something important?

"Ah, I see the pieces are falling into place, then."

"He did not give me the necklace in an attempt to win my favor," Grace said, her mother's silver-chained pendant in her mind's eye. "No, the doctor gave it to me for safekeeping. It was yours, not my mother's."

"Smart girl," the Queen complimented her, though the snide tone of her voice stripped her words of any true kindness. "The doctor liked to poke about in my things while I rested after receiving a medicinal sleep aid. When he found the necklace, he knew right away where to look for my true identity—because you had seen fit to tell him all about the pendant's origins. Your mother's necklace was gone, of course, traded or gambled away to a long line of wastrels, no doubt. And so your husband stole mine and passed it off as your mother's.

"I cannot blame you for failing to realize the mistake earlier. After all, the necklaces are only distinguishable one from another by the initials. Your mother's were SLH, for Sibyl Louise Hastings, while mine are STH for Serendipity Theodora Hatch. A very subtle difference—only one letter. But one you may have used to identify me. That is, if you'd known what to look for."

The woman was right. Grace hated to admit it, but there it was. She'd not bothered to remove the necklace from its velvet jeweler's pouch since the doctor had returned it to her some years before. The proof had been in her possession all along.

"Why?" she asked the Queen, genuinely curious. "Clearly you were a member of the ton. Why would you sacrifice your life in order to work for an organization such as the Kingsmen?"

The Queen flushed with annoyance. "I did not sacrifice my life to work for the Kingsmen. I sacrificed my life to *create* the Kingsmen. As to why? I did it for love, Mrs. Crowther."

24

"You missed out on all the fun."

Concealed behind a stack of wooden crates on the deck of the *Resurrection,* Langdon watched as a bulky Kingsmen, his belt bristling with weapons, addressed Marcus.

"Buttons," Mitchell said in reply.

The man glared at a group of Kingsmen as they bounded up the stairs. "Back down with ye," he yelled at them, gesturing toward where they'd just come from. "Those Hills Crossing boys will be here soon enough."

The Kingsmen eyed Buttons, then the gangplank.

"Don't even think—"

The six Kingsmen rushed him, knocking him off his feet before bounding down the gangplank and into the dark night.

"Did I miss something?" Marcus asked, stepping closer to his fellow Kingsmen.

The man rolled over and rose on all fours, pushing himself to stand. "Someone's been spreading the news that the King is dead—and the Queen is the killer. That doesn't sit well with some of the boys, who say she's barking mad. Been plenty of deserters, and us expecting Clark's men anytime. Bloody cowards."

Buttons threatened a new group of men who appeared on the stairs, his knife drawn. "Go on."

The men gave him a wide berth as they ran for freedom.

"And the Queen?" Mitchell asked, watching the Kingsmen retreat. "Is she still aboard?"

"She may have gone, though I doubt it," Buttons answered, kicking a Kingsmen backward as he climbed the stairs. "This is the only way off the ship and I've not seen her leave. Must be below deck."

"Many thanks," Marcus told the man, then hit him hard with a wooden belaying pin.

Buttons went down like a sack of potatoes. Marcus nudged him with the toe of his boot, but the man remained completely still, not responding. "Come. We will find the Queen."

Langdon left his hiding place and stepped over Buttons. "And Grace?" Both he and Marcus swerved to avoid a fresh crop of Kingsmen pounding up the stairs.

"God, I hope so."

Marcus shoved and fought his way down the stairwell and Langdon followed, doing the same. The men came more quickly now.

"Keep your head down," Marcus warned. They turned left down a short hall.

Langdon stuck close, taking one sharp, assessing glance around before tucking his chin lower. "Is that the King's man, there, at the end?"

"Oh God," Marcus answered.

Langdon kept his head down as they strode toward the King's cabin. "Is that Isle?"

"Unfortunately, yes."

"I'd turn back 'round if I were you," a booming voice sounded.

Langdon lifted his gaze upward until he could see the face that belonged with the voice.

Marcus's eyes went to Langdon, then back to the large man. "Thank you for the suggestion. But I believe we will do otherwise. Now, move out of the way."

"You're a funny man, Mitchell," the man growled in response.

Marcus slammed his fist into the giant's jaw.

Isle barely flinched. "Shoulda done as I told you to," he warned, then reached out and grasped Marcus by the neck with one meaty hand, lifting him off his feet.

Marcus flailed, but his punches did not faze the giant.

Langdon slammed a fist into the huge man's gut, then again when the man continued to remain upright.

Marcus's face was turning a brilliant shade of purple.

The giant looked to be hardly breaking a sweat.

Langdon grabbed the stiletto from his boot and palmed the hilt. With a swift, practiced move, he drove the razor-sharp blade into the giant's gut and sliced upward, straight to the heart.

The man's hand opened and Marcus fell, staggering as he landed.

"I do hope you've found the right cabin," a familiar voice called out from behind Langdon.

The giant collapsed onto the floor into the growing pool of his own blood.

Looking over his shoulder, Langdon saw Niles and at least a dozen other Corinthians coming toward him, weapons drawn.

"About bloody time," Mitchell said, his voice ragged.

Niles raised his sword in a blur of movement and before Mitchell could blink, the point rested dangerously close to the pulse in his throat. "I will deal with you later."

"Where are the rest of the men?" Langdon asked, reaching out and lowering Niles's weapon.

He looked at Langdon and raised his eyebrow in inquiry. "Above, seeing to the Kingsmen who are fleeing like rats from the proverbial sinking ship."

Langdon nodded. "There seems to be some question as to who is in control of the Kingsmen. King or Queen."

"Well, let's find out. Remember, we need him or her alive," Niles warned before handing his sword to his friend.

Langdon gripped the hilt in his hand, the weight of the steel familiar. He did not bother acknowledging Niles's warning. Instead, he kicked the frame of the broken, closed door as hard as he could.

The already battered wood gave way, ripping clean off the hinges and landing with a crash inside the cabin.

A feminine scream sounded from a corner of the room.

Langdon charged inside, followed by Niles and his fellow Corinthians. The Queen held Grace at the back wall, a knife blade too near his love's slender throat.

A man Langdon assumed must be the King lay on the floor in front of the two, an impossible amount of blood pooling beneath his body.

"Did you deny me my justice on purpose?" Langdon asked the wild-eyed woman. "Or was it done unwittingly? Either way you will pay, I promise you. But I would prefer to know, all the same."

"He is an imbecile," the woman said in Grace's ear, her voice laced with disgust. "The King lies dead at his feet and still he cannot see what is, quite literally, right before his eyes. Tell him, Mrs. Crowther, if you would."

Grace looked only at Langdon. Her eyes held fear, but also determination. "There never was a King. All these years, a Queen pulled the strings."

Langdon gritted his teeth. His mind warred with the immediate need to free Grace from the madwoman's grasp and the unquenchable desire to free himself from the past. "You mean to tell me that you, my Queen, are the true leader of the Kingsmen?" he asked, allowing an air of disbelief to color his words. "Surely a woman capable of running the most dangerous of criminal organizations would not find it necessary to hide behind a man, would she?"

The Queen visibly stiffened with rage at his apparent doubt and placed her blade against Grace's skin. "Come now, you are stupid, but not completely without wits. Your sex believes mine to be the weaker—a fact that both plagued my efforts while helping as well. It is true that hiding behind the King was necessary. No man would willingly work for a woman. And so I put Adolphus on the throne while I operated behind a veil of secrecy, holding the reins of power.

But do you know, not one man ever suspected me of being involved. Not one. Which was convenient, considering my place in society."

"Not one man until the doctor, that is," Grace added, her voice no more than a whisper.

The Queen's mouth pursed with irritation, while her eyes flashed, glittering with madness. "Unbelievable, isn't it? Of all the so-called gentlemen of my acquaintance, and all the skilled criminals as well, it was the worthless Rupert Crowther who discovered my secret."

Langdon narrowed his eyes at the woman; the leashed fury from the Corinthians standing behind him was palpable in the disheveled cabin. "But my men and I know the truth now, too. Why would you go to all this trouble only to reveal yourself to those who will most certainly bring you down?"

"Because of love," the Queen answered, an unhinged cackle of satisfaction escaping her lips.

Langdon felt Niles, relieved of his sword only moments before, begin to draw on his back. A plan. The two of them had been reduced to such tactics in the past. Outlining a plan silently, sightlessly. It left an agent feeling somewhat childish, but it had proven effective.

"Love?" Langdon asked, pretending to be riveted to the Queen's words while he secretly followed Niles's directions.

"Does that surprise you?" she asked, an almost sentimental air to her tone. "It did Mrs. Crowther as well. But I assure you, I too was young once. And just like you, I fell deeply in love. Which is why I know you will do nothing that might bring harm to Mrs. Crowther."

She shifted the knifepoint until it rested directly over Grace's pulse.

Langdon started forward but was held back by Niles.

"You see? Love is powerful—so much so that it will make you do foolish things. Will even drive one mad if given enough time."

The Queen's smug condescension gnawed at Langdon's self-control. But he managed what he hoped was an admiring expression anyway. "You know me too well, my Queen. Love has indeed impacted my ability to think clearly. I am glad to know I am not the only fool."

The smile that spread across the woman's thin lips enraged Langdon. Still, he bided his time, knowing it was only a matter of minutes until Grace would be free.

"My dear man, love has its way with even the mightiest of mortals. Do not make the mistake I did and assume you are weak. It is not you, believe me. You are the brave one. It is the object of your affection who fails you. The man I loved tortured me with innuendo and false dreams. And when I was completely under his spell he cast me upon the rocks. Mrs. Crowther would do the same to you if given half a chance. Therefore, I will spare you the heartache," the Queen said, her tight grip on the knife visibly relaxing as she reveled in her wisdom being acknowledged. "You will provide me with the means to leave the country safely. And in return, I will take Mrs. Crowther with me. I will not kill her, you see. She will live out her days as my maid. And you, Mr. Clark, will be freed from a future that would truly be worse than this prison."

Langdon nodded in apparent deference to her intelligence, though the woman's chillingly mad line of reasoning was horrific. "You would do that for me? And all you require in return is safe passage?"

He watched closely, and at last saw the Queen's grip about Grace's waist ease. "And the funds to live in a manner befitting a queen, of course," she replied, her chin dropping at a flirtatious angle as she appeared to sense victory.

Niles tapped just below Langdon's shoulder blade.

Langdon flung himself low and forward, reaching for Grace.

The distinctive soft hiss of displaced air from Niles's stiletto sounded in Langdon's ear and he looked up just as the blade pierced the Queen's forearm and pinned her to the cabin wall.

Langdon caught Grace's legs at the thigh and snatched her from the Queen, rolling with her wrapped in his arms, away from the danger and across the cabin floor.

The Queen let out an otherworldly scream of rage. She reached up and pulled the knife from her arm and the wall, spinning toward the open porthole. "You will regret ever having crossed me," she lashed out, a stream of red blood spreading over her arm and splashing her skirt. She leapt up and out through the porthole, only the bottom half of her visible. Langdon shoved to his feet and lunged for her, grasping at her skirt as she disappeared.

The fabric tore, leaving nothing but a scrap of

embroidered muslin in his hand. Langdon stuck his head out the porthole and peered into the dark water, watching as the woman's head suddenly bobbed up.

Torchlight flashed, illuminating a small boat as it pulled alongside the *Resurrection*. A man hauled the Queen out of the water and shoved her into a sitting position aboard the skiff.

"The King?" the man yelled to Langdon, his voice unmistakable.

"You have what you came for," Langdon answered Carmichael. "It is done."

꽃 ⚘

Henry Prescott, Viscount Carmichael, sat in his office at the Young Corinthians Club. Everything in the room was familiar and dear to him. The desk, made of sturdy, strong mahogany, had been his superior's, and his superior's superior before that. The well-worn Persian carpet beneath his feet was one he'd crawled upon as an infant. The candelabras that perched upon the serviceable fireplace hearth once graced the mantel of his family's Warwickshire property. Even the ink pot held precious memories, being the very one his father had employed to write a fairy tale for his son.

No one else knew what the contents of the room meant to Carmichael. And he'd designed it that way. Even the many conversations with his fellow agents that had taken place within the four walls were catalogued within his heart, his Corinthians the only family he had left.

Henry looked across his desk at Lady Serendipity Hatch. She'd once been familiar to him as well. Never as dear as those memories that cradled him within his Corinthian office. No, never dear. But fond? Yes, he would use such a term.

Not now. Henry had come in contact with Serendipity over the years since their awkward moment in the garden. Seeing each other on occasion was practically unavoidable, both being members of the ton. At least he had never thought to stay out of her path, their past hardly warranting such behavior.

Clearly, she had felt differently.

"You are surprised?" she said, breaking the uncomfortable silence that had stretched between them since two agents had brought her into his office.

"I am," he confirmed, her glittering, fixated stare more unnerving than any Henry had faced before.

She batted her eyelashes, flirting as if they were young lovers conversing at a ball. "I must confess, I am as well. I never would have guessed you were the sort who would relish a job."

"Is that so?" Henry asked. He began to slowly twist his signet ring around his finger, the act bringing him a measure of calm. "And why is that?"

Lady Serendipity smiled with condescension. "Our kind was not meant to work, Henry. It upsets the natural balance of things."

"And you?" he asked, carefully measuring his tone. "One would argue you've worked harder than all of my men put together. What of that?"

She lowered her gaze to his desk and picked up a crystal figurine that had once belonged to his mother. "You know the answer to that question, Henry."

"But I would prefer to hear it from you, Lady Serendipity," he countered, dreading what she might reveal.

She settled back into the leather chair, her chin held defiantly high while a faint flush colored her cheeks. "I had no other choice. When you decided against asking my father for my hand in marriage, I refused to entertain any other offers. I felt certain you would come to your senses eventually, and so I waited. Before I realized it, time passed too quickly, I was too old to marry and my cousin had inherited the whole of Papa's fortune. I was forced to consider alternative sources of income, which is when I conceived the plan to create the Kingsmen."

The woman was delusional, that much Henry could confirm without a second opinion. The very idea of marrying her had not entered his mind until the night she'd waylaid him on the terrace at the Filburns' ball. He'd felt badly about hurting her and spent a significant amount of time considering whether there was any truth to her claim that he'd given her ample reason to believe he cared for her.

His conclusion? He had not. There was only one girl for him and she'd agreed to marry another. And that girl was not Serendipity Hatch.

"Did you mourn Lady Cecelia Afton?"

Her question shocked Henry, but he remained calm, a skill he'd honed over years of Corinthian service. "I did, as every last member of the ton did as well."

"Not every last member, no," she replied, holding the figurine up in order to examine it more closely. "As you know by now, I am the person who ordered her death. And do you know why? Oddly enough, it had absolutely nothing to do with the Young Corinthians. That connection was simply an added bonus. No, I killed her for love. Your love."

Henry felt bile rise in his throat, but he continued to stare at Serendipity, even as his vision began to blur. "I do not understand."

"Come now, Henry, we are adults," she replied, returning the figurine to the exact spot on the desk where she'd found it. "I knew you loved Cecelia. And when she accepted Afton's proposal? Oh, I cried, knowing how much it must have upset you. I could have healed you, Henry. I waited for you to realize . . ." She paused, her gaze pinning him with sudden, startling clarity. "But you never did, you see. I knew that the only way we could be together was if Cecelia was gone. And so I had her killed. And I waited."

Henry had never experienced an overwhelming need to harm a woman. Plenty of men, yes. Mostly criminals, though the occasional peer made himself a deserving candidate.

But now he felt a nearly uncontrollable rage to destroy.

Henry wanted to cut out Serendipity's evil heart and throw it in the ocean, where it could not take root—could no longer do harm.

He wanted her to experience the same pain she'd inflicted upon Cecelia and Afton, Sophia, Dash, Nicholas, and Langdon. And every last victim of the Kingsmen.

Henry wanted his heart gone, too. He would not

have to wait long. Cecelia's death had taken half of the organ. And the realization that he'd played a part in her murder would do away with the rest.

"You waited in vain, Lady Serendipity." His words held no inflection, his voice ice cold.

They seemed to break the spell she'd fallen into, though. Serendipity looked at him now with clear, lucid eyes. "And why is that?"

"I never loved you, Lady Serendipity. Nor would I ever have come to. Before today, you were nothing more to me than an acquaintance I had unwittingly upset. And now?" Henry stopped. He folded his hands in his lap and adopted an air of absolute indifference. "Now you are a criminal—one who will hang for your many crimes. That is all you will ever be to me."

"You lie," she hissed, her agitation visible. "After everything I have done for you?"

"Everything you have done for yourself, Lady Hatch," he corrected her, choosing to use her proper name. "You are a selfish, unstable, wholly deceitful woman. Why you would have ever believed I could love you, I do not know. But I will tell you one more thing: you can stop waiting."

Lady Serendipity opened her mouth as if to scream. No sound emerged, only a choked intake of breath.

"Beals," Henry called to one of the Corinthians who waited outside the door.

The agent appeared just as Lady Serendipity grabbed the crystal figurine, smashed it against the desk, and lifted the jagged, broken edges toward her throat. He knocked it out of her grasp and yanked her upward, securing both of her hands behind her back.

"There was no simple path to release for your victims, Lady Hatch," Carmichael told the woman, fighting to maintain his civility. "Nor will there be for you."

25

Three weeks later
DEVON, ENGLAND

"May I open my eyes now?" Grace asked, pretending to lift a corner of the scarf from her eyes.

"Absolutely not," Langdon answered with mock horror. "You will ruin the surprise!"

Truth be told, Grace had never been one for surprises—though the dramatic turn her life had taken since meeting Langdon could be called the greatest surprise of all time. It had been three weeks since they'd captured the Queen. The Corinthians were in the process of dismantling the Kingsmen and Langdon had written letters to Dash, Sophia, and Nicholas telling them what had happened.

Grace had moved out of Aylworth House and into the accepting arms of a formidable trio of women known as the Furies. The sisters were three women with such significant ties to the ton that no one, not even Langdon's polite if distant mother, could question the appropriateness of Langdon and Grace's marriage.

And word had arrived from Marcus. In no more than three sentences, he'd told Grace of his impending voyage to America where he would most surely find a wife to love and share his life with in time. He'd wished her all of life's blessings and signed it, *Your trusted friend, Marcus.*

There were moments late at night when Grace would awaken in her bed and sit up, peering into the darkness in search of the landscape painting that had hung in her room at 3 Bedford Square. She had not found it yet, and was beginning to feel relatively confident she never would.

"I must confess, I am not normally fond of surprises," Grace admitted to Langdon as the coach rolled to a slow stop. "Especially not after a rather long road trip."

One day in a coach could make for an adventure. One week in a coach could drive a person mad. Mrs. Templeton had not even allowed Grace to know which coaching inns they were occupying, let alone where they might be going.

"Ah," her friend sighed, then cleared her throat in an effort to mask the sound of . . . Of what, precisely?

"Are you pleased, Mrs. Templeton?" Grace asked, sitting up and leaning toward the woman who sat across from her. "Or disappointed? Because I would say pleased, but I cannot be sure."

"You will know soon enough, my lady," the dear woman answered mysteriously.

The sound of the coach door opening pricked Grace's interest and she turned her head toward it as if staring blindly in the right direction would help her decipher her whereabouts.

Mrs. Templeton's skirts rustled and the coach gently swayed, suggesting the woman had gotten out.

"Langdon?" Grace asked, turning her head to her left, where Langdon sat. Or had sat. She reached out and encountered his thigh. "Now may I take the blindfold off?"

She heard him chuckle.

Then she pinched him on either side of his knee, where she knew him to be terribly ticklish.

"All right," he yelled, letting loose a charming and full-bodied laugh. "I promise you, it is almost time."

The coach door shut once again and the wheels began to roll, gravel crunching beneath them.

"What have you done with Mrs. Templeton?" Grace asked, entirely confused by the woman's departure.

The coach gently swung to the right as if taking a turn.

"You will see her soon."

"I do not know that I will be able to see anything ever again," Grace teased, sure they were now going down a gentle hill. "I've been a prisoner in the dark for such a long time now. Who is to say I haven't been blinded by my ordeal?"

Langdon's arm wound about her shoulders and he pulled her close, landing a sensual kiss on the shell of her ear. "Ordeal? Has it really been such an ordeal to travel with me? You seemed rather satisfied with the trip thus far when I visited your room last night."

"Mmm . . ." It was all Grace could manage to utter as he conjured memories from their night together. She had been quite satisfied—three times, if she wasn't mistaken.

The man had a rather good point.

"Shameless," she muttered. "Absolutely shameless."

"And rather enjoying it, if you must know," Langdon replied, loosening her fichu. "Blast."

Grace furrowed her brows in response to the odd turn in his tone. "I am sorry?"

"Oh, it is nothing," Langdon assured her. "We are here, is all."

Grace ripped herself from Langdon's side, nearly falling back when the coach came to a stop. "Now?"

"Almost," he replied, then pulled her close and kissed her on the lips. "All right, now."

He unknotted the silk scarf and removed it from Grace's eyes.

She opened them slowly, the bright sunlight pouring through the coach windows almost too much for her to bear.

Almost.

Somewhere between claiming she did not like surprises right before they dropped Mrs. Templeton off and now, Grace had developed something more than guarded curiosity. She was excited.

"Slowly, love," Langdon urged.

The driver appeared and opened the coach door, blocking out the intense light. "My lady," he said in greeting, offering her his hand.

"Thank you," Grace answered, taking advantage of the moment and opening her eyes a touch further. She put her hand in his and stepped down, using her right hand to shield her eyes.

"Wait for me," Langdon said.

Grace could not. She released the driver's hand and walked slowly toward what looked to be a cottage. A

golden thatched roof sat atop the small stone structure. Two windows just below the eaves winked at
the world, while four more were featured along the
front of the main level. Snapdragons guarded the
stone walkway and served to keep the tidy patches of
grass in line. Beds of daisies and hollyhock, bluebells
and poppies dipped back and forth in the pleasant
breeze. Honeysuckle grew heavy and twined about
the eaves of the home, as if it were delicate lace adorn-
ing a gift.

Langdon came up behind her and encircled her
waist with his arms. He leaned in and whispered in
her ear, "Do you like it?"

"What is it?" Grace countered with her own question as she stared at the perfectly situated cottage.

"Yours," Langdon answered, releasing her waist
and coming to stand in front of her. "It is all yours.
Of course, I hope you'll agree to share it with me. But
if not, I believe there may be room in the main house."

He pointed beyond Grace's shoulder and she
turned. A stately mansion stood off in the distance, a
sea of rolling green hills and trees separating the two
buildings.

"Audley Estate," she breathed, remembering back
to when she'd stayed the summer with her parents at
the familial property. Her father had lost the home a
short while after in a card game and they'd never returned.

She looked back at the cottage and narrowed her
eyes, attempting to remember its existence. "Is this
the groundskeeper's cottage?"

"It *was* the groundskeeper's cottage before I bought
Audley and all of her lands and outbuildings," Lang-

don answered, taking Grace's hand in his and pulling her down the stone walkway. "Thankfully, some local craftsmen agreed to fix the old girl up—and in record time. And now she is yours. A simple cottage, tucked away in Devon. That is what you wanted, was it not?"

Langdon produced a key from his pocket and handed it to Grace.

"Not quite," she said, stepping forward and grasping the doorknob. The key fit easily into the lock and the door opened wide.

Grace walked in first, slowly, as though she entered a holy place. She tugged Langdon in, too, and then closed the door behind him. "This—you," she said, standing on her toes and kissing him on the mouth, "are what I want—are all that I need for the rest of my days."

She kissed him a second time, deepening the exchange as her tongue searched for his.

Langdon responded in kind, teasing her until Grace could not stand for them to be clothed any longer.

"The bedroom?" she asked simply, too stirred for coyness.

Langdon unwrapped her arms from about his neck and stepped back until not one measure of his body touched hers. "This will have to wait."

"What on earth for?" Grace asked, stunned by his statement.

"For after the wedding, my love."

Grace suspected she would regret embracing surprises by the end of the day. "And when will this wedding take place?"

"Today," Langdon answered rather sheepishly. "In

less than two hours, actually. I cannot wait any longer for you to become my wife. Please do not be angry with me."

"What am I to do for a dress?" Grace asked, dazed by the newly announced plan. "Won't your mother be quite upset to miss the occasion? And I've yet—"

Langdon leaned in and kissed Grace quiet. "I have arranged everything. My mother is here, as is Mr. Templeton and Master Chow and his daughter. Your dress is upstairs and your ring is in my brother's possession as we speak."

"He is here?" she asked, pressure forming behind her eyes.

Langdon nodded. "I understand now, you see. Love, no matter what, will not be denied. And I will be eternally grateful to my brother and Sophia for having the courage to act on theirs. If they had not, I never would have met you. Marry me, Grace. Marry me today."

Grace looked up through her tears at the man she loved. "I will."

⚜

"Well, my work here is done."

Langdon stood on the balcony situated off the back of Audley House, admiring the view. He stirred at the sound of his brother's voice, a sense of sadness overtaking him. "And what work is that?"

Nicholas came to stand next to him. "Mother is absolutely frothing at the bit over this, and I quote, 'slap-dash ceremony.' Really, brother, you should have remembered that Mother always comes first."

Langdon watched Nicholas from the corner of his eye. "You came."

"Was there ever any doubt that I would?" his brother asked, staring out at the expansive lawns of Audley Estate.

"Doubt?"

Both brothers turned toward the house this time and found Sophia walking toward them, her steps slow but purposeful. "Nicholas would not have missed your wedding for anything in the world. Otherwise, he would have had me to answer to."

Langdon smiled at Sophia as she came to stand next to Nicholas. He reached out and embraced her, then whispered, "For which I will always be eternally grateful."

"As it should be," Sophia subtly teased.

Langdon released her and chuckled. He filled his lungs with the fresh country air, and then expelled it slowly through his nose, contemplating his words. "I should not have kept you from pursuing the King. Actually, that bit made perfect sense. But I used it to punish both of you. And for that, I am truly sorry."

"Neither of us blamed you," Nicholas replied, carefully keeping his eyes on the horizon. "You'd been hurt by two of the people you care most about in the world. Some men would not have showed such restraint."

Langdon could see Grace's cottage from where he stood, the cozy thatched roof showing yellow in the summer sun. "I did not realize what it meant to be in love, you see. I could not understand why you two would sacrifice so much in order to be together."

"And now?" Sophia asked, the familiar, soothing sound of her voice pleasing to his ears.

"I loved you—still do," Langdon began, resting his palms against the stone railing. "But as a dear friend. My feelings for you are nothing compared to what I feel for Grace. The difference is something you can only comprehend after having found the one person in the world who makes you whole."

"Rather romantic for you, isn't it?" Nicholas teased, nudging Langdon in the ribs with his elbow.

"Do not dismiss what I have to say simply because it makes you uncomfortable," Langdon said to his brother. "I see it in your eyes, Nicholas. You are a changed man."

"Let us hope so," Sophia added, elbowing Nicholas in the ribs this time.

Langdon turned and sat down on the stone railing, facing his brother and Sophia. "Sophia found you— the true you. Not the man you wished the world to believe was the real Nicholas. They ate it right up, though, did they not? Your antics and devil-may-care attitude supplied endless entertainment for the ton. But she knew better—did all along, I suspect. She unearthed that little boy and his broken heart. And she has put you back together, as no one else ever could. She loves you beyond measure—scars and all. You are the man you always thought she deserved."

"You are meant to make your bloody bride cry on the wedding day," Nicholas replied dryly then swiped at his eyes, "not your brother."

"Well, yes, it is my wedding day. Therefore I am making the rules," Langdon replied, his own emotions threatening to get the better of him.

"You always loved me beyond measure, too—even more with the scars, I would venture to guess," Nicholas muttered as he looked down at the toes of his boots. "Do not think that I've forgotten that. And I will spend the rest of my days living up to yours and Sophia's expectations for me—because I know now that I can. She is my other half, Langdon. Just as Grace is yours."

Sophia took Nicholas's hand and brought it to her mouth, placing a loving kiss on his palm before releasing it.

"Look at us," Langdon said, offering his hand to his brother. "Two of the luckiest bastards in all of England. Who would have imagined that?"

Nicholas refused his brother's hand and instead hugged Langdon, thumping him on the back. "No one, I can assure you."

"This is where you three are hiding, is it?"

Nicholas released Langdon and turned to face the house.

"You are attempting to evade our mother, aren't you?" Langdon asked Dash as the man stalked toward them.

Dash offered his dear friends an impish grin. "Of course I am. She came quite close to discovering me in the library. Damned shame, too, as Audley House is packed to the rafters with a veritable treasure trove of priceless books. Poorly organized, though, so let us do our best to keep Elena occupied or we may be here far longer than I'd originally planned. Such disorganization would prove too irresistible a challenge for my dear wife."

Langdon laughed at Dash's warning, happiness

washing over him. He and his brother understood each other now in a way they'd never managed before. It had taken trial and tribulation, anger and resentment to remind them of their unbreakable bond.

And in a short while, Langdon would marry Grace in front of him and their dearest friends.

"Langdon Lucius!"

And his mother, of course.

"Lucius?" Dash exclaimed, then burst out laughing. "No wonder you refused to tell me your middle name when we were young. I would have teased you relentlessly."

"Laugh if you will," Langdon warned his friend as he stood up. "I am a grown man now. Such teasing would not bother me at all, I assure you."

Dash turned to Nicholas and Sophia, confusion creasing his brow. "Tell me, what rhymes with Lucius? Does anything come to mind?"

"Confucius?" Nicholas offered helpfully. "Putrious?"

"That is not even an actual word," Langdon complained.

Dash looked at him with evil glee. "Isn't it? What say you to 'moostrious'? I believe it has something to do with animal husbandry. Specifically, when working with bovines."

"Oh yes, he is telling the truth," Sophia joined in gleefully. "I myself have done some reading on the topic. Quite interesting, moostrious."

His mother's diminutive kid boots clicked along the parquet flooring as she neared.

"I say you have not changed one whit," Langdon replied sarcastically.

"Coothrious," Nicholas announced. "Or uncooth-rious, depending upon the situation."

"Nor have you, little brother," Langdon accused Nicholas.

"Not in the important ways, no," Nicholas replied, smiling at him. "We have not. Nor have you. Now, shall we stage a blindman's bluff?"

"Well, that does not rhyme with Lucius in the least," Dash offered, then reviewed Nicholas's words. "I remember something about a blind man . . . You two would—"

Langdon and Nicholas grabbed hold of Dash simultaneously, each dragging the bottom of his coat up and over his head until he could not see a thing.

"Langdon Lucius! I am calling you! Right now!"

"She always did have a gift for the obvious," Nicholas said dryly.

"You cannot mean to leave me like this?" Dash asked from under the makeshift straitjacket.

Langdon and Nicholas stood back and admired their work. "Oh, that is precisely what we had in mind."

"Never fear, Dash," Sophia replied, waving the brothers off before beginning to free their friend. "I will face the lion's den with you."

"Ever the truest friend, Sophia. As for you two, you bloody . . ."

The brothers did not stay long enough to hear the entirety of Dash's lament. Instead, they hopped over the side of the stone rail and landed in a bank of hydrangea bushes.

"Sophia, there you are. Dashiell? What on earth are you doing out here? With your coat in disarray?"

Langdon cringed at his mother's shrill voice.

Nicholas stifled a laugh.

"Lady Stonecliffe, how lovely to see you."

"But you cannot see me," their mother objected.

"That is precisely my point."

"Is it dishonorable to feed him to the lions?" Langdon whispered to his brother.

"God, yes," Nicholas confirmed. "Now come, you've a wedding to prepare for."

And with that, the two Bourne brothers crawled toward the side of Audley House, staying low to the ground for fear their mother might see them.

26

"Oh," a woman's voice breathed reverently behind Grace and Mrs. Templeton. "You look beautiful."

The two women swung about to see who had made the kind, if unexpected, observation.

Grace looked at two women staring at her. "I am sorry?" she asked, somewhat unnerved by their sudden appearance.

"No, we are the ones who should apologize," the petite pregnant one corrected her. "Sneaking about your cottage is beyond the bounds of propriety."

The taller woman with dark hair held up her finger to add, "Though 'sneaking' is not the word I would have used."

"Well, I was sneaking," the shorter one muttered.

"My ladies, I do not mean to be impertinent," Mrs. Templeton said, placing a protective hand on Grace's shoulder, "but who are you?"

Grace watched as the two grew even more embarrassed. Neither of them could tear their gaze from her, as if they were peering into a mirage.

"Well, you will never forget making our acquaintance, that I have no doubt," the mahogany-haired one said wryly. "I am—"

"Lady Elena," Grace finished for her, admiring her

deep umber eyes. "And you must be Sophia," she continued, turning to the second woman.

"Our reputation precedes us?" Lady Elena asked, her diminutive elbow poking Lady Sophia in the ribs.

Grace smiled at the woman's wit, remembering how Langdon had described her. "In a way, yes. Langdon has spoken of you both, often over the last few weeks," Grace assured her, adding, "with great affection."

Lady Sophia continued to gaze at Grace intently. "I apologize, Lady Grace. It is just that—"

"You are everything we would have wished for Langdon?" Lady Elena interrupted her friend.

Lady Sophia nodded in agreement. "You must think us mad."

"Mrs. Templeton, would you give the three of us a moment alone to talk?" Grace asked her dear friend.

Mrs. Templeton secured the final button on Grace's gown then stood back to admire her. "Of course, my lady," she agreed, taking one last lingering glance before curtsying and leaving the room.

Grace gestured to a settee and two silk-covered chairs in the corner. "Shall we?"

Lady Elena led the way, choosing one of the chairs. Lady Sophia sat next, taking the far end of the settee. Grace followed, sitting down next to Sophia.

"Now, ladies, you should know I am a very practical person," Grace began, gently arranging the skirts of her pale blue gown. "I am also honest to a fault. So I must tell you that the very idea of deciding one person is perfect for another without any real information is . . ."

She hesitated, wanting terribly to be accepted—

even loved—by Langdon's dear friends, but also needing to remain true to who she was. Grace would not re-enter society, even on such a small scale, playing by the ton's rules.

"Mad?" Lady Elena suggested. "And you would be right. Which is why I must tell you that there have been many, many letters sent across the whole of England in the past two weeks—all having to do with you."

Oddly enough, this did not put Grace's mind at ease. "Is that right?"

Lady Sophia reached out tentatively and offered her hand to Grace. "You know the entire story concerning my mother?"

Grace looked at the woman's hand and considered the kindness in her voice. She'd known Lady Sophia would be a woman of honor and strength—Langdon had told her as much. What she did not expect was to like her almost immediately.

The day was growing more peculiar—and, in a very surprising way, delightful—as it wore on. Grace put her hand in Lady Sophia's then nodded. "He did. Every last detail," she answered truthfully, wanting no lies or half-truths between them.

"Then you understand the four of us are family," Lady Sophia continued, casting a glance at Lady Elena and adding, "Now five. You are to be the sixth—and Langdon's wife, no less. It is not an exaggeration to say that out of all of us, Langdon is the most deserving of love."

Grace looked earnestly at Lady Sophia. "You all suffered equally—some would say you the most."

"Yes, but Langdon was the one expected to fix

everything," Lady Sophia replied, squeezing Grace's hand as if to underscore her point. "To keep the three of us safe—and sane, if at all possible. It was a nearly unachievable responsibility that he shouldered gladly. Not one of us—not myself, nor Dash, nor Nicholas— would be here today without Langdon. So you see why it was vital we discern whether you were indeed deserving of him."

Lady Sophia's reasoning made perfect sense. Even if Grace *had* been the one under suspicion. "Yes, of course. But I still do not understand where the letters come in."

"The Furies, Lady Grace," Lady Elena offered, absentmindedly patting her round belly. "Those three women would have made excellent spies—actually, they *do* make excellent spies, as they've been watching you very carefully. There is not one detail about you we do not know."

Grace looked at Lady Elena, then at Lady Sophia, contemplating the information. "Well, while your methods were rather underhanded, I cannot say that I would not have done the very same thing in your position. A bit of espionage, though wholly devious, is from time to time necessary—even when it comes to matchmaking."

"You *are* quite practical," Lady Sophia said.

"And brutally honest," Lady Elena added with satisfaction.

Grace smiled at the two women, the beginning of a friendship taking root in her heart. "Well, I do not know. What did the Furies tell you?"

Mrs. Templeton returned just then, a letter in her

hand. "A boy just delivered this from the manor house."

Grace released Lady Sophia's hand and stood as Mrs. Templeton crossed the room to her and handed over the missive.

"Well, my ladies, is she everything you would have wished for Lord Stonecliffe?" Mrs. Templeton asked.

"More," Lady Sophia answered, smiling at Grace. "Much more."

Grace returned the woman's smile with a heartfelt one of her own as she opened the letter.

> *Meet me in your garden in one hour.*
> *This is the final surprise, I promise!*
> *All my love, Langdon*

"Is everything all right?" Lady Elena asked worriedly.

Grace brought the letter to her lips and kissed it. "Everything is perfect."

❦

"I must say, yours is a request I've not had before," the Reverend Nutley said to Langdon, then batted away a bee with his hand.

The two men stood in the garden behind Grace's cottage. The sun was wearily making its way to the other side of the world, leaving the sky in brilliant shades of oranges and blues. All was quiet around them except for the low, rhythmical buzzing of the persistent bee. A light breeze blew from the north, carrying the scent of clematis and rose across the intimate stretch of cultivated land.

"Does it displease you?" Langdon asked Reverend Nutley.

The reverend's thin face appeared to grow longer as he ruminated on the question. "No, it does not displease. I will admit it confounds me, but it does not displease."

Langdon removed his coat and set it down upon a stone bench. "The wedding you will perform up at the main house this evening is for my family and friends. While the one you will oversee here in a few short minutes is strictly for me and my fiancée. Can you appreciate a man's desire to wed in peace and quiet contemplation?"

The reverend silently watched Langdon untie his cravat. "I can."

Langdon unwound the strip of fabric and threw it on top of his coat. "Do you also understand how a man might choose two weddings over arguing with no less than five individuals who would be very put out by not being present for his nuptials?"

"Say no more," the reverend replied, turning his attention to Langdon's feet. "Now, the only question remaining is your state of dress. You do realize you've forgotten your boots, yes?"

Langdon followed the man's gaze. "I do, Reverend Nutley."

The reverend quietly cleared his throat. "All right, then." He looked up from the ground, then uttered an admiring "Oh." He smiled. "Your bride, I believe, Lord Stonecliffe."

Langdon slowly turned around. Grace stood at the

far end of the garden path, the first rays from the set-ting sun caressing her from head to toe. He started to walk toward her, his steps barely audible as he pad-ded along the stone walkway.

With every step he took toward her, Grace grew lovelier. Her hair was down, the blond tresses cascad-ing down her back and a wreath of daisies encircling her head. Her skin, sun-kissed and luminous, called to Langdon's senses, begging for his touch.

The dress he'd ordered from Madame Bissett fit perfectly. He'd even managed to pick just the right shade of blue to complement her coloring. The frock's silk skirt modestly hid her ankles and almost covered her feet.

Almost.

Langdon smiled at the sight of her toes wriggling in the grass.

Grace's laughter drew his eyes upward.

"We match," she said, holding out her hands.

Langdon reached the end of the stone walkway and took her hands in his. "Isn't this how you always pic-tured your wedding day?"

Grace kissed the fingers on his right hand and then the left. "Sans shoes? No, not at all. You?"

"Lord, no," Langdon replied, closing the distance between them. "There was always shoes. And hun-dreds of guests—some of whom I cared for, many of whom I did not. And pomp. And circumstance. It was absolutely dreadful."

Grace smiled sweetly, then feigned a seriousness that did not reach her eyes. "Yes, shoes featured in mine as well. Dreadful," she replied, looking up at Langdon. "What on earth are you up to?"

"We are going to be married. Here, in your garden, in front of Reverend Nutley and a particularly persistent bumblebee."

An adorable crease formed between Grace's eyebrows. "And the shoes—or rather lack thereof?"

"Do you remember when I found you in the garden at Aylworth House?" Langdon asked, releasing Grace's hands and wrapping his arms about her waist. "Barefoot and basking in the sun?"

Grace appeared to consider his question. "Oh right. I could not help but take my shoes off. The sun practically begged that I do so."

"It is one of my very favorite aspects of your personality," Langdon said. "You do not give a hang what others think—and yet, you are the most regal, most wise and wonderful woman I've ever had the good fortune to know. You defy everything I ever thought I knew about life. I fought you at first," he explained, lost in her violet eyes. "Change is painful—admitting I was wrong was *very* painful. And then I gave in—and my life truly began."

Grace stood on tiptoe and placed a gentle kiss on Langdon's lips. "All because of my bare feet?"

"All because of your bare feet," Langdon repeated, sure he'd never been happier in his entire life.

"You are my home, Langdon Bourne," Grace said, her voice beginning to tremble. "And my heart. I had given up on ever discovering the good in life—the pure and uncomplicated truth of it all. Love, Langdon. You are the very definition of love to me."

The faint noise of Reverend Nutley clearing his throat caught their attention and Grace peeked over

Langdon's shoulder, a sigh of wonder escaping her lips.

Langdon turned so that both faced the reverend and discovered what had made Grace sigh. The sun had finally ambled beneath their view and a glorious, shining streak-filled sky stood in its place.

"Shall we meet our future, Grace?"

She turned into his embrace, placing her cheek on his chest. "I thought you would never ask."

ACKNOWLEDGMENTS

Lois Dyer, Jennifer Schober, Junessa Viloria

Turn the page for an excerpt from

THE SAINT WHO STOLE MY HEART

By Stefanie Sloane

A Regency Rogues Novel

Published by Ballantine Books

1

"You're *quite* tan."

Honorable Nicholas Bourne looked across the card table at Lady Sophia Afton with a devilish grin. "Yes, well, exposure to the sun does tend to cause such things." He lifted his crystal tumbler in salute before draining it in one quick swallow.

"Nicholas," Sophia said reproachfully, in the same disappointed huffing of breath she'd exhibited while still in pigtails. "You're bluffing."

"I'm shocked," Dashiell Matthews, Viscount Carrington, objected, settling back against the gold patterned sofa. "Not Bourne," he admonished, a sly grin forming on his lips.

Next to him, Langdon Bourne, the Earl of Stonecliffe, stifled a laugh. "Come now, Sophia. Must you always be so suspicious?"

"Really, Mrs. Kirk," Nicholas commented as he looked at Sophia's companion with mock disapproval. "I'm greatly disappointed. The poor girl hasn't the first clue when it comes to scientific facts regarding the result of sun exposure on one's skin. What do you have to say for yourself?"

A quiet, intelligent woman, Mrs. Lettie Kirk had been hired as Sophia's nanny shortly after the death of Lady Afton. And when her charge had outgrown the need for such things, she'd been persuaded to stay on as Sophia's companion, though it took very little to sway the woman, for she loved the girl as her own. She shifted her willowy frame in the chair across the room and adjusted her spectacles. "Lady Afton received the finest education a young woman could hope for, Mr. Bourne."

Sophia turned to Mrs. Kirk and arched an eyebrow. "Thank you, Lettie, for enlightening the man. But we both know the bluff I refer to is in his cards, not the sun in the sky."

She turned back to Nicholas and drummed her fingertips on the table. "Show me your cards."

"And *so* forward! Mrs. Kirk—"

"Now," Sophia ordered, pinning Nicholas with a lethal glare.

Nicholas threw down his cards, feigning outrage. Shoving back in his chair, he rose abruptly and carried his glass to the mahogany sideboard where the decanter sat, already nearly empty. "Do you steal away at night to a gambling hell and lighten the pockets of cutthroats?" he asked, pulling the crystal stopper out and pouring the rest into his cup.

"I needn't bother with such things," Sophia replied, her eyes narrowing as she assessed his cards. "Your behavior tells me all I need to know."

"What on earth is she talking about?" Nicholas asked, his words slurring slightly.

Sophia winced as the syllables slid into one another. "It's of no importance," she answered blithely, stacking the cards in a neat pile. "What matters is that you lost. I'll collect my winnings, now, if you don't mind."

Dash listened to the banter, letting his mind wander. He'd not set foot in Stonecliffe House since the night before Nicholas Bourne's departure for India. It hadn't changed a bit, the dark, masculine touches put in place by Langdon still evident throughout. Their mother had retired to the country upon her husband's death, eager to make room for Langdon and the wife and family she'd confidently assumed he'd acquire once he'd taken on the title.

Said wife and family were still breathlessly awaited by the Dowager Duchess. From what Dash knew of the woman, she'd wait as long as she had to, duty and responsibility far more important than dying ever could be.

"Yes, do pay up. I'll not have you besmirching the name of Bourne by denying what rightfully belongs to Sophia," Langdon chimed in, the cigar in his fingers giving off a mellow, smoky glow.

Nicholas finished off the brandy and leaned against the sideboard. "No, we wouldn't want that," he said sardonically, folding his arms across his chest. "Now, Sophia, these winnings. Remind me, what is it that we were playing for?"

"A promise," she answered so quietly that Dash thought he misheard her.

Nicholas stared at Sophia, his brow furrowing. "Well, that's rather vague, isn't it?" he replied, shifting his feet. "What, exactly, did I promise you?"

"Anything that I asked," she said, smoothly pushing back in her chair and standing. "Lettie, I'm chilled. Would you please fetch my wrap?"

Mrs. Kirk closed the book she'd been reading and rose. "Of course, Lady Afton," the companion replied. She walked from the room, gently closing the door behind her.

"Well, one lady alone with three men. This is scandalous," Nicholas jeered, waggling his eyebrows at Sophia. "Which I fully support, of course."

Dash couldn't put his finger on precisely why, but he knew a squall was brewing. He could feel it. "I'm eager to hear of your Indian adventures, Bourne," he interrupted, hoping to throw the storm off course. "Were there tigers? Oh, and cobras, of course. Wouldn't be a proper trip without a few snakes."

"My mother's death," Sophia said, as if Dash hadn't spoken. She twitched the silken skirt of her dress into place. "I want to talk about my mother's death. And how we're going to catch her killer."

Langdon stubbed out his cigar in a crystal ashtray and abruptly stood. "We promised to never speak of it—we all did, Sophia. I can't see the point in dredging up the past. It would prove far too painful for you."

Nicholas slumped against the sideboard, his composure markedly compromised. "Hell, Sophia. I'd no idea you'd ask for something so . . ."

"Yes?" she demanded, crossing her arms over her bodice. "What is it to you, Nicholas? What is it to *any* of you?" She pierced each one with a tormented gaze. "I know what it means to me . . ." she paused, clearly close to crying.

Dash didn't want to hear any more. All those years ago, Lord Carmichael had made the children promise to never speak of the tragedy. He'd assured them that doing so would only make the death harder to leave behind. They needed to forget if they wanted to move on, he'd reasoned.

Proper honor and respect was always shown for Lady Afton, but no one was ever able to explain what happened. No one even tried—not even Lord Afton. Or so it had seemed to him.

That is until his father and Lords Carmichael and Stonecliffe had invited Dash, Langdon, and Nicholas to join them and become members of the Young Corinthians, a clandestine spy organization that operated within the cavalry's Horse Guards. Nicholas had refused while the other two had gladly seen to their duty. Subsequent access to the files concerning Lady Afton's death had forced Dash and Langdon to accept that the less any one of them had known when they were children, the safer they all had been. The killer had made a habit of preying upon Corinthian agents and their families. No one had been safe.

The same was true today. Dash clenched his jaw as he thought back on all of the lies he'd told. The Corinthians had never come close to finding the killer, but Dash had kept the truth of the situation from Sophia. He'd played his part so well over the years that the guilt had nearly disappeared.

Or so it had seemed.

"Listen to Langdon, Sophia," he said. "He's right. It's ancient history. It would do more harm than good."

Sophia swallowed hard, not allowing one tear to fall from her eyes. "My dear, diplomatic Dash. Listen to yourself, would you? Hasn't there been enough harm done by the silence?"

She uncrossed her arms and walked toward him, reaching out to tightly grasp the settee. "Where did you go, Dash? Can you tell me? You've played at life so skillfully that I hardly remember who you were before my mother's death. Who are you, Dash? You're afraid. You know it and so do I."

"Dammit, Sophia, where is this coming from?"

Dash lashed out, a sudden sense of exposure and vulnerability twisting in his soul.

"You'll not talk to Sophia in such a manner," Langdon ordered, his hard stare judgmental.

Sophia pushed away from the settee and rounded on the earl. "And why is that, Langdon? An overgrown sense of propriety?"

"I believe you're in need of rest. I'll call Mrs. Kirk—"

Sophia threw up her hands angrily. "This isn't fatigue, Langdon. It's a wretched, growing disease. And it's ugly and disruptive—and out of your control. When will you accept the truth?"

"She's gone, Sophia. I would do anything to change that fact—anything for you . . ." Langdon replied, his fists flexing at his sides.

"Then help me," she begged. "Help me find who did this to her. To us all."

"You cannot go chasing after a killer, Sophia," Nicholas ground out, frustration coloring his tone.

Sophia walked toward Nicholas until her skirts brushed his boots. She rested her palms on his coat, just above his heart. "Not by myself, no," she answered, her voice shaking. "Nor will you find peace all alone." She glanced meaningfully at the empty brandy bottle.

Nicholas stared at Sophia, as if he wanted to listen. Wanted to obey. Then his expression turned cold. He backed up and threw his crystal glass against the wall and watched as it splintered into a thousand pieces. "You've the wrong man, Sophia."

Mrs. Kirk came rushing into the room, Sophia's wrap in her hands. "I heard a crash, Lady Afton. Are you all right?"

Sophia lowered her shaking hands and folded them tightly together. "Right as a line, Mrs. Kirk. Right as a line."

Dash took a deep drink of the piquant brandy and contemplated her words. God, the woman *was* right. She deserved to know who killed her mother. They all did.

DORSET
Two weeks previous

"Elena."

Miss Elena Barnes, the only child of Henry Barnes, Baron Harcourt, wrinkled her nose in unconscious protest when her father's voice intruded upon her reading.

"I saw that."

Elena smiled with warm affection. "You always do."

"And yet," he replied, taking a seat next to her on the chilly stone bench piled high with brocade pillows, "you continue to give yourself away. Attempting to deceive me is a hopeless habit, if there ever was one," he added amiably, settling his small frame comfortably on the makeshift settee and sighing with relief.

Elena slipped a satin ribbon between the pages to mark her place and reluctantly closed her book. Her gaze moved past the folly columns to the lake beyond and the white stone of Harcourt House shining brightly in the distance. "Really, one would think twitching my nose would be far easier to hide, even from you, considering that fact that everyone seems to agree that I always have my nose in a book."

Her father turned to her and cleared his throat, his eyes twinkling with wry disbelief.

"Oh, all right," Elena ceded with a smile, looking at the dear man. "It is true that I spend much time reading. It's my favorite indulgence. But must Lady Van Allen mention it at *every* dinner party? Even Lord Van Allen sighed when she brought it up again, and he never hears a word the woman says."

Her father reached out and took one of her hands in his, the weight and familiar feel acting as a gentle balm to Elena's stinging pride.

"Actually, I believe he does hear every word," she amended. "But it's not like the man to reveal that he's heard her comments, which only proves my point. Really, I have no illusions about my status as a bluestocking. Nor does anyone else in Dorset—or the whole of England, I would venture to guess. Perhaps even the entire world, though I would have to consult Lady Van Allen on that point," she finished, winking conspiratorially.

Last evening's spring gathering had gone well and exactly as planned—with the glaring exception of Lady Van Allen's comment. The turbot had been braised to perfection, the wine her father's favorite, and those in attendance the best of friends. Elena adored every single person present, including Lady Van Allen, a bosom friend of her mother's before the baroness's death.

It was this very connection that drove the well-intentioned woman to say such things, Elena reminded herself. Lady Van Allen's conviction that Elena would eventually find her prince was both endearing and vexatious. Elena was all for perseverance. She thought it a commendable trait in the right situation. But when it came to her marital status, one would have to be an absolute lackwit to hold out any shred of hope for a happy announcement in the *Morning Post*.

She was five-and-twenty. If there'd been a prince for her, he'd long ago gone in search of a far more fair damsel, Elena thought philosophically. She calmly met her father's gaze, and then pointedly turned her attention to the fine day.

Brilliant yellow daffodils and creamy Lady Jane tulips bloomed in clusters about the folly. A sea of bluebells spread out before her, their minuscule heads bobbing on the breeze. And just past the lake, a doe and her speckled fawn nibbled at the sweet spring grass.

Elena contemplated the beauty of her pastoral home. She was content, in her own way. Hours spent relegated to the ranks of older women and wallflowers in ballrooms during her one season had firmly beaten down any hopes she may have harbored for a life in London. She'd been plain. And even worse, curved where she should have been straight. Heavy, when she should have been light. None of which had mattered a whit in Dorset.

But in London, *everything* about her appearance and comportment was taken into consideration.

And the women of the ton had judged her harshly—as if her inability to attract a man somehow made her completely undeserving of kindness or friendship.

She discreetly eyed a long curl of her brown hair where it lay against her shoulder, thoughtfully studied the formless moss-green muslin gown that hid her generous curves, and finally looked at the leather-bound book in her lap.

Bluestocking. Elena could still recall the first time she'd heard a fellow debutante call her that. She'd questioned whether the funds used to sponsor a young woman's season wouldn't be better spent on the poor. The room had fallen eerily quiet at her temerity, like a Dorset winter's morn after the first snowfall.

Elena mentally shook herself from the cold, crystalized memory. She'd left London shortly after. Turned tail, some surely said. Elena, in her darkest moments, might agree.

She'd been fully aware that returning to Dorset permanently would, most likely, end any chance of a suitable match. Again, perseverance was all well and good. But Elena was no fool.

Her father stretched his legs, the effort causing him to wince from pain.

The movement drew Elena from her musing and she slipped the cashmere shawl from her shoulders to tuck it around her father's. "What on earth possessed you to risk inflaming your gout by venturing this far afield? It is spring, but still cold enough to do you harm."

"The lure of seeing you smile was too great to resist," he replied cryptically.

Elena narrowed her eyes. "Come now, I do so all the time. Surely you could have waited until dinner."

"Oh, but this smile . . ." Lord Harcourt paused, grinning knowingly, "This smile will rival that of Euphrosyne."

Elena's heart leapt at the mention of the Greek goddess of joy. Her father knew better than to invoke one of her favorite mythological characters without just cause. "You've my complete attention. Please, amaze me with your news," she proclaimed eagerly.

Reaching into his waistcoat, he drew out a letter. He slowly opened the thick, cream-colored paper and began meticulously smoothing out the folds—every last one of them.

"You torture me for the fun of it, don't you?" Elena admonished, craning her neck in a vain attempt to read the inverted script.

Lord Harcourt chuckled and mercifully handed the letter to her. "Just a touch. You do make it so easy—and enjoyable. No one would blame me."

Elena righted the letter and began to read. The elegant handwriting was unfamiliar, but soon enough, the names mentioned within the lines began to make sense.

As did the message itself. Thrilling, fantastic, perfect sense.

"Am I to understand . . ." Elena asked, carefully setting her book on the bench between them before abruptly standing with the correspondence in her hand.

"I'm afraid I won't be of much use until you complete your sentence, my dear."

Elena reread the letter, turning in slow circles as she did so. "That the fifth Viscount Carrington has died—"

"Rather a sad fact for you to be so happily contemplating, wouldn't you say," her father interrupted to point out.

"Oh, of course," she agreed remorsefully, stopping in front of him. "He was a dear friend, was he not?"

Her father grinned again. "That he was, Elena. And he'd lived an interesting life, which is a blessing, indeed. I'd venture to guess the man is sitting at the right hand of the Almighty at this very moment, happily setting to work on one puzzle or another, as he was wont to do."

Elena realized he'd only been teasing her further and frowned at him before continuing. "Am I to understand," she began again, "that the fifth viscount Carrington died and his son has offered you the late lord's entire collection of antiquarian books?"

Lord Harcourt appeared to be contemplating her words. "Yes," he finally confirmed.

"Including the Paolini?" she ventured, not stopping to scold him as she held her breath.

"Including the Paolini."

Giacomo Paolini's *Abecedary Illustrations of Greek Mythology* dated back to the fifteenth century. A single copy had survived. And it resided in the Carrington library.

Elena felt the rush of excitement bubble from her belly to her chest, and finally her face.

"Ah, that is the smile I was waiting for," her father said, standing with some difficulty.

She automatically offered her arm just as the sun's rays began to slant toward the horizon. "When will you go?"

"Go where, my dear?" Lord Harcourt asked as he allowed Elena to assist him down the steps of the folly.

"To Carrington House in London, of course," she replied distractedly, her mind already contemplating where the valuable tome would be placed in the library at Harcourt House.

"Oh, there. Yes, well, you see, I won't be."

Elena stopped, forcing her father to do the same. "What do you mean? Lord Carrington is expecting you."

He gestured ahead to where a cart and horse waited, and they set off once again. "That may be, but I can hardly travel with this gout plaguing me so. You will have to go in my stead."

"Father, is that really necessary?" Elena countered. "Could we not send Mr. Ghent after the book—that is, books?"

Lord Harcourt patted his daughter's hand. "And are you aware of my estate manager's knowledge of such things, my dear?"

"No," she admitted, already anticipating what would come next.

"Mr. Ghent knows no more of priceless books than a robin does," her father replied. "He's a good man, Mr. Ghent, but not the sort one sends to collect such valuables. Your expertise is needed, my dear."

Elena could hardly argue. She would not risk her father's health by insisting that he travel, and she'd not risk the safety of the books by employing Mr. Ghent.

Besides, there was no one more uniquely qualified to catalogue the tomes than herself. Their own library was a thing of beauty, if Elena did say so herself. From the time she could toddle along with the help of her dear nurse's hand, the baron had welcomed Elena into the enormous room that housed his most prized possessions. She'd come to love not only the books themselves, but the respectful process that was required for the care and safekeeping of the delicate volumes. They were an extended family of sorts to her, each one with its own unique place in her heart.

And Lord Carrington's books? Could she leave them in the hands of an unschooled individual? Elena envisioned rare books being tossed hither and yon, thrown into trunks without the benefit of even the most basic of lists to distinguish one collection from the other. It was too much to bear.

"I see," she answered practically, relishing the warmth of the sun's fading rays. "Of course, I'll go. We've no other choice, do we?"

"No," her father confirmed, patting her arm reassuringly.

Elena looked again at the letter in her hand. She'd met Dashiell Matthews once, which had been quite enough for her. She couldn't recall much about him, but she did remember the man had caught the attention of eligible females within the length and breadth of London—and quite a few ineligible ones as well. He was tall and broad, with golden hair and a face that could only be described as beautiful.

If you liked that sort of thing, Elena thought, feigning disinterest.

"And so I shall go," she agreed resolutely. They reached the aged farm cart and Elena allowed the groom to lift her onto the seat. She attempted to smooth her wrinkled skirt, ultimately accepting defeat and folding her hands tightly in her lap.

Returning to London had not been in her plans—ever.

But neither had acquiring Paolini's *Abecedary.*

She would travel as soon as possible, catalogue and pack the books, then return to Harcourt House before her father had time to miss her.

Simple. Straightforward. Just as Elena preferred.

✤

"Good God," Dash muttered under his breath as he watched the landau bearing Elizabeth Bradshaw, Marchioness of Mowbray, pull to a stop in front of Carrington House.

Several heavy leather trunks were lashed to the conveyance, leaving Dash to wonder if there'd been room for the marchioness. He narrowed his eyes and peered through the window, fully expecting to find the interior filled with the familiar boxy shapes of yet more trunks.

Instead, he discovered a pair of bright green eyes watching him above a mouth that curved upward in a mischievous smile.

A footman dutifully opened the lacquered carriage door and lowered the steps, extending his hand. Lady Mowbray graciously accepted his aid and stepped from the carriage onto the pavers. She pulled her deep crimson pelisse tightly about her narrow shoulders and beamed at Dash.

"Lady Mowbray," Dash addressed the handsome older woman, walking to her side. "My dear lady, it's delightful to see you. And looking as beautiful as always, I must say."

The marchioness turned her cheek and allowed Dash to chastely kiss her soft, scented skin. "Yes, you must say, as I'm wearing a new gown. But 'delightful to see me'? Come now, my lord. Our shared history assures we may speak plainly, does it not?"

"You question my sincerity?" Dash asked with amusement, offering Lady Mowbray his arm. He waited while she adjusted her gloves, and then led her toward the wide, solid steps of Carrington House.

"Always," she confirmed, gracefully adjusting the pale yellow scarf tied jauntily about her neck. "That is why I'm your favorite aunt."

The irresistible woman was not his aunt, strictly speaking. But she may as well have been. Dash could not recall a time when Lady Mowbray had not been poking about his affairs, firmly asserting that her role as his mother's dearest friend gave her the right to do so. Not that the woman needed permission—at least not to her way of thinking. She could be incredibly opinionated and pushy, but Dash loved her all the same. Lady Mowbray knew him better than almost anyone else in his life. And so he overlooked her many annoying habits.

Though the number of trunks did give him pause.

"Now," the marchioness began, patting Dash's arm. "When does Miss Barnes arrive? I cannot wait to make her acquaintance. She is rumored to be quite intelligent—perhaps even as sharp as you, my boy."

The hair on Dash's neck prickled at the woman's words. "Do not even think on it," he warned.

"Think on what?" she replied innocently, gracefully lifting her skirts as they mounted the stairs.

Dash shook his head slowly in disbelief. "You know exactly what I'm talking about. Your attempts to secure a wife on my behalf are legendary."

"I would hardly call them legendary, my boy—"

"Lady Emma Scott?" Dash interrupted. The very mention of the woman's name quieted the marchioness.

A footman opened wide the oaken front door and stepped aside.

"That was simply a bit of bad luck," Lady Mowbray countered, sweeping into the foyer ahead of Dash. "How was I to know she was acutely allergic to flowers?"

Dash groaned and released her arm. "Precisely. Which is why you've no place dabbling in such matters—ever," he answered. "I do adore you, but come now. You've behaved so well since the infamous Scott scene. I thought you'd learned your lesson."

"Really, my lord, you haven't a clue as to how the female mind works, do you?" the marchioness answered blithely and patted him reassuringly on the arm.

Lady Mowbray handed her pelisse to a waiting servant and removed her poke bonnet. "Now, I would like to retire to my room. I would prefer to be settled before Miss Barnes arrives so that she might have my full attention. After all, it is my duty as her chaperone to provide instruction and guidance to the girl, is it not?"

Dash groaned a second time as the marchioness handed him the hat.

"We're in agreement, then. Splendid," she replied, clapping her hands together. "Tell me, where is my chamber?"

Dash stared at the bonnet in his hands. "The west wing. Bell will accompany you."

"And Miss Barnes? Will she be housed in the east wing—with you?" Lady Mowbray inquired innocently.

Dash gripped the hat in a death hold and cleared his throat. "Bessie . . ." he said warningly.

"Really, my boy. It's merely that the east wing affords a superior view of the city."

"Go," Dash commanded, pointing to the stairs.

"Yes, I believe I'll retire now," she replied amiably. "Bell, if you please."

Dash watched Lady Mowbray ascend the stairs until she disappeared down the hall to the western half of the house, realizing only after she'd gone that he'd fisted the blasted bonnet into an unrecognizable ball.

"Good God."